Devilishly Wicked

Devilishly Wicked

KATHY LOVE

BRAVA

KENSINGTON PUBLISHING CORP.

www.kensingtonbooks.com

BRAVA BOOKS are published by

Kensington Publishing Corp.
119 West 40th Street
New York, NY 10018

All Kensington titles, imprints, and distributed lines are available at special quantity discounts for bulk purchases for sales promotions, premiums, fund-raising, educational, or institutional use.

Special book excerpts or customized printings can also be created to fit specific needs. For details, write or phone the office of the Kensington special sales manager: Kensington Publishing Corp., 119 West 40th Street, New York, NY 10018, attn: Special Sales Department; phone: 1-800-221-2647.

BRAVA and the B logo are Reg. U.S. Pat. & TM Off.

ISBN-13: 978-0-7582-6589-0
ISBN-10: 0-7582-6589-1

First Kensington trade book printing: November 2013

10 9 8 7 6 5 4 3 2 1

Printed in the United States of America

First electronic edition: November 2013

ISBN-13: 978-0-7582-7914-9
ISBN-10: 0-7582-7914-0

Chapter One

"Go ahead, beg. Beg for it."

Tristan fought back a growl. Beg. Damn, he would so beg Peaches. He'd get down on his knees, without hesitation.

"Good boy." Her fingers stroked Tristan's coconspirator. Her black lacquered nails sank into his hair and it wasn't the first time Tristan had been jealous that his fellow demon got to enjoy her touch. Her affection.

Tristan shifted, peering through the decorative shrubbery, and when she lifted her head and looked in his direction, he shrank back against the building, hoping she hadn't spotted him. The brick wall was cold against his back, but did nothing to cool his ardor, or his imagination, which ran rampant with naughty, sexual scenarios. All of them included her hands stroking over his body like she'd stroked her "good boy."

Damn, he was so hard. Painfully hard.

"Yes," Tristan could hear her croon, "such a good, good boy."

This time, he couldn't suppress his groan. Even her throaty voice turned him on. He stepped forward again, peeking once more through the greenery.

Dear Lucifer, the whole scene had become even more arousing. Now she leaned over her "begging good boy," the pose drawing her black leather skirt taut over her rounded ass and full hips. Her ample breasts swelled over the neckline of her corset-style top, her skin almost translucently pale against the black, brocade material.

Shit, she was like a gothic wet dream. Tristan's wet dream.

"My good, good boy."

Tristan reconsidered. He didn't want to be her good boy. He wanted to be her very bad boy. But he did want that same kind of adoring attention from her, his sexy dominatrix with a sultry voice and a cherub's face.

"Oh, no. What's going on with your collar?" she cooed. "Hmm, this seems too loose. I don't want you getting away."

Tristan's eyes locked on to her fingers back on his colleague, fussing with the collar around his neck. Her finger slipped under the collar and around the edge, testing the tightness.

How could Tristan find that simple action so sensual? He was a demon of lust, so in truth, many things turned him on. But there was something different about Peaches. And this scene.

Shit, what he wouldn't do to be wearing that collar. And he sure as hell wouldn't try to get away.

"Oh, yes, this needs to be tightened."

Her nimble fingers worked the collar, slipping it open, then rethreading the end back through the buckle, pulling it tighter.

Tristan had to close his eyes again as she pushed the prong through the hole, that image too close to what he wanted to do to a part of her body with a part of his.

Demon of lust or not, the sight of someone tightening a collar had never affected him like this.

"There, that's nice and snug. No getting away for you."

His coconspirator would have to be an idiot to want to get away from this sexy woman. Tristan opened his eyes to watch her turn and lightly tug the leash she'd had hooked on her wrist.

"Come on, good boy. Come this way."

She pulled the leash again lightly, but her action wasn't met with the response she wanted.

"Oh, being a stubborn boy now, huh?"

She *tsked* and returned to her stubborn charge.

"No being naughty now, my dear," she warned, her tone still gentle. "If you get me in trouble, then I won't be so nice. So come on."

She pulled again on the leash. Nothing. Still disobedient.

Tristan knew what he'd want her to do to him if he was disobedient. He groaned again.

This time, Peaches straightened, looking in his direction. He remained still. What would happen if she realized he was spying on her?

She wouldn't punish him in any way he'd enjoy, that was for sure. She'd avoid him even more than she already did.

She stared in his direction for another moment, and then bent down.

"Come on, silly," she said, her tone not as cajoling as it had been. "I have to get back to work now. The potty break is over."

She scooped up his colleague, taking advantage of his diminutive size.

"I know you don't want to go back," she said to the little, white fluffy dog she cradled in her arms. "I don't want to go back either."

Tristan suspected he knew exactly why she didn't want to go back to work. Him. The idea really didn't please him, but Tristan knew Peaches always tried to avoid him. Not easy, since she was his personal assistant. But she did her best anyway.

She nuzzled her cheek against the dog—the dog that was actually a hellhound and Satan's minion. Never before had

Tristan been jealous of a dog. Never had he been jealous, period. A demon of lust didn't need to be jealous. There was always another piece of ass out there.

But he was pretty certain that the tight feeling in his chest accompanied by the general sense of irrational irritation was jealousy.

He was jealous of the attention a hellhound was getting on his pee break.

This wasn't good. Peaches shouldn't be avoiding him; Tristan should be avoiding her.

But something about his curvy, eccentric personal assistant fascinated him. Fascinated him too much.

Peaches—or rather Georgia Sullivan—was a distraction, and that made her dangerous. Very dangerous.

"You really think this is the woman who can help us?"

The two men watched as the woman in question walked up to the building in a pair of red patent-leather platform heels that were clearly intended as a fashion statement. No woman would wear them for comfort, although "fashion" might not exactly be the accurate term either. But they did make a statement. She carried the white fur ball that Gabriel recognized as Finola White's little lapdog.

Finola wasn't even her boss anymore, but she was still doing Finola's bidding, obviously. Interesting. He guessed giving up the power she'd once wielded was difficult. Especially for someone like Finola, who had abused it with such delight.

"I'm telling you, Tristan McIntyre is highly attracted to her." Elton, the Demon Intelligence Agency's top seer, spoke with utter certainty.

Gabriel tilted his head, trying to understand what Tristan could possibly see in the woman. Not that he didn't trust Elton. Elton was DIA's best seer for a reason. He had an amazing ability to sense and see many things: demons, the possessed, the damned, even normal humans' reactions to other humans. If he wasn't so damned good, Gabriel suspected the older man would be long retired by now. But the DIA needed him, and he knew it.

Still—this woman?

She wasn't ugly exactly. In fact, she was really rather interesting looking with her funky, dark-rimmed glasses and black hair streaked with both red and pink. She had an hourglass figure, although it definitely leaned toward the chubbier side. And in this world of high fashion, she would be considered downright fat.

Gabriel supposed she did have a certain style, in her black leather skirt and top that was somewhere between a blouse and corset.

The clothes, the shoes, the hair, and the bright red lipstick were over the top, and he could almost applaud her for embracing her own look in a world of fashion clones—all too thin, too dedicated to the trends, and too willing to do whatever they had to do to be a part of the fake, shallow, and soulless organization that was *Hot!* magazine.

Literally soulless.

Still Gabriel found himself saying, "I don't know."

"I'm telling you, she is the perfect one to be our mole. Tristan can't resist her, and I can tell you she is trustworthy."

Well, trustworthy was key. After recent events during which one of their demon slayers had been recognized and one of *HOT!* magazine's editors had been whisked away never to be seen again, the demons now realized that someone out there knew who they were and what they were doing: trying to take over the human world via the fashion industry.

The DIA had to make a move quickly now, and they needed people on the inside to help. But bringing in a stranger would be impossible at this stage of the game. The demons, specifically the head demon, Tristan McIntyre, the newly appointed head editor of *HOT!* magazine, would be suspicious of any new face. And the DIA already knew he was watching the mail room with an eagle eye.

The DIA's cover was perilously close to being blown. They had to move fast.

"But you said she doesn't have a soul contract on her. What's the benefit for her in helping us?"

Elton cast him a sidelong look. "Are you so jaded that you don't think a human would be willing to fight evil without having something in it for them?"

Gabriel guessed that was a pretty jaded attitude. But unfortunately, he'd seen it to be true too many times. Everybody wanted something.

"Will she even believe us?"

Elton looked at him askance. "Well, you don't have to tell her the demon situation from the start. But you *can* tell her that her boss is dangerous. Sticking close to the truth should work. You and Eugene are both smart. You'll think of something."

"Okay," Gabriel said, knowing he had little choice but to trust Elton's judgment. "I will go tell Eugene that I'm going to make my move tonight."

Elton nodded as if he'd known that would be his decision. Then again, right now, they didn't seem to have too many options. They had a few operatives still planted in the magazine, but none of them was close enough to Tristan to get the real dirt and find out his demon weaknesses.

And this woman was Tristan McIntyre's personal assistant. That placed her very close to him.

"Okay, I'll go talk to Eugene now," he said, still hesitating. He didn't know what the head of the DIA was going to say about this choice. Somehow Gabriel didn't think Eugene would be convinced either.

He sighed and levered himself away from the wall to

head down to the mail room, where Eugene worked under the guise of manager.

"She will do it," Elton repeated, obviously sensing Gabriel's reticence. He was the seer after all.

"Okay." Gabriel just hoped she'd be able to handle the task. A job like this would require subtlety and discretion. This woman didn't exactly give the impression of embodying either of those traits.

He walked into the back employee entrance of the *HOT!* building.

He sighed and said softly to himself—or maybe he was sending his concern out to the universe, too—"Here's hoping you are truly the right woman for this job, Georgia Louise Sullivan."

The same two things always went through Georgia Sullivan's mind as she stepped off the elevator and into the *HOT!* lobby. Why had she ever thought she was the right type of woman to work at a place like this? And if she thought she could find a job that paid half as well, she'd be out of here right now.

But today, she was also thinking that her feet were killing her, and she should not have eaten that pastry for breakfast. What was that saying, "Past the lips, straight to the hips"?

She looked over at the gorgeous, blond receptionist whose svelte figure suggested that she'd probably had a healthy breakfast. A half of a grapefruit or maybe, if she was feeling really famished, an egg white omelet, sans cheese or sausage or fried onions and peppers, of course.

The blonde stood to greet a man who approached her desk, and Georgia studied her tall, lithe body in her perfectly fitted pencil skirt and tailored blouse.

Forget that, this woman didn't eat breakfast. She rolled out of bed and headed straight to the gym for Pilates or spin class or some other form of exercise Georgia had only read about in magazines like *HOT!*, but had never done in real life.

Not that she hadn't felt pressured to go to classes like that—aerobics, Pilates, Zumba. She'd even signed up for a couple, only to find excuses to skip them. Of course, excuses weren't hard to come by with this job. Overtime was standard.

But that still didn't mean she couldn't eat better, and work in some exercise every day. But there was the perverse side of her that was determined not to change to fit into this world. She was going to stay true to herself, which meant true to her taste, her style, and *her* size.

Which she had to admit was easier to feel confident about when she wasn't surrounded by size two, supergorgeous creatures who made her feel like Miss Piggy.

Not that she didn't genuinely like her eclectic style, or Miss Piggy for that matter, because she did. She loved fashion—clothes, shoes, accessories. She'd even always dreamed of working in the fashion industry. But somehow she'd always imagined that she would singlehandedly convince the world that "real" women were just as fashionable and sexy as the half-starved models that filled the pages of *HOT!*

How very naïve of her. Downright silly actually.

She didn't fit in here, and hadn't since day one, which made for an uncomfortable and rather lonely work environment.

Still, in some misguided attempt to bond with her fellow coworker, she smiled at the receptionist. The woman looked her up and down once, then turned her attention to her ringing phone without smiling back.

Georgia grimaced. Honestly, she should be used to this. She was the ugly stepchild of the beautiful *HOT!* family.

And anyone who might be nice or interesting was over-worked, harried, and too wrapped up in his or her job to be social. All in all, working for *HOT!* might be prestigious and pay well, but it wasn't the fun dream job she'd imagined. And not just because she had junk in her trunk.

She hugged her only pal to her chest. At least, she could count on Dippy to accept her.

Georgia pushed open one of the large double doors that led to the offices and cubicles of the magazine's other employees. She picked her way through the bustling hallways, not moving too quickly, even when her current outfit received a few more once-overs and raised eyebrows.

To be fair, some people didn't give her dubious looks, but neither were they friendly. Everyone was too focused on their work to be warm and fuzzy. And she found that weird, too. The employees here had a shared interest—the love of fashion. And considering this was the number-one fashion magazine to work for, Georgia just thought there should be an excitement in the air. A wonderful creative vibe. Hell, she knew people who would probably sell their souls for a job like this, and yet, everyone seemed almost . . . depressed. It was like a hive of worker bees, going through the motions of keeping the queen bee happy.

The queen bee had even been replaced, and still the atmosphere hadn't changed.

Of course, Georgia had her own mixed feelings about the shift of power from the supreme diva, Finola White, to her once assistant editor, Tristan McIntyre.

Finola had been pure hell to work for—demanding, irrational, often downright mean, but Tristan, well, he was a different type of difficult. Her main issue being that she was ridiculously attracted to the man, who was so not going to be interested in a woman like her. He definitely went for the supermodels and actresses, women with perfect faces and perfect figures who looked perfect with his own stunning good looks. It was all a bit nauseating.

But worse than her pathetic crush was the fact that he was totally aware of her hopeless attraction to him, and always seemed to be toying with her because of it. He flirted, but Georgia wasn't delusional enough to think his interest was genuine. It was more a patronizing, "Aren't you cute in your hopeless infatuation."

Which was just another thing that made working at *HOT!* awkward and difficult.

But in the end, none of that mattered. She couldn't walk away from this job, as lonely, demanding, and often ego-shattering as it might be.

"Peaches."

Georgia closed her eyes.

Couldn't she at least make it to her desk and get herself as mentally together as she could before she had to deal with him? The insincere flirting that still managed to make her stupid, wayward heart race was way too cruel a start to a Monday morning.

The little dog she still held in her arms squirmed, and she realized she was holding it too tight in her nervousness. She loosened her hold, stroking the dog's soft fur, and pulled in a deep breath, telling herself, as she did every day, that she could handle this. Handle him. And handle her utterly juvenile reaction to him.

Slowly, she turned to find her boss, Tristan McIntyre, standing only inches from her. It was something he always did. She suspected it was only because he knew it made her uncomfortable. She automatically took a step back.

He smiled crookedly, again making her think he knew full well what he was doing to her. And he was enjoying it.

His eyes, the greenest gaze Georgia had ever seen, like new leaves in spring or freshly mown grass, so green that she often thought they couldn't possibly be real, moved over her.

He raised a dark eyebrow, that smirking little smile still in place.

"You've gone with yet another interesting ensemble today, Peaches." He, of course, pronounced *ensemble* with a French accent. Pretension was as natural to him as breathing. And stupidly, she even found that attractive.

Georgia never knew if his comments were a compliment or an insult, but she took her usual stance and tried to accept it gracefully.

"Thank you, Mr. McIntyre."

He smiled again, this time a little wider. "When will you ever just call me Tristan?"

God, he loved to toy with her, but she again refused to give him the response he wanted.

As it turned out, he made answering unnecessary. His green gaze moved to the little dog in her arms.

"Why do you have that mutt?"

"Ms. White asked me to—"

"Ms. White should not be asking you to do anything. You no longer work for her. You work for me."

"I understand," she said, although she really wasn't sure how she could disregard Finola White's demands. Finola White was still Georgia's superior, at least around here, and Georgia wasn't about to challenge that. Finola White could still be scary and mean. But it was best just to agree with Tristan right now.

Play the game. Play the game.

She leaned down to place the dog on the floor. The little animal scampered away, disappearing under her desk. Smart boy. She wished she could slip away and make herself scarce, too.

When she straightened, she got the feeling Tristan's gaze

had been on her rear end, but she couldn't be sure. Still, that shivery feeling prickled her skin and made it hard for her to swallow.

But she cleared her throat and managed to find her voice.

"Do you have the lists of daily duties ready for me, sir?"

He studied her for a moment, those green eyes of his gazing over her slowly, making her feel that she wanted to shift under his scrutiny. To move farther away. But she stood fast on her red-patent, dolly platform heels.

"Yes, I actually left it on your desk. It looks like a relatively light day."

Georgia would have laughed if she wasn't so shaken. There was no such thing as a light day when it came to working for *HOT!*—even under Tristan McIntyre.

Under Tristan McIntyre. She felt herself blush at her own off-color train of thought.

Yikes, Georgia, get a grip.

He took a step toward her, and despite herself, Georgia crossed her arms in front of her. It was a not-so-subtle barrier between them.

Tristan raised an eyebrow, giving her an almost admonishing look; then he moved past her. His broad shoulder just barely brushed hers as he walked by.

"I'll be in a meeting with Finola—or rather, Ms. White, if you need me."

Georgia didn't turn to watch him leave. She didn't need to; everything about the man was committed to her memory. There was the stylishly mussed cut of his dark hair, the gait of his walk, the way his expensive clothing fit his lean, muscular body perfectly.

She remained where she was until she knew he was gone. And only then did she head to her desk, which took up a majority of Tristan McIntyre's reception area.

She turned sideways to slip behind the large semicircular desk and dropped onto her desk chair. She sat there for a moment, willing herself to calm down, but her heart thudded almost painfully in her chest.

"Dippy," she called, wanting something else to focus on to help calm her. But the little dog didn't appear. He must have followed Tristan into the back office. She didn't know if she should be offended that the little fluff ball had left her for the dark side.

Not that the little dog was any real protection. She took another deep breath, then pulled her chair in and focused on her list of duties. But her attention didn't make it through the first few tasks.

Why couldn't she just remain calm and not let this man get to her? She knew the flirtation was just a game for him. An amusement, because she was so easily flustered by his attention. She knew exactly what he was doing, so why did he still have this effect on her? Even after all these months working for him? Even before that, when she'd worked for Finola White, she'd seen him daily. And he'd been a flirt then, too. With everyone.

She reached for the legal pad with the list of handwritten tasks covering several lines. Tristan's handwriting was neat, precise, but still had a certain flare.

Her skin tingled just looking at it.

And this, this was the real torture of her job. This ridiculous, uncontrollable, undeniable, and overwhelming attraction to her boss. To a boss who could be a model himself.

Talk about totally hopeless.

Chapter Two

Tristan McIntyre smiled as he made his way through the catacomb of glass walls to his office. He could always count on his personal assistant's reaction to him to start his day off right. Since the first time he'd met Georgia Sullivan, her reaction had never wavered.

She wanted him. Her desire for him filled the air, and he drank it up like the morning's first cup of coffee. In fact, he craved it just like a caffeine addict craved his coffee fix.

His smile widened as he recalled how her desire surged and intensified as he'd flirted with her. Making the regular coffee into a double espresso. Strong, dark, and hot.

Oh, yeah, he loved playing with her. As a demon of lust, he needed that kind of reaction. Thrived on it.

But his bliss faded as he realized someone was following close at his heels. His smile flipped to a frown. Damned Dippy.

One thing he'd learned, perhaps a little too late—hellhounds were relentless. And when it came to trying to get what he wanted, Dippy was like a dog with a bone, literally and figuratively.

But the pesky ball of fur didn't say anything. He just settled on his haunches, watching with his beady little eyes while he waited for Tristan to open the office door.

Tristan did, pushing open the glass door, before he realized Finola White sat at his desk, the highly polished white acrylic command center that had once belonged to her. And from the way she lounged in the desk chair, she obviously thought it still did.

He sighed. Caught between a demon and a hellhound—so, so much worse than a rock and a hard place.

And this was another reason he needed the little moments of fun with his personal assistant. Because the truth was, being the leader of a demon rebellion was not all that it was cracked up to be. Especially when he had to work with two underlings who refused to accept they were indeed his minions.

He walked into the room, bracing himself for more complaints and defiance and general drama, and he wasn't disappointed.

"Tristan, power doesn't suit you. It's clearly caused you to lose your mind."

Tristan dropped his briefcase onto *his* desk, giving her a pointed look, waiting for her to move. She settled deeper into the chair and crossed her arms over her chest.

Dippy, who was technically her dog but also Tristan's co-conspirator, wandered to his doggy bed, watching the two of them. His doggy expression showed that he was no more pleased with Tristan than Finola was.

Ah, another fun day at work.

He gave her another look, this one filled with silent warning.

"You are in my seat."

She made a face, one somewhere between a sneer and a smirk, but then slowly levered herself out of the white leather chair, making sure to keep her movements unhurried.

Tristan waited, not giving her the satisfaction of showing any reaction whatsoever. That was one thing he'd perfected to an art during his time under her reign: utter indifference.

Oh, he was irritated, sick of dealing with her insubordinate, often downright childish behavior, but she'd never get the satisfaction of seeing that. Because she would love it, if she could. She wanted to aggravate and annoy him. She wanted to make his life hell.

Finola White had not taken losing her position well. She was furious. But that wasn't Tristan's problem. If she'd done her job correctly, Tristan wouldn't have been able to usurp her position.

But Finola had been more interested in herself, her indulgences, and living the high life than doing the work Satan wanted from her. Tristan wasn't going to make the same mistakes.

Oh, he was definitely all about taking advantage of the luxuries and status and worldly pleasures that being the editor-in-chief of a prestigious fashion magazine could offer him. But he was also going to make damned sure the demon realm was invading the human one as he did so.

Finola had been a loose cannon, letting power go to her head. Tristan planned to stay grounded and focused, even while he was being decadent as hell. Which would definitely be a tricky balance for a demon of lust, but he'd figure out a way to handle his desires. A way to keep his focus on the task at hand.

World domination.

But the first thing he needed to do was get his insubordinate inferiors under control.

He moved behind the desk and collapsed in the chair, making a show of basking in the comfort of the cushioned, supple leather.

Finola grimaced again, but perched on the edge of a much less comfortable chair on the other side of the office.

"So," Tristan said, "please do explain how you've come to the conclusion that my mind has been lost."

Finola glared at him, and then finally leaned back in the chair, taking an indifferent stance herself.

"You know full well what I'm talking about."

Tristan pretended to ponder the possibilities, and then widened his eyes with feigned realization.

"Oh, you are referring to the fact that I'm relocating you to the mail room."

"I will not work in the mail room. In fact, I will not set foot in the mail room."

Tristan again pretended to consider her words.

"Actually, you will. Because not only did I, your master, tell you that you have to work there. But I'm very certain that *my* master, the Prince of Darkness, will back me on this plan. After all, I'm not sending you down there just to make your life hell." He smirked. "I have a very important job for you in the mail room."

Finola rose, her usually pure alabaster skin actually flushed in anger. Her hands were balled at her sides, and for a moment, Tristan thought she was going to stamp her foot like a bratty child not getting her way. Of course, that wouldn't be the first time he'd ever seen her do that.

But instead she said in a rougher tone, and her usually melodic voice took on a hissing quality, "This will never work. Don't you think the mail room employees will be highly suspicious of the editor-in-chief of the magazine suddenly working down there?"

"The *ex* editor-in-chief," Tristan corrected. "And yes, I'm sure they will. But that suspicion might work in our favor, putting any traitors on edge and causing them to make a stupid mistake. We already know a demon slayer was working down there. We have to make sure there are no other rebels working at *HOT!*, looking to stop our mission."

Finola glared at him, but didn't speak.

"So you see," Tristan continued, "being sent to work in the mail room is actually an important task. And quite flattering, really."

Finola didn't move, nor did the rage flashing in her eyes lessen. In fact, she'd gone from looking like a petulant child to a murderous demon.

Tristan was unaffected.

"I do not deliver things," she stated. "I'm the person things are delivered to."

Tristan nodded. "I understand. But unfortunately now, you are the person who does what I tell you to do."

If looks could kill, Tristan knew he'd be dead. But looks couldn't, not even a demon's. And frankly, he felt far too good to be concerned with her look of hate. Finola would be out of his office and out of his hair. Nothing could be any better.

He reached for the phone and pressed the intercom button.

"Georgia, could you come to my office, please?"

He released the button and then looked back at Finola.

"It really isn't a punishment," Tristan told her, even though they both knew that it was, but he also was serious about the fact that he wanted her paying attention down there.

In that regard, Finola wouldn't have been his first choice. She was too self-absorbed to be aware of anything outside of herself. That's how the demon slayer had infiltrated *HOT!* in the first place. But Tristan did need her away from him, and he did need someone down there, keeping an eye out for other disturbances.

So the mail room really was the best place to put her.

A soft knock sounded at the door, and Tristan waved Georgia into the room.

"Georgia, I'm going to need you to help get Ms. White situated in the mail room."

Georgia's dark eyebrows pulled together over the funky frames of her glasses. She clearly found his request odd and bewildering, but unlike Finola, she simply nodded.

"Of course, sir."

Another reason he liked his assistant. There was no disobedience from her.

Tristan felt his body react, remembering her moments with Dippy this morning. Could she be both dominant and submissive? Damn, he'd love to find out. But he suppressed the thought, not any easy feat, and turned his attention back to Finola.

"The mail room manager, Eugene Saint, already knows that you are relocating down there, and he'll get you situated."

Finola didn't respond. No sarcastic comment, or nod, or anything. Instead, she just looked at Georgia, and raised an eyebrow as if to silently say, "Are we going?"

Georgia, in turn, glanced toward Tristan, and he nodded. Both women left the room.

Tristan sighed. "Eugene Saint—you really are going to have to be a saint to deal with Finola White."

"I'm starting to think maybe I need to be a saint, too," said a deep, growly voice from beside his chair.

Tristan looked down to see Dippy sitting at his feet. Finola still didn't know her pet was actually a hellhound, so Dippy never spoke in front of her.

The dog narrowed his dark eyes. "You've managed to get rid of Finola, so when are you going to transform me to human, and introduce me as your new assistant editor?"

Tristan looked down at his cohort, who had been a major part of Tristan's play to take control of *HOT!* and the demon rebellion. Now he was little more than a fluffy, white thorn in Tristan's side. Not much more appealing to deal with than Finola, frankly. Maybe he could send Dippy to the kennel.

And to think, his day had actually been quite enjoyable for a minute there. Tristan sighed. He should have known that it couldn't last.

"Do you need to stop by your office for anything?" Georgia asked tentatively, really wishing she didn't have to speak at all.

"No," Finola snapped, her usually melodic voice flat.

Georgia decided she didn't need to say anything more, not if she didn't want to get ripped a new one.

She did not like Finola White, but she had to admit, this must be very hard for the woman. The great Finola White was now going to be working in the . . . the mail room? Talk about a demotion. Georgia almost felt sorry for the woman. Almost.

Georgia looked at Finola out of the corner of her eye. The woman wore her signature white, today a draping, white blouse with white skinny jeans. On her feet were white snakeskin boots.

Georgia was sure that outfit had cost thousands of dollars and now she was supposed to go to the mail room, put on one of their royal blue smocks, and start sorting mail.

It didn't make sense. But then again, there were many things that happened at *HOT!* that defied reason.

Finola White in royal blue. She couldn't even picture it.

"I should be the head of *HOT!*" Finola muttered.

Georgia instantly dropped her gaze to her feet and made sure she kept her face blank, not wanting to give the woman any reason to react to her. But Finola seemed focused on herself, *shocker,* and her comment had just been a lament to the universe in general.

"I will make his life a living hell," Finola muttered, and her voice took on a strange, almost unnatural quality.

Or at least Georgia thought it did, but she must be imagining that, right?

She suppressed a shudder despite herself. She must have imagined it. Still, Georgia was not sorry to see Finola gone from the office. The woman scared her. She was . . . not right. And while Finola wasn't her direct boss anymore, Georgia still felt as if she had to answer to the woman. It would be nice to not have to deal with her much at all.

But Georgia wasn't about to celebrate yet. It was best to remain silent and stoic. The less interaction with Finola White, the better. She'd learned that very quickly under her employment. If she could just make it through this trip unscathed, she might be free of the super diva.

Now that idea almost made her smile.

As they walked through the offices of *HOT!*, Georgia noticed that all the employees still reacted to Finola in much the same way Georgia did by keeping their gazes downcast and scurrying out of her way.

Finola White had been a huge presence at the magazine. So huge that Georgia still didn't see how Tristan's punishment would really work. Finola would never do anything useful for the mail room. Nor would she fit in. And Georgia would be very surprised if she even stayed long enough to go down there. She had to be just leaving the building. Period.

But when they entered the elevator, it was Finola who hit the button labeled LL. The mail room was as far down in the building as a person could go.

Rather symbolic, Georgia thought. Finola White had fallen from her all-powerful position in the company straight to the lowest.

Neither said a word as the elevator shimmied and shuddered, not stopping on any of the other fourteen floors on the way down.

On the way down. Georgia again couldn't miss the symbolism. This had to be Finola's idea of hell. Or at least that was Georgia's guess.

Finola, with her pale skin, white blond hair, light gray eyes, and all-white attire could sort of be seen as angelic. But Georgia knew Finola White was hardly an angel.

She risked a sidelong glance at the tall, elegant woman in white. But why was she actually going to the mail room? Why didn't she just walk out? She could surely get a job at another magazine. She was an icon after all. But apparently Finola was as trapped as Georgia. Probably not for the same reason. Georgia highly doubted Finola had financial issues, but she was trapped by something.

The elevator slowly bobbed to a stop, and the silver door slid open, revealing a room bustling with employees.

Georgia waited for Finola to step off, but she remained rooted to the elevator's laminate-lined floor.

Just as the door would have shut again, a man appeared. He was the epitome of average: average height and average build with rather nondescript brown hair and features.

Well, except for one, his eyes, which were a vivid blue— so dazzlingly brilliant, Georgia thought they must be contacts or something. Although, this guy didn't seem like the type to wear cosmetic lenses.

"Ms. Finola White?" he asked in a voice that Georgia would neither describe as particularly deep, nor particularly high.

Finola lifted her chin. "Yes."

"I'm Eugene Saint. Mr. McIntyre told me you would be joining us today." He extended a hand. "It's wonderful to finally meet the woman I've worked for all these years."

Georgia's gaze turned to Finola, not sure how that comment would be received. Was it really a good idea to point out that Finola had once been in power? And now she was here?

But to her surprise, Finola actually smiled and stepped off the elevator, accepting the man's extended hand, her long, pale fingers stroking his palm as they shook.

And to Georgia, it seemed as if Finola's touch lingered. She was a beautiful woman in her own unique, pale way. Maybe she would find a way to fit in down here. Quite well.

"I'm pleased to be here," Finola said, her smile appearing sincere, but Georgia knew it couldn't be. Inside, the diva had to be writhing at the idea of being expected to work here, amongst average people like this guy. Finola was all about beauty and wealth and prestige, not an average Joe like Eugene Saint. But again, she probably had a plan on how not to work. She was using the one thing women had used as their power since the dawn of time.

Although, Georgia couldn't tell if this man was affected by Finola's flirty attention or not. He was inscrutably unexcited.

"Please," the man said, waving a hand toward the mail room. "Let me show you around."

Finola bowed her head. "Thank you."

Georgia knew she wasn't keeping the bewildered frown off her face, but never, *never* would she have expected Finola to be so accepting of this man or a tour of the mail room. Never mind that she had to stay here and work.

Georgia found herself following the couple, too confounded to do anything else. But after a few steps, Finola stopped and looked back at her.

"You are no longer needed."

Georgia stopped instantly. This was the Finola she knew. The one with icy, pale eyes, who snapped orders as if she'd been born doing so.

But then Finola glanced back to Eugene, that sweet smile returning.

"Eugene seems to have everything under control down here." She looked back at Georgia, some of that sweetness slipping again. "So please tell Tristan that I'm all settled and everything is just great."

Georgia nodded, still dazed. Finola was going to take this graciously? Really? That made no sense. She had to be up to something. Georgia didn't believe for a minute that Finola would simply be satisfied with manipulating the mail room staff so she could get out of doing any work. She had something bigger and badder planned. She had to.

"Okay," Finola said, her tone just a tad harder. "Run along. We're fine here."

Georgia nodded again and headed back to the elevators. She stared at the couple until the metal door closed, her last glimpse that of Finola laughing, quite merrily, it appeared.

Chapter Three

"It's time for me to properly join you in this takeover."

Tristan fought his urge to groan with annoyance. They had been discussing this for twenty minutes now. Did he have to repeat everything yet again? Dippy really was an irritating little lapdog, always yapping about what he wanted. Never giving it a rest.

Maybe the kennel wasn't such a bad idea. Hellhound or not, he didn't have opposable thumbs. A cage would surely be impossible for him to escape from.

But alas, Dippy was Satan's favorite lapdog. And knowing Dippy, he'd find some way to escape and tattle. Satan believed every word the little mongrel yapped.

Which Tristan could admit had been very useful when he'd needed the mangy mutt. But now he found the dog a real pain in the ass. Sort of like one of those sweet-faced little puppies you adopted as a Christmas present for the kids, only to realize you were now stuck with an animal that wasn't nearly so cute when the reality of the incessant barking and constant care kicked in.

Okay, the analogy wasn't exactly accurate, but it was close enough. Especially the incessant barking. In-cess-ant.

"Dippy, I've told you repeatedly, we have to wait until the time is right. We don't want Satan realizing we set this whole thing up. To have me in command, and you as my second."

"It's been months," Dippy said. "I think you could easily approach Satan now. Telling him what an asset I've been."

Tristan knew he could do that, but he didn't have any intention of sharing his power with a hellhound. Ever.

"Give it another few weeks."

Dippy growled, a low rumbling in his tiny, fur-covered chest. "I'm not waiting much longer. I can still influence Satan on my own. And by the way, I don't recall there being any plan that you would be first in command and me second. I thought we planned to run this takeover together. Fifty/fifty."

"I'm talking about now," Tristan lied. "We are still running this demonic takeover together."

But not for long. There had to be a way to show Satan his favorite hellhound was not to be trusted. But how? He wanted to be rid of both Dippy and Finola. That was his true plan. He just hadn't figured out a permanent solution to deal with both annoyances.

But at least Finola was stuck in the mail room for now. Maybe he could send Dippy away to be groomed, and instead he could be "accidentally" put down. Could a hellhound be euthanized?

"I'm serious," Dippy said, standing on his hind legs and digging at Tristan's knee with his front paw. "I won't stay like this indefinitely."

Tristan lifted a finger to his lips and pointed toward the office door. Georgia was making her way through the glass maze back to his office.

Good timing, Peaches.

Dippy looked over his fuzzy shoulder to see Georgia and jumped down.

"This isn't over," he growled before settling back on his dog bed.

So, so true, but Tristan didn't reply, instead focusing his attention on Georgia. He waved her into his office as soon as she appeared outside the door.

Georgia entered, a strange, almost bemused expression on her face.

"Did Finola give you any trouble going to the mail room?" he asked.

She shook her head. "No, and she is being shown around by the mail room manager now."

"Excellent," he said. Then he couldn't stop himself from asking, "How did she seem about the new position?"

"She seemed . . . fine."

Tristan's smug smile faded. "She was fine? No tantrums? No rude behavior to the other employees? No idle threats?"

Georgia shook her head again, looking as surprised as he felt.

This couldn't be right.

"Not at all," she said. "She actually seemed . . . pleased to be there."

It was Tristan's turn to look baffled. Finola was simply accepting her fate? That was not like her.

He managed to focus his attention on Georgia, which normally wasn't difficult, but her revelation had startled him. Even she knew Finola going quietly to the mail room was not right.

"Thank you," he finally said.

She nodded. "Did you need anything else?"

This would typically be the time when he'd make some lascivious comment, then breathe in deeply her reaction to him. But right now he was too distracted.

"No, thank you," he repeated. Then, just as she was about to leave the office, he quickly added, "Actually, could you please take Dippy with you?"

Georgia instantly smiled at the small dog. For some reason, she actually liked the little creature. Then again, the dog didn't *talk* to her.

"Sure," she agreed, her smile still wide and natural. Small dimples accented each side of her rosy, bow-shaped mouth, and Tristan found himself reacting to the sight.

Such kissable. Lickable. Nippable lips.

She leaned forward and patted her knee, making a kissing noise to call the dog to her, almost as if to taunt Tristan. But she didn't know his thoughts.

Tristan admired the pale cleavage that swelled over her top. And his eyes went back to that ass. That full, round ass.

Damn, he loved her body. And her face.

"Come on, boy," she called sweetly to Dippy.

And her voice.

"Come on, silly," she coaxed with an indulgent laugh.

For a moment, Tristan was actually jealous again of the four-legged beast. Dippy got held against that ripe, curvy body on a regular basis. What wasn't there to be jealous of?

As if he could read Tristan's mind, Dippy trotted over to Georgia, coming up on his hind legs as if to say, "Hold me."

Dippy even glanced back at Tristan. Oh, that little mutt was rubbing it in.

But instead of scooping him up, she petted his head and then straightened. The lovely smile remained on her lips, but only for the dog. "Want to come with me, sweetie?"

Dippy pranced around her like a real dog would at the suggestion of such an adventure.

She nodded toward Tristan, her smile fading, and left the office with Dippy following behind, although the dog paused long enough to look back at Tristan and lift his leg.

Tristan watched as the beast urinated on his office door.

Tristan gritted his teeth, but didn't react otherwise. Just like Finola, Dippy wanted a reaction, and Tristan wasn't going to give it to him. Not now anyway.

Instead, he pondered what Georgia had told him. Finola was fine with being in the mail room. That was so not the reaction he'd expected. Infuriating her was the reason he'd sent her there. Well, as well as making it difficult for the rebels, if there really were any more down there.

Finola would definitely make things hard for them. He'd thought Finola would make things hard for the whole mail room. So why was she accepting her fate so placidly?

Unless she was up to something. And of course, she *was* up to something.

Tristan fought back a groan. Of course, she was up to something. But what now? And couldn't he enjoy banishing her, even for a day?

"That damned bitch. What are you planning now?"

Yeah, being the head demon wasn't nearly as much fun as he'd imagined.

Just then the scent of dog urine reached him.

Not fun at all.

Gabriel watched from behind his sorting machine as Eugene showed Finola White, *the* Finola White, probably one of the nastiest and most unpredictable demons he'd ever encountered, around the mail room.

It was unnerving to have her in their space, right in the midst of the DIA operatives, and right above their main offices, which were another floor below them. A floor no one at *HOT!* even knew existed. And one none of the demons could enter, because the offices were encased in copper. Demons could not cross over copper. But still, having the enemy so close was unsettling, and always dangerous.

He continued to watch as Eugene led her to a sorting station and waved over Dave, who posed as Eugene's mail room assistant, but who was in fact Eugene's right-hand man in the agency.

The three talked for a moment, and Gabriel noticed Finola was all smiles. As Dave talked to her, probably about sorting mail, she flipped her hair and leaned her head close to Dave's, seeming to listen intently.

Gabriel didn't buy for a moment that she was really interested in learning the proper way to sort and stack mail. Nor did he believe she'd ever do the work. So what was she up to?

Eugene said a few more words to Finola, then left her alone with Dave, and headed back to his office. Gabriel waited a moment, and then followed his supervisor.

"Come in," Eugene said as soon as Gabriel knocked.

Gabriel stepped into Eugene's small office. The man already sat at his desk, waiting for his computer to boot up.

"Is everything okay with her?"

Neither of them had to clarify who "her" was.

"She seemed to be quite content to be down here," Eugene said, his expression, as usual, unreadable.

"And you aren't suspicious of that?"

Eugene looked away from his computer to meet Gabriel's gaze. "I didn't say that. We all know we are going to have to watch her closely."

Gabriel nodded, relieved to hear that Eugene hadn't somehow fallen prey to Finola White's charms and pale beauty. Or to her demon guile. She was a predator on every level.

Gabriel started to ask if he could just handle her. After all, he'd been slaying demons a century before the DIA even came into existence, but he also knew the DIA no longer approved of the killing of demons. Now, it was generally accepted that demons could be reformed. Not that he'd ever met a reformed demon himself.

But either way, he knew Eugene would never approve the request.

"The DIA will handle Finola," Eugene said. "In truth, I

was more interested in meeting Georgia Sullivan. She is the one who we are going to recruit to work with us, right?"

"Yes."

Eugene studied him for a moment, and then turned his attention back to his computer screen.

Gabriel waited, knowing from past experience that Eugene probably wasn't done talking. Plus, Gabriel wanted to know more about his boss's thoughts. One would think the head of the DIA would be very, very concerned about the presence of a powerful demon in their midst, but he was more interested in Georgia Sullivan. Why?

"I think she will be good for the task," Eugene said, in his eerie way of seemingly answering an unspoken question. Although, Gabriel should be used to that by now. "I get a positive feeling from her. And I think she will be extremely useful in getting to Tristan McIntyre."

"Good," Gabriel said. "Although, I will admit, I'm not as sure myself."

"She's perfect. She's exactly right to appeal to Tristan McIntyre."

"Really?" Gabriel still had his doubts about that one. True, Tristan was a demon of lust and all women would likely appeal to the demon in some way or another. But in this world of high fashion, where the demon was surrounded by gorgeous women on a daily basis, how would a quirky, quite frankly chunky, woman like Georgia Sullivan stand out?

"She's different," Eugene said, again answering Gabriel's unspoken question.

"He will be drawn to her individuality. And I believe we can trust her. She has a good soul."

Gabriel nodded, not sure how Eugene could tell all that from one brief meeting, in which he hadn't even seen his boss actually speak to the woman, but he hoped Eugene was right.

* ★ *

"Well, little Dippy," Georgia said, unhooking the dog from its leash and hanging the leash back on the coat rack beside her desk, "it was still nice to go for a little walk, even if you didn't need to go potty."

The dog wagged its small, nubby tail and seemed to smile. She smiled, too.

Then she took a shawl off the coat rack hook. She left it here at work, just in case she got cold while at her desk, but right now she dropped it on the ground beside her chair.

Dippy stood a few feet away, regarding her.

"Come on," she said, pointing to her shawl. "Lie down."

The dog wandered closer, looking from the shawl to her.

"It's okay," she cooed to the animal. "It's just an old shawl. You can sleep on it. It's not like it can't be washed."

The dog hesitated a moment longer, then settled on the cloth, tugging at it with his teeth and paws to get it arranged just so.

Georgia smiled, watching the animal get comfortable.

"You are such a cute little thing."

"Why, thank you."

Georgia started at the unexpected voice. She looked up to find Tristan approaching her desk. She hadn't expected to see him again so soon. She hadn't gotten to anything on the list he'd given her. She hoped that didn't upset him. She could already tell he hadn't been pleased about her description of Finola's reaction to the mail room.

"Oh, were you talking to that mutt?" he said, with a grin.

He didn't look upset now. He looked gorgeous.

Georgia tried to answer with some kind of decorum, but instead only managed a croaked little "Yes."

Tristan's smile deepened, and she knew he was pleased by her flustered response. He did so enjoy torturing her.

"I don't get it myself," he said, leaning forward to peer over her desk at the dog.

Dippy growled as if he understood.

Tristan didn't acknowledge the sound, instead focusing his intense green gaze on Georgia.

"Peaches, I'm going to need your help on a very important task today."

Georgia automatically reached for the list, and again jumped when Tristan's hand came out to stop her. His long, masculine fingers curled around her much smaller, much softer hand.

"This task isn't on your list," he said, and she could swear he actually purred the words. It was a deep, seductive purr that made every nerve ending in her body tingle.

Georgia's eyes met his, and her heart threatened to beat right out of her chest.

"Okay," she managed to say, proud the word came out normal, and not a sad little croak.

Then his hand, still holding hers, curled even tighter, and he tugged slightly.

"I need you to come with me."

Georgia's heart leapt again, painfully. Why was it everything this man said sounded flirty and seductive? He really hadn't said anything forward, or even unusual, yet she felt like every word, every comment, was designed seduce her.

Of course, it had to be her own desires making her feel that way. Heaven knew, she wasn't the type of woman Tristan McIntyre would want to seduce. He went for women as perfect and polished as himself. And he certainly had his pick of those at *HOT!* Models, actresses, every perfect woman in the world, right here for his choosing.

She was irritated with herself that she was even hopeful he was flirting with her. Let's face it, if he was, it was just some egotistical game he was playing. "The watch your

chubby assistant blush and look pathetically hopeful game."
And damned if she didn't fall for it every time.

She cleared her throat and told herself to calm down.
"What task do you need help with, sir?"

His gaze lingered on her for a moment, a gaze that
seemed filled with silent innuendo; although she told herself she was imagining it. This man did not want her, not as
anything other than a personal assistant. At his beck and
call—only for work.

"I need you to come shopping with me."

Georgia hadn't expected that.

"Shopping?" Her gaze moved to his perfectly tailored,
extremely expensive suit. "I don't think you need me to
help you shop. Besides, I don't think I exactly share your
taste."

She gave a pointed look down at her vintage rockabilly
ensemble.

Tristan smiled at that, his own gaze roaming over her.
"No, you don't. But I am quite fond of your taste."

She could have sworn his gaze dropped, just for an in-
stant, to her cleavage, but she decided that was also her own
warped desire for him. Leave it to her to be longing for sexual harassment from her boss.

Ack. Get a grip, girl.

"But I'm not talking about clothes shopping. I need you
to come help me find new office furniture. All of this is
going."

Chapter Four

"Which one would you pick?" Georgia frowned at her boss, and then looked between the two desks. Both were large, made of heavy, dark wood and ornately carved with Chippendale legs and decorative knobs and drawer pulls.

They were both very cool, very gothic, and so not very Tristan McIntyre.

She looked back at him, perplexed. "They are both beautiful, but—"

"You're right," Tristan said, cutting her off. He waved to the sales clerk, who already hovered nearby, sensing a big sale.

Smart man.

"I'm going to take both of these." Tristan pointed to the desks. "And the chairs, too, I think." He looked at Georgia questioningly. "What do you think? Do you like the chairs, too?"

Georgia nodded, bemused. They were gorgeous, matching the desks perfectly with high backs and ornately carved armrests.

"Yes." Tristan smiled. "We will take those, too." He instantly began looking again. "I'm not done."

"Yes, sir," the salesman said, practically rubbing his hands together. Georgia knew he was mentally calculating his commission. She would be.

"Peaches," Tristan called, moving on to another display, "look at this one."

Georgia followed, knowing she probably looked like a bewildered child tagging along after him. Or a pathetically lovelorn employee.

"Isn't this fabulous?" He smiled at her, and for a moment she forgot her confusion and could think about nothing but how beautiful his smile was. Was it really possible for a man to be that beautiful?

She had seen dozens of male models in the *HOT!* offices, and none of them were as stunning as Tristan. Maybe she was being overdramatic—she did have a bit of a flare for that—but his looks seemed almost otherworldly. Looks like his just didn't happen in nature.

"Do you think I should get this one?"

Georgia's dreamy appreciation disappeared, her confusion returning.

It took her a moment to comprehend what he asking her. She stared at the desk in question. This one was bigger than the last two, and truly medieval.

"It's lovely—"

Tristan started to raise his hand to beckon the salesperson again, but she caught his wrist before he could call the man over.

"It's lovely," she repeated, determined to get her thought out this time. "But why are you buying all of this furniture? It isn't your style."

Tristan's gaze moved over her; then he tilted his head, looking so damned adorable it had to be criminal. "What is my style, Peaches?"

Georgia pulled in a breath, bracing herself for more of his flirting, his torturous flirting. Okay, she could admit he did seem to be flirting with her, and maybe all of it wasn't her imagination. Maybe it was such a part of his nature, he couldn't help himself. She still couldn't take it as genuine attraction to her. He just couldn't help himself.

Still her body hummed at his attention.

Again, leave it to her to like the disingenuous flirtations of her boss. Talk about a crush that was doomed on every level. A therapist would have a field day with that one.

Because you never received affection from your father, you are desperate for any male attention you can get. Or something to that effect, even though she and her dad had a wonderful relationship. Given that it had been just her father, her grandmother, and herself when she was growing up, she'd say she was probably closer to her father than most daughters. So she couldn't blame that relationship.

Georgia was more inclined to think she was just a masochist.

Time to stop the fantasies, and remember that someone like Tristan McIntyre would never be interested in a quirky, chubby chick. He went for the size-two beauty queens. Georgia amused him, only because she reacted to his attention. If she didn't, he'd get bored and leave her alone.

So remember, she told herself, his flirting is insulting, not flattering. Remember that, Georgia Louise Sullivan.

There was absolutely no reason for her heart to be thumping painfully against her ribcage. Except for disgust.

Yeah, that's what she was feeling. Disgust.

"What's my style?" he asked again, and Georgia realized she hadn't answered him.

"Your style is expensive," she said, managing to sound calm and businesslike. "It's sleek and contemporary. Clean lines and exclusive designs."

"Well, these pieces are definitely expensive," he pointed out. Then his gaze dropped to his wrist. Her fingers still clung to the cuff of his shirtsleeve.

She instantly released him, and he smiled knowingly.

"Very true," she said, surprised she sounded so unaffected, even though her fingers seemed to tingle where she'd touched him, "but it's just not what I would have expected you to buy."

"Don't you like it?"

"I love it. But this is *my* style. Of course, I'd love it."

Tristan's gaze moved over her, that slow roam that made her flushed and fidgety, despite her mental pep talk. "And I've told you repeatedly that I happen to like your style."

Georgia gave him a skeptical look, even as a tiny part of her hoped he was being honest. So he might not be genuinely attracted to her, she rationally knew that, but surely it was okay to be flattered that he might honestly like her taste?

He tilted his head in that sexy way of his. "I don't know why you won't believe me."

Her vintage versus his Versace?

Yeah, he was toying with her about this, too, and she was giving him the reaction he wanted.

She could be such a little fool. And curse her fair skin. She could feel the heat creeping into her cheeks, and knew that he could see her blushing.

"I do," he repeated. "And I like this furniture. The *HOT!* offices need a makeover, and this is exactly the type of change I want."

Well, if that's what he wanted, then she certainly wasn't going to stop him. She did love everything he'd chosen. But then again, her own apartment was decorated like a place stolen from the pages of a gothic novel—with a little old Hollywood and French bordello tossed in.

"Besides," he mused aloud, turning back to study the latest desk that had captured his interest, "Finola will absolutely hate it."

Ah, now the sudden shopping spree made sense. This was Tristan establishing for everyone to see, quite literally, that he was the one in control. He was the one making the decisions and calling the shots. Not Finola.

Frankly, Georgia could sort of understand that. She had found every moment of working for Finola White pure hell. She suspected it hadn't been any better for him. Georgia would want to make it clear who was in charge, too, if she were him. Finola probably needed to be reminded of that on a daily basis.

"You know what?" he said almost to himself, and then gestured for the sales clerk to join them again. "I'm going to take everything in this section."

"Ev—everything?" the salesman sputtered.

Georgia nearly choked, too. She looked around. He was talking about six full room sets with desks, chairs, settees, credenzas, rugs, lamps. She couldn't image how many thousands of dollars that had to be.

"Yes," Tristan said as if he was just buying a couple of pieces at a discount warehouse rather than an exclusive furniture store. Then again, Georgia supposed it wasn't a big deal. He was the editor-in-chief of the most successful fashion magazine in the world.

"And let me get a half dozen of those suits of armor."

"A—a half a dozen. Absolutely." The clerk looked as if he was about to have an apoplectic seizure.

Tristan cast a look around the showroom, and then nodded his head, obviously satisfied with his work here.

To Georgia's further surprise, he moved to her side and placed a hand on the small of her back, the action familiar and personal.

She told herself to move away, but her silly legs wouldn't obey. His large hand felt so good, warm, and strong against her.

"Can you have all of this delivered the day after tomorrow? Thursday?"

The salesman nodded, and Georgia was certain this man

would agree to anything to clinch the deal. Of course, she didn't blame him.

"Excellent."

Tristan and the clerk went over to the checkout counter to settle up the bill. Georgia wanted to follow, curious to hear what the grand total was, but her manners forced her to stay away. Not to mention, she'd probably see the receipt when the items were delivered. Most things went through her anyway.

Instead, she only half-attentively browsed. She was stopping here and there to look at a piece, when a lamp caught her attention. It was a sculpture of a voluptuous woman scantily clad, and over her head she held a glowing globe. Her eyes were closed and her face serene. There was a certain appealing strength in her serenity and her utterly feminine form.

Georgia looked at the tag. "The Goddess."

That was a perfect name for her. Then she looked at the price. Yikes. Apparently, goddesses didn't come cheap.

She lingered a moment longer, then moved on.

"Ready?"

She turned from looking at a set of bookends of two knights jousting, creating the illusion that the jousting sticks were piercing straight through the books.

"Yes."

Again, Tristan placed a hand on the small of her back and directed her toward the exit. She debated whether she should move away, but decided there was no way to do so without it being obvious and awkward.

Besides, the touch was probably one of habit. She could see him walking like this with models and designers and other important females in the industry as they discussed business or entered an exclusive party. He probably wasn't even aware he was doing it.

Unlike her, who felt, yet again, as if her heart was going

to bounce out of her chest and onto the floor. Her toes curled in her platform dollies as she allowed herself to enjoy the heat and strength of his touch. Even though she'd just told herself she wasn't going to let him affect her.

But good golly, his hand felt so good.

She stumbled slightly, focused more on the feeling of that large, masculine hand than actually walking. Said hand slid across her back and around her waist to steady her.

"Are you okay?"

Holy moly, no. No, she wasn't, because now she was pressed directly against his side, and she could feel his lean muscles and even more heat.

"I'm sorry," she managed to say, "I'm a klutz on the best of days, and I suddenly felt a little dizzy."

She expected a cocked eyebrow or knowing look. But instead, he just continued to keep her tucked against his side, and he stated, "Well, then we'd better get you something to eat."

"I— I don't think that's it," she told him, finding it hard to focus on anything but the movement of his body against hers.

"Did you have a decent breakfast?"

She thought about her pastry. It was a cheese Danish. Cheese was healthy, kinda, sorta, right?

"It wasn't too bad," she lied.

"Mm-hmm."

She immediately felt a little insulted. Just because she was a little fluffy, or maybe a lot fluffy for the fashion world, didn't give him the right to assume she'd had an unhealthy breakfast. And of course, he would also automatically assume she was hungry now.

"I've seen you eat before," he said.

Oh, here we go. Here came the lecture about watching one's weight, and he was probably going to go into some spiel about the benefits of a macrobiotic diet or some other diet that she could never do. She was a five-time Weight Watchers dropout. She sure as hell wasn't going to be able to stick with a diet of tofu and wheatgrass. Or something equally unpleasant sounding.

"And I know you always eat on the go. Grabbing a bite here or there. And usually not enough of anything to even sustain a bird. You need to sit down and actually enjoy a meal."

Oh. Her irritation instantly deflated. But a bird? Clearly, he could see that wasn't true.

"So we are going to go to my favorite place."

Chapter Five

When Tristan pulled his Bentley Supersport into the small parking lot of the place that was his absolute favorite restaurant, he could tell Georgia was thinking this must be some kind of a mistake. But he parked and shut off the ignition. She looked around as if some posh little bistro must be hidden around there somewhere. But no.

"This is it? Your favorite restaurant?" She stared at the neon sign, with part of the name burnt out so it read ILLIE'S BAR AND GRILL.

"Willie," he clarified, just in case she missed the darkened W. "It's my absolute favorite."

She looked at the bar again, then back to him. "Really? This doesn't seem like your style."

Tristan didn't respond; instead, he slid out of the car and came around to open her door.

"Isn't it time to admit that maybe you don't really know my style?" he said, offering her a hand.

She ignored it, using the car door to lever herself out of the low-slung seat. The action wasn't easy and required her to hike up her tight skirt a bit more than she would have liked, if her reddened cheeks were any indication. But she did manage to pull herself upright without any aid from him. Of course, not before revealing a healthy glimpse of her thigh-high stockings and the bare, creamy skin above them.

Tristan held back a groan. He couldn't hold back his arousal though, and just hoped his suit coat hid that fact.

Embarrassedly, she adjusted her skirt, and then shot Tristan a glance. His eyes locked with hers, and he knew he hadn't managed to hide his desire for her. But instead of saying anything, he held out a hand, gesturing to the building's doorway.

"Right this way."

She hesitated for a moment, and he wasn't sure whether it was because of his lustful look or the looks of the establishment. He decided to assume it was Willie's and not him.

"I know it doesn't look like much, but this place has the very best heroes in New York. And killer onion rings and fries, too. Not to mention, excellent ice-cold beer."

"Heroes?" she said, picking her way carefully over the uneven and cracked asphalt. Tristan automatically moved his hand to the small of her back to steady her. He felt her stiffen slightly as she had the other times he'd touched her, but as before, she didn't move away. He was glad about that.

He looked down at the potholed pavement, making sure she didn't accidently step into one of the gaps, only to find himself admiring how her shoe straps looked circling her dainty ankles.

And the curve of her calves. Which led up to those creamy thighs. Damn.

"Heroes?" she repeated, shooting him a quick quizzical look before returning her attention to the ground.

"Sandwiches," he said rather absently, trying to get control of his lust. "You know, subs."

"Oh," she said, shooting him another look, this one sheepish with a slight smile. "I guess I should know that term, huh?"

"You've never heard of heroes?"

"I guess maybe I have," she said, sounding a little vague herself. Like she was distracted, too. By him? He hoped so. He shouldn't have to suffer through this desperate longing alone. "But we just call them subs in Ohio."

They reached the door, and he opened it for her. "You are from Ohio? I thought you were from Georgia."

"Nooo," she said, and then laughed. "Georgia is just my name, not my name *and* location."

"You have a great laugh."

Georgia stumbled as she took a step over the threshold, and his hand curled around her waist to steady her.

"See, klutz," she said after a moment, her voice a little breathless and her pale skin pink again.

Damn, he wondered if her voice would sound that way in bed, if her skin would get flushed with desire rather than embarrassment. Pink all over. With darker pink around her nipples and dusky pink, moist skin between her thighs.

This time he did groan.

"Oh, no," she said, pulling out of his hold. "Did I hurt you?"

"Hardly," he said, his tone wry, which he could see confused her. Could she really not know the effect she had on him?

She studied him briefly, and then turned her attention to the restaurant. She walked ahead of him into the large, warehouse-style room. One side was set up as a bar with neon lights, tall round bar tables, a long shiny wooden bar, stools, and three pool tables.

The other side was partitioned off by a half wall and frosted panes of glass, where people could sit down to eat.

Tristan's hand returned to her back, because he had to touch her again, even innocuously. He steered her in the direction of the restaurant side.

"Two," he said to the woman standing at the hostess station, surveying a seating chart. She automatically reached for two menus before looking up to see them. When she caught sight of him, she dropped the menus, fumbling to retrieve them.

Vaguely, he was aware of the hostess's attraction to him. But her desire was a pale comparison to Georgia's heady scent. The hostess's scent was like a poor knockoff of an expensive perfume, whereas Georgia's was the real deal, and worth every penny.

"Welcome," the woman said, still clearly flustered by Tristan. But she recovered enough to offer him a coy smile.

Tristan didn't return the look.

"Right this way."

Tristan nodded his thanks, then allowed Georgia to go ahead of him. He watched the sway of Georgia's hips and that perfectly rounded derriere. He imagined taking her from behind. Would she struggle at first, if he just bent her over? Or arch her back and give him exactly what he wanted. He discovered both options excited him.

He nearly made a moan of disappointment as she slid into the booth the hostess directed them to. He missed the view already.

Tristan took a seat across from her, and discovered he was just as pleased to take in Georgia's amazing cleavage and truly lovely face.

After a moment, he realized the hostess still lingered. He raised an eyebrow in silent question. The hostess shifted, seeming to realize she didn't have anything else to say. So she simply mumbled, "Enjoy your meal," and then walked away.

"Does that ever get tiring?" Georgia asked with a smile. But he noticed it didn't quite reach her dark brown eyes.

"Does whatever get tiring?"

"The adoration from women as soon as they see you?"

Ah, she was jealous. He rather liked that idea. His Peaches being possessive.

"I didn't notice," he said, which wasn't quite honest. He had noticed, but he didn't care. He just wanted Peaches' adoration.

At the moment, he amended. Peach was currently his flavor of the month.

"Isn't this place great?" he said, not wanting to talk about other women.

Georgia looked around, and then nodded approvingly. "It's definitely pretty cool. Still not your sty—" She caught herself.

Tristan smiled. "I'm telling you, Peaches, a whole lot of things about me would surprise you."

"Oh, I have no doubt about that," she agreed, and it was her turn to sound wry.

But before he could question her about what she meant, exactly, she looked down at her opened menu and asked, "So which hero is your favorite?"

"I like 'The Works.' "

She found it on the menu. "Wow, that really is the works. Everything but the kitchen sink. That thing has to be enormous."

"It is," he agreed. "But I'm not really into moderation. I have a great fondness for overindulgence." He gave her one of his pointed looks and instantly she blushed.

She returned her attention to her menu.

"I should have known your home state from your resumé," he said suddenly.

She looked back up, surprised. "You were the one who hired me? I always assumed it was Finola."

He laughed at that. "Since you worked for her, I'd think you would have realized she didn't do anything for herself. Not when others could do it for her."

"I-I—" She clearly didn't know the correct response. Georgia was a smart lady. She knew he was telling the truth, but she also knew any negative response could be unprofessional and potentially come back to bite her. So, instead, she changed the subject. "Did you hire her other personal assistants by just looking over their resumés, then calling to tell them they had the job? No interviews or anything?"

"Well, the way Finola went through assistants, it hardly seemed worth the effort."

"Well, there goes my theory that I was hired sight unseen because my resumé just popped when compared to all the others," she said with a slight smile that hinted at the dimples framing her pretty lips.

"Maybe it did," he said, smiling back.

She made a face. "Well, you clearly don't remember a thing about it, so that sort of kills that notion, doesn't it?"

"Well, one thing is for certain," he said slowly, straightening his silverware, "you are definitely my favorite personal assistant. And like I said, I hired many."

Georgia didn't say anything, and he looked back up at her.

She had blushed again. He loved her easy reaction to him. And even though he knew she thought it was just one of his lines, he was being honest. She was by far his favorite. He hadn't even mustered up a mild attraction to most of them.

Hmm, now that he thought about it, he wondered why. What made her different?

"Hi, there." A waitress appeared at the edge of their booth, smiling at Georgia first. But as soon as her attention turned to Tristan, Georgia might as well have been invisible.

"Would you like to hear the specials?" she said, her voice low. This one was definitely more seasoned than the hostess, and she wasn't going to have any trouble going for what she wanted.

Normally, Tristan would have gone along with the waitress's interest. It was easy, and he was, after all, a demon of lust. But today, her attention just irritated him. He wanted to focus on the woman he was sitting with. He wanted to have Georgia to himself.

"No need," Tristan said, his tone unusually curt. Again, not how he usually treated a woman who was openly attracted to him.

The young blonde's face fell.

"Want to try my favorite?" he asked Georgia, all that curtness leaving as he spoke to her. He didn't wait for her to answer.

"We're going to have two of The Works with the onion rings. Plus a side of fries. And two of your Willie's pale ales. Tall."

Again, the blonde looked thoroughly disappointed that he was so concise. Then out of sheer jealousy, the waitress raised an eyebrow in Georgia's direction. "That's a lot of food. Far more than I could ever eat."

Tristan didn't miss the pointed jab, and from Georgia's deflated look, neither did she.

"Well, the lady here," he said in an acerbic tone, "is humoring me, since this is my favorite place. Although, I'm beginning to wonder why. The service isn't what I remember."

The blond waitress had the good grace to look worried.

"I'll be right back with your beers." She hurried away from the table and straight to the bar.

Georgia watched the waitress's departure with a mixture of relief and sympathy.

Peaches was too kindhearted. The waitress had been blatantly rude to her, yet his sweet assistant felt bad for her.

The idea that Georgia might possibly be used to comments like the waitress's bothered him. He couldn't say why. That comment wouldn't affect his mission to have this woman. So why did he really care about Georgia's potentially wounded ego?

He didn't want to contemplate that, so instead he said, "You popped."

"I— popped." She immediately turned her attention away from the unimportant waitress and down at herself. She touched the lacing on her corseted top, as if she expected it to have popped open.

Which would be nice. He'd love to see more of those luscious breasts of hers.

"As soon as I saw you—*you* definitely popped."

It took her a moment to understand he was referring back to her comment about her resumé. Then as expected, she blushed.

Now she busied herself with straightening her silverware. "Well, I'm sure I definitely wasn't the usual applicant. Multicolored hair, funky glasses, vintage wear."

"No, you weren't. Frankly, you were more interesting and quite refreshing."

She stopped spacing her knife and spoon the perfect few centimeters apart.

"Interesting and refreshing." She smiled wryly. "That's a nice way to put it."

Tristan sighed. "Do you ever just take a compliment?"

Honestly, it was starting to bother him. He was so damned attracted to this woman. Couldn't she see that? Feel it?

She stared at him for a moment, but then went back to fiddling with her spoon.

"Sorry," she said, then mumbled something about "going along with his games," but he didn't quite hear what she said, because the waitress returned at the same time.

"Here you go." She set down two large glasses of beer, then waited.

Really, this chick wasn't going to be put off easily, was she?

Tristan lifted his glass to his lips and took a testing sip, even though he'd had the same ale dozens of times.

"It's great, thank you," he said dismissively.

"Can I get you anything else?"

Tristan shot the woman a look. He might have appreciated this woman's persistence another day, but definitely not at the moment. "I think we're good right now."

The waitress lingered just a moment longer as if she was trying to think of something else to say, but apparently nothing came to her.

"Well, just let me know if you think of something," she said with a sweet smile. "My name is Chrissy—if you need anything."

Her eagerness actually made Tristan feel a little disgusted. Did *Chrissy* not see he was here with another woman?

Tristan thanked the waitress again and she finally left, probably heading back to the kitchen to tell the cook he needed to get a rush on those sandwiches and onion rings.

"She's just trying to get your attention," Georgia said, reaching for her own beer.

His dark brows jutted together as he frowned.

"What?" she asked.

"Trying too hard," he stated.

"She's actually quite pretty," Georgia said.

Was she really trying to convince him to be interested in the rude, pushy waitress? That idea pissed him off—for a reason he didn't entirely understand.

"The hostess is pretty, too," Georgia added. "And she was flirting with you as well."

She was trying to get him interested in one of the restaurant staff. Someone other than her. Well, he wasn't going to be that easily distracted.

He returned his attention to Georgia and shrugged. "I guess I didn't really notice. I'm preoccupied with other company."

She stared at him for a moment, and then to his surprise she laughed.

He smiled, but gave her a quizzical look. "What's so funny?"

"I appreciate your kindness in trying to make me feel special, but we both know I'm not really your type, so there is no need to play that game with me. I'd totally understand if you wanted to get a number or two while you are here. After all, they're lining up to give them to you."

She jerked her head in the direction of the hostess podium. Several female staffers and even one male employee, covertly, or not so covertly, looked in their direction. They almost comically tried to look busy when they realized Tristan had noticed them.

Almost comical, but he wasn't amused by Georgia's dismissal. He was certain she had been jealous of the hostess, but now, he didn't feel that energy. He didn't even feel much of her usual desire for him. Why? What was going on here?

"All day you've been insisting you know my style," he said, feeling very annoyed. This lunch was not going as he'd envisioned. "So you should know that humility is definitely *not* my style. That being said, you asked me a question, and I told you the truth. I didn't really notice those other women's reactions. Actually, I did notice, but I'm not interested."

Georgia nodded, immediately looking down again, clearly intimidated by his harsh reaction. Which wasn't really the response he'd wanted either. Honestly, he'd wanted to spend the afternoon with the woman who'd been driving him to distraction from the very moment she'd teetered into his office on a pair of her ridiculous platform heels.

Was that too much to ask? To have a break from demon rebellions, insubordinate employees, talking canines, and stress to simply enjoy the company of a woman he found so damned attractive he couldn't think straight?

He started to open his mouth, to tell her just that, when

he realized, while he did consider her his right-hand woman, she was still a mere mortal, unaware of the war waging around her. If Peaches was reluctant to flirt with him now, imagine if she knew the truth?

The waitress arrived with their food, but this time she didn't hang around. Maybe it was because she was busy, or maybe because she'd finally gotten the hint. Either way, Tristan was glad to be alone with Georgia.

He was determined to feel his Peaches' attraction again. It couldn't really be gone.

"I can tell you one thing that's very much my style," he said, reaching for the bottle of ketchup as he talked. "A sexy woman in thigh-high stockings."

She looked up from the pile of food in front of her. She didn't say anything as he poured ketchup beside the mound of fries. He set the bottle down, and then sucked a little excess of the red condiment from his index finger.

She watched the action, her dark eyes huge behind her frames.

Suddenly, he felt her desire like a rush of hot air from a radiator. Her scent filled his nostrils, even blotting out the smells of their delicious food.

He smiled smugly. Oh, she could pretend to not want him. She could pretend she didn't care if he wanted someone else. But only for so long.

He didn't ponder too closely why a sense of relief mingled with his smugness.

"Would you like me to tell you what I like to do to a woman in thigh-high stockings?"

Georgia immediately shook her head, and it was his turn to laugh.

Chapter Six

Georgia shifted in her seat, wishing she wasn't so damned obvious. She felt like she might as well be naked, sitting across from her boss.

She was so stupidly attracted to him, and she knew she wasn't hiding it. She'd tried. She had even tried to draw his attention to the other women here. But he wasn't having any of it.

He enjoyed messing with her too much.

And it always worked. His suggestive words had her thoroughly aroused. Georgia shifted again, feeling the dampness between her thighs. But she forced herself to ignore that and to focus on her food. The sooner they ate, the sooner she could get away from this evilly seductive man.

"Tasty, huh?" he said as she took a bite of her sandwich. She couldn't answer right away with her mouth full, so he waited for her to finish chewing, his green eyes locked on her lips.

Even that seemed designed to be suggestive, flirty.

Finally, she swallowed and wiped her lips with her paper napkin.

"You love to mess with me, don't you?"

He shot her an innocent look. "What do you mean?"

She didn't answer. Instead, she took another drink of beer.

He chuckled, damn him. It was far too easy for him to make her react. Far too easy.

"I don't mean to make you uncomfortable," he said after she set down her glass. "But I do love how easily you get flustered by my attention."

Well, that was pretty honest, she realized.

He took a sip of his own beer.

"Actually, I do enjoy messing with you. It amuses me very much," he said, surprising her again with his honesty. "But I suppose it is inappropriate for an employer to flirt with an employee."

"Yes," she said flatly, "it is. It's actually called sexual harassment."

Tristan leaned back in his seat and regarded her seriously. "I'm hoping that isn't actually a threat, Georgia."

Georgia squirmed a little under his stern gaze. It hadn't been a threat. The truth was she hadn't even thought before she'd said it. She'd actually been thinking more about the fact that everything she'd believed about his attention was true. He did find amusement in her reaction to him. Just as she'd always thought. She'd been absolutely right: he was entertaining himself with her silly reactions to him. Her pathetically transparent reactions.

And that hurt a little. Or maybe a lot.

But hey, what wouldn't be funny about a woman like her blushing and fidgeting under his flirty attention, especially when she knew he'd never really be interested in her? She was sure it would be quite an entertaining joke, if she wasn't the butt of it.

But she managed to push her wounded ego aside and meet his gaze.

"No, it wasn't a threat."

Pursuing a lawsuit had never crossed her mind, to be honest. After all, she didn't think she'd win it. Tristan McIntyre and *HOT!* wielded too much power. And who would believe someone as powerful and drop-dead gorgeous as Tristan would sexually harass *her*? Especially surrounded by the plethora of beautiful women he was. Some of the world's most beautiful women.

And he was making lascivious comments to his size fourteen, goth/rockabilly personal assistant in her wacky framed glasses and vintage store clothing? No one would buy that.

But more than that, she'd never considered the idea of sexual harassment, because she was too busy not making waves. Because she needed this job. Period. She couldn't hope to walk into any other magazine or periodical and start at the salary she was making at *HOT!* And she needed every dime of that money. Otherwise, she would have quit on her own, long before Tristan became her boss.

Tristan regarded her for a moment more, and then nodded. "Good. I'm glad we don't have a problem."

He returned his attention to his food.

She did the same, although not with the same enthusiasm he did. She wished she could just merrily eat her lunch, feeling that everything was hunky dory. Instead, she was feeling—she was feeling hurt. Talk about a stupid reaction.

"So what do you think?"

She blinked up at him. "What do I think?"

He smiled, just a straightforward, non-flirty smile, but her damned heart did a cartwheel in her chest.

"About the food?"

"Oh." She forced a polite smile. "It's very good."

In truth, she couldn't have told him what anything tasted like. Nor could she really tell anyone what Tristan talked about for the remainder of the lunch. Every now and then, she'd pick up something about the redecorating of the *HOT!* offices, or other comments about work, but through it all, Georgia just nodded, pretended to listen, picked at her food, and stewed.

The more she thought about it, the more it really chapped

her ass that he could simply say, "Oh, yes, I totally like messing with you—it amuses me," and expect her to have no reaction.

Oh, he expected her to react to his flirty words and naughty smiles, but telling her that he was toying with her—now that she was just supposed to accept with no response at all.

"Excuse me."

Georgia snapped out of her bitter reverie as Tristan stood.

"I'm going to use the restroom," he told her. "If the waitress comes back, ask for the check."

She nodded, although she irrationally wanted to snap at him and tell him to get the check himself. Which she knew would have been a silly response, but she was annoyed.

She watched as he walked across the room. Several female heads turned as he passed. The hostess even hurried over to ask him if she could help him with anything. He shook his head and pointed toward the restroom sign, but not without bestowing one of his charming smiles on the young woman.

More irritation filled Georgia.

The waitress appeared, looking around expectantly for Tristan. Of course.

"We'll take the check," Georgia told her, instantly regretting her harsh tone. It wasn't this girl's fault that Tristan McIntyre was insanely attractive and he knew it.

Another few minutes passed and Tristan stepped out of the bathroom. Again, appreciative female gazes were on him, but he simply strode back to the table, unaware of their looks. Or at least not acknowledging them.

"Did the waitress come by?"

Georgia nodded.

He slipped back into his seat, and then frowned at her plate.

"You didn't eat much. Is something wrong?"

Before she could catch herself, she snapped, "What? Does something have to be wrong for the chubby girl not to finish her lunch?"

Tristan frowned, although his green eyes widened. He was surprised and confused.

And she didn't blame him. She certainly had never spoken to him that way before. She hadn't dared, so what had gotten into her now?

But the waitress came up with their bill, not giving Tristan a chance to ask Georgia what the hell was wrong with her. But Georgia was sure this was just a small reprieve before that question came.

Why hadn't she just kept her mouth shut? What was the point of acting like a silly, petulant child?

Tristan glanced at the check and handed the waitress a hundred dollar bill. "Keep the change."

The waitress beamed. She certainly didn't think he was a jerk, which somehow made Georgia feel even more stupid.

"Are you ready to go?" he asked Georgia, his tone calm with no hint of confusion or anger.

She nodded, sliding out from the booth. They both walked to the car, although this time his hand wasn't on the small of her back, waiting to steady her as she picked her way over the cracked asphalt.

But he did open the car door for her, and she slipped onto the leather seat. She waited nervously as he walked around the car and got inside, his large form seeming to eat up all the space in the car.

He didn't speak as he turned the key and the car purred to life. Nor did he say anything as they pulled out of the parking lot and headed back in the direction of *HOT!*

The silence ate at her, making her more and more uncomfortable, and when they finally reached the parking garage of the *HOT!* building, Georgia couldn't take it anymore.

As Tristan parked in his reserved parking place, she turned to him, nervously blurting out, "I'm sorry for being so rude back there. I—I don't know why I said that."

He glanced at her, his expression unreadable. Then he got out of the car.

Georgia's stomach sank. This was it. She'd managed to keep her job while working for Finola White, but now she was going to lose it. She could not lose this job.

She reached for the door handle, but Tristan was there, opening it for her. This time when he offered her his hand, she accepted it, deciding no good would come of refusing him again.

His hand was warm and strong and he helped her out easily. Then he promptly released her fingers.

He studied her for a moment, his expression still indecipherable.

"Thank you for helping me pick out the furniture," he finally said. "Head back to the office. I have some other errands I need to run."

Surprised that that was all he was going to say, she could only nod.

She walked away from him, pausing at the door that led into their building and the elevators up to the *HOT!* offices. He was watching her, but when she looked back, it was his turn to nod at her.

She still couldn't read anything he was thinking, and that scared her, but she just went into the building and back to her desk.

After a moment of nerves and worries, she decided the best way to secure her job was to get back to work and start checking the items off her list.

By six o'clock, the list was completed and Tristan still

hadn't returned. That didn't help her nerves, but she told herself not to borrow trouble. She'd worry when she knew she had something to worry about.

Plus, she had plenty of other things that needed her attention.

Still, while standing on the subway, jerking and jostling toward home, she wondered if she'd have a job tomorrow morning. She needed this job.

But when she stepped into her apartment, all thoughts about *HOT!* and its infuriating editor–in–chief disappeared.

"How is she?" Georgia asked softly as soon as she entered her small kitchen to find her neighbor Ellen fixing two cups of tea.

Ellen automatically reached into the cupboard to get a third cup.

"She's been pretty good today. Just one little bout of confusion, but overall, today was a good day."

Georgia smiled, maybe her first genuine smile of the day, and left Ellen to head into the living room.

"Hi, Grammy," she said, still smiling as she entered the room.

Her frail, sweet-faced grandmother set down her knitting and smiled back at her. Georgia could immediately see that today definitely was one of her good days. Recognition was clear in the old woman's hazy blue eyes.

"Georgie, how was your day?"

"Ah, never mind my day, Grammy. HHHhhhow was yours?"

Her grandmother picked up her knitting. "Well, I'm almost done with your hat."

Georgia admired it, amazed at the detailing her grandmother could still do even with her gnarled fingers.

"It's beautiful, Grammy."

Her grandmother looked very pleased, but then she

frowned. "I don't remember what I did with the mittens though. I thought I made them."

"You did," Georgia immediately assured her. "I have them in my room."

"Oh, right," her grandmother said as if she remembered, but Georgia knew she didn't. But that was just a small memory lapse. Just a blip compared to some days.

This was the person Georgia was working for. She was determined to keep her grandmother here living with her as long as possible. And Georgia needed the money she made at *HOT!* to do that.

Chapter Seven

"Where were you all day?"

Tristan pulled in a deep breath, willing himself not to actually kick the little four-legged harpy. Shit, with his luck, Dippy would call PETA himself and report Tristan if he did. Even demons were wary of PETA.

"I had some errands to do," he said absently, but his mind wasn't really on his nonexistent errands or his canine co-conspirator's disgruntled demeanor.

"Where is Georgia?"

She usually didn't leave for the day without checking in with him. Tonight, she hadn't even called to make sure he didn't need anything before she left. He checked his watch, and it wasn't even eight p.m. yet. She'd worked much later and still checked with him before leaving the office.

"I don't know," Dippy growled. "I imagine she is home. But you need to stop fixating on your emo personal assistant and focus on this takeover. Do you even know how things are going in the mail room with Finola? Shouldn't you be more worried about that than your assistant? Georgia Sullivan doesn't have the power to bring this whole revolt down around your demonic ears. Finola White absolutely does."

Tristan dropped his briefcase next to his desk and headed to his computer.

"Are you listening?" the hellhound demanded.

Tristan turned on his computer, waiting for it to boot up. As much as he hated to admit it, he was. And he'd already come to these same conclusions while driving around all afternoon.

He was far too obsessed with Peaches. He couldn't even argue with a damned dog about that.

He'd wanted to lead this demonic invasion, and now that he was heading it up, all he could think about was bagging his emo assistant.

"Technically she's not emo," Tristan found himself saying. "More rockabilly goth, I'd say."

Dippy growled again. "Damn it, Tristan, I don't give a shit if she's an emo, mod, hipster, or effin yuppy. We need to get this takeover moving. Have you completely forgotten that we need to prove ourselves to Satan?"

That should be pretty hard to forget, shouldn't it? Satan was—well, Satan. That did tend to make him memorable. Yet Tristan hadn't been focused on their boss.

"I'm perfectly aware that I— we need to prove ourselves." He honestly was, and he had to figure out how to get his focus back.

He had even had to admit to himself, while on his drive, that he hadn't truly gone to buy furniture to make the office his domain. He'd just wanted to get away from this place and be with Georgia. Why?

He'd originally told himself it was the stress of Finola and Dippy, but ultimately he'd had to admit the truth.

"I find her . . . distracting," Tristan admitted, almost as much to himself as to Dippy.

"So get rid of her. You know firsthand personal assistants are a dime a dozen. You don't need her."

Tristan immediately shook his head. "No. I do need her. We need her. She's loyal. And good at her job. She's become my right hand here."

"Maybe you should use your right hand, and get rid of the damned hard-on you have for her," Dippy muttered. "Then maybe you'll be able to focus on your damned work."

Tristan had done that. It didn't help.

Then he paused. Use his right hand. That was it. Why hadn't he thought of that before? There wasn't anything particularly special about Georgia, except that he hadn't had her. Once he plucked this piece of forbidden fruit, and took a few bites, his desire, his curiosity would be quenched.

Of course. That was it. He just needed to fuck Georgia and she'd be out of his system; then he could focus on the task at hand.

And he intended to set this plan in motion tonight.

He opened a file titled "Employee Contacts," only to find it empty. Yeah, as if Finola had kept track of such things. He looked toward his old office, realizing he had all those numbers on the computer in there.

He stood and headed to that computer with Dippy on his heels.

"What are you doing?"

He didn't answer the mutt until he sat down at his old desk and punched the button to turn on the desktop computer.

"I plan to take care of this problem. ASAP."

"Very good," Dippy growled.

Tristan ignored the animal. After a moment, he found the file he was looking for; Georgia's number was listed. Score.

He immediately pulled out his cell phone and programmed Georgia's home address into it. Why didn't he already have it in his phone?

Because Georgia was usually here. Yeah, it was so not normal for her to not be here.

He glanced at the address again, committing it to memory; then he rose.

"Where are you going?" Dippy demanded, scampering behind Tristan's determined strides.

"To pick some forbidden fruit," Tristan said. "And this time, it's not an apple but a peach."

"I'll come with you." Dippy fell into prancing steps behind Tristan.

Tristan paused. "I don't think so. I can definitely handle this one on my own."

Who knew hellhounds were little sexual deviants?

"You go check on Finola."

"How?"

"You're a hellhound," Tristan said. "I'm quite sure you can figure out how to get to her."

"We don't even know if she's still in the building," Dippy pointed out.

"Then just wait for me to return."

"And when will that be?" the dog growled.

"Not long." Okay, that was probably a lie. Somehow, Tristan didn't think a quickie was going to get Georgia out of his system. But give him a night, and he'd have this obsession under control.

Tristan stopped beside Georgia's desk and looked down at his canine shadow.

"Seriously, Dippy," he whispered, so no one passing by would realize he was conversing with a dog, "you need to stay here."

Dippy sighed. "Fine." He sat, looking peeved, but at least obeying.

"Very good," Tristan said, relieved that for once the little pest was listening. "Hold the fort. I'll be back soon."

He heard Dippy muttering as he walked away. Something to the effect that holding the fort would be easier with opposable thumbs.

Tristan knew it would be, and that's why he didn't plan for Dippy to ever have them.

"So? Did you speak with her?"

Gabriel shook his head. "Georgia Sullivan was out of the office for most of the day. With McIntyre. Then she left early—well, earlier than usual. Should I go to her home?"

Eugene shook his head. "No. She's already going to be unnerved about what you have to tell her. It would be even more disturbing to have a stranger show up at her door to tell her. We'll have to wait until tomorrow."

Gabriel nodded, but he wondered how Eugene could be so patient and calm, especially with Finola White in the mail room. Having her around, even for one day, was a vivid reminder that the DIA operatives needed to do their jobs as quickly as possible and get these demons under control.

"Eugene?"

And speak of the devil. The blond-haired, alabaster-skinned, and icy-eyed devil.

Both men turned to see Finola standing in the doorway. Why was she still here? Gabriel had no doubt that she had never stayed so late when she was the head of the magazine. So why so late now? Did she suspect something about the mail room already?

"Eugene— I mean, sir." She smiled sweetly.

"Can I help you, Finola?"

She smiled, this time more sheepishly than sweet. "Yes. I'm sorry to interrupt, but I need to ask you for help again."

Gabriel was shocked to see that Eugene actually returned the demon's smile. Now that he saw the easy upturn of his boss's lips, Gabriel realized he rarely saw Eugene smile. It seemed odd that when he did, it would be at a demon. Especially this demon—the one who had been their nemesis since they'd started this battle.

And on top of that, Eugene's smile looked genuine, not forced in the least. Gabriel looked back and forth between the two. Worry, tight and unpleasant, spread through his chest. Was Eugene actually falling for this demon's tricks? She did have an attractive human form, in an unusual and exotic way. And she did know how to be charming. But it was all just a façade. It was a mask hiding what lay beneath—pure evil.

"What seems to be the problem now, Finola?" Eugene sounded perfectly patient and kind. Maybe even a little sympathetic.

Gabriel stared at his boss. Did he truly feel that way?

"Well, I was just finishing up sorting my mail, but I got confused again on what order I'm supposed to organize everything on the cart," she explained with a flip of her long hair and another sheepish smile.

Eugene nodded as if sorting mail was actually complicated. "I'm currently in the middle of something," he said.

Yes, like trying to thwart a demonic takeover, Gabriel thought wryly.

"But Gabriel here should be able to help you," Eugene finished.

Gabriel shot his boss a startled look. No, he didn't want to interact with this evil creature. He again wished he could just resort to the old ways of dealing with a demon.

Lop her head off and call it a day.

But those times were gone. Now the DIA believed in demonic rehabilitation, and Gabriel had seen it work, with lesser demons. And certainly with the possessed. But he still had his doubts it could work with more powerful demons, like Finola. And even if it could, that didn't mean Gabriel wanted to be directly involved with the demonically challenged.

He saw himself more as an enforcer brought in if all other attempts at rehabilitation failed. He was ultimately a demon slayer.

But he was also subordinate to Eugene, so he found himself nodding. "I can help."

He couldn't muster a smile, however.

Finola's pale gaze shifted to him, sweeping over him from head to toe, and he got the feeling she completely assessed him with that quick once-over. He also saw keen intelligence in her icy eyes. That startled him.

But then she masked that flash of intelligence behind the tilt of her head and a flirty smile.

He'd been watching her now for some time, and when she'd been in control of *HOT!* and the takeover, he'd only seen the decadent, spoiled creature who loved her own comfort and wealth. He'd seen a self-indulgent diva, and he realized now, in part, that had been exactly what she'd wanted him to see. What she'd wanted everyone to see.

But she'd been ousted, and she was pissed, and now he saw in those pale gray eyes that she didn't intend to stay in exile. She had a plan. The wheels were turning, and she was dangerous.

Did Eugene see that, too?

When he looked back to his boss, Eugene nodded his head, but Gabriel couldn't tell if that was somehow an answer to his unasked question. It couldn't be, could it? It had to be a simple nod of approval that Gabriel was agreeing to deal with her.

"Why don't we head back to your station, and you can show me," Gabriel said, gesturing for her to lead the way.

Finola's shrewd gaze warmed. Well, as much as her eyes' iciness could warm. She smiled broadly, to hide that calculating coldness.

"Thank you so much."

He bobbed his head, finding that his disgust made it hard to speak.

She led the way back to her station, which was covered with mail that she clearly hadn't touched. Demons were notoriously lazy, unless they were working toward something they really wanted.

She beamed him with another smile. And she was working on something she wanted right now. But what was it?

"I don't know why I can't remember how to do this." She sighed, looking down at the strewn pile of missives. "It seems so simple when others explain it to me. And I hate to keep you here so late. Were you about to go home?"

She flipped her hair again. Then, almost seductively, she brushed her fingertips over one of the manila envelopes.

"Not quite yet," he said, ignoring her attempt to flirt. "Okay, let's go through it again."

He showed her how to sort the letters by the recipient's location, bundling them with rubber bands, and arranging them from lowest floor to highest on the cart.

She made appropriate comments and noises to show she was paying attention and comprehending. Several times she brushed against him under the guise of getting a better view of what he was doing. Each fleeting touch made him cringe on the inside. He wouldn't show her any reaction whatsoever.

"That's pretty much it," he told her, stepping away from her as she leaned in again to thoroughly study the bundle of envelopes he'd just placed on the metal cart.

"Okay. It's very simple," she said, giving him another feigned, "I'm so silly" look.

"Yes, it is," Gabriel said flatly, not giving her the ego stroke she expected, but her smile didn't slip.

Instead, she reached for several of the envelopes, scanned the addresses, and then organized them as he'd done.

Good, she had it. And he was out of here.

He had started to walk away, when she stopped him.

"Do you like working down here?"

He turned back to her, narrowing his eyes. Why was she asking?

"Yes, I do."

She nodded, reaching for a rubber band. Her perfectly manicured fingers curled around one of the beige bands like the talons of a bird snatching up a worm.

She paused, and then tilted her head as she regarded him. Her pale gaze held his. "I'm surprised. You seem too intelligent, too ambitious, for a job like this."

"You got all of that from me teaching you how to sort mail?"

She smiled again, but this time, he noticed her grin didn't look nearly as sweet. It was more— a smirk.

His skin prickled with awareness. She was up to something. The air suddenly seemed heavier, laden with a palpable energy.

"I just— just get this feeling there is something more you want."

His eyes remained locked with hers, but after a moment, he looked away. Breaking her gaze had required physical strength on his part. She was definitely up to something . . . but more than that, she was *doing* something. More energy surrounded him, thick and suffocating.

"I'm fine working here," he said resolutely, but he didn't meet her eyes again.

"I'm sorry to pry. I just get these feelings about people sometimes, and the feeling I got from you seemed to be a vibe of dissatisfaction. Like you are missing something. Or searching for something."

Gabriel found her words as unnerving as her gaze had been. His skin prickled again, and he backed away from her, needing to put more space between them, even though there was now a good five feet and a metal table separating them.

"I'm not sure why you would feel that way," he said, trying to sound casual, even uninterested. He was anything but. Her words unsettled him, even though they really said nothing in particular. In fact, it was a rather vague observation that could probably apply to a majority of the population. Yet still, he felt as if she'd somehow pulled them directly out of his mind.

But how and why? He hadn't been thinking anything like that. Missing something? Searching for something?

She had to be saying things, hoping something would stick and freak him out. Demons were always playing mind games. He knew that.

"Well, I'll let you get to your work," he said, deciding dismissing her was the best plan right now, until he figured out what she was up to and why he was feeling so—so strange.

He began to walk away again, but again her words stopped him.

"Wait, you aren't searching for something. You are searching for *someone*."

Her words hit him like a sucker punch to the gut, but he still refused to look at her, or to show any reaction, period.

Searching for someone.

What did she know about him? What could she sense or see?

This time, he didn't have to meet her gaze to have that . . . almost . . . almost invaded feeling. But he did need to get away from her. He strode away, not stopping until he was on the other side of the room, back at his own desk, separated from her by desks and machinery and people.

He dropped down onto his chair, his knees weak. His hands shook as he busied himself with turning on his computer. When he finally looked back toward Finola's workstation, she was working, but he could see a small, smug smile curling the corners of her ruby red lips.

And in that moment he knew something for certain about Finola White. She was a much more evil demon than he'd realized. And much, much more dangerous.

Chapter Eight

Sweat slicked his palms. Sweaty palms, him? This was crazy. When did a demon of lust ever get nervous about talking to a woman? Talking to anyone, really?

Still Tristan found himself standing outside Georgia's door, hesitating to even knock.

What was wrong with him?

He raised his hand, but paused again. How would she react to him just showing up at her door?

Seriously? He was here to seduce the woman. Who cared if she was a little startled to see him there? She'd soon be naked and writhing underneath him.

What if she quit after that? He knew Peaches had a backbone. She might blush and act self-conscious under his attention, but that wasn't because she lacked determination. Would she really continue to work at *HOT!* after diddling the boss?

Hell, a woman didn't dress the way she did and not have self-assurance. Peaches was audacious, even if she didn't always seem to know it. And he loved that. His cock hardened at the very thought of her over-the-top clothes and makeup and hair.

But maybe he should wait. Maybe he needed a better plan. He did need her at the job just as much as he needed to be buried deep inside her.

He glanced down at the tented front of his Armani trousers. Okay, he needed to be deep inside her pretty damned badly.

He might find her accidental confidence sweetly sexy, but in this case he didn't think it would help his cause. Hell, he might have a hard time even seducing her. It was a rare admission for a demon of lust.

Instantly, his cock hardened more and pulsed in his tailored pants at the thought of his Peaches defying him. Not giving him what he wanted.

Suddenly, his nerves didn't matter. He had to see her.

He rapped on the door loudly. Silence greeted him. Was she not home yet? Was she avoiding him?

He raised his hand to knock again when the door opened. He was greeted by a startled Georgia. Her wide eyes shifted from him to his raised fist. He immediately dropped his hand to his side.

"Tris— Mr. McIntyre," she said, her voice breathy, her dark eyes still huge.

"Will you please call me Tristan?" he said as he had many times before, but this time it wasn't a flirty suggestion. It was a plea.

"Okay," she said, clearly too surprised to see him to argue. "Why— why are you here?"

"You didn't check in with me before you left." Damn, that sounded almost pathetically forlorn. As if she'd abandoned him.

"No, but I left a note on your desk. You didn't see it?"

Tristan shook his head, realizing he'd been so wrapped up in finding her address, he hadn't even noticed.

"I'm sorry," she said, "I should have called you directly."

"Yes, you should have," Tristan agreed, his tone harsh because of his irritation with his own preoccupation.

He needed her. He'd never *needed* a woman like this. To the point of total distraction.

He'd sped over here, nearly wrecking his car in the crazy New York traffic. He was even double-parked. All of that was—well, desperate. He did not like feeling desperate.

But she clearly misunderstood where his annoyance was aimed.

"I'm sorry. I-I hope this doesn't mean that—" she paused, her face pale with what appeared to be worry bordering on panic.

Why was she so upset?

"I just hope—" She stopped again, and he couldn't understand what had her so worked up. He was the one who was acting like a crazed maniac.

"I—" she started again, when a loud crash echoed from inside her apartment.

Her eyes widened, and her nervousness turned to real fear. Without hesitation or a word to him, she spun and rushed back into her apartment.

Tristan debated for half a second whether he should follow her, and then hurried inside himself.

Even though Tristan didn't take the time to inspect her place closely, he still saw that the rooms were decorated with her unique style. There was furniture that was somewhere between shabby chic and French boudoir and lots of deep, sensual colors, reds and golds and deep oranges.

But he was more curious about what could make her hurry away from him like that. She clearly had thought she was in trouble, so it surprised him that she'd dare leave during their conversation.

And from the sound of the noise, she wasn't alone. Suddenly, he realized that he didn't even know if Georgia lived by herself. Maybe she had a roommate. Or a boyfriend. Or a husband.

The idea stole his breath like a sucker punch to the stomach. No, she couldn't have a husband. She would wear a ring. Peaches was loyal, she wouldn't hide her commitment like some people did. She'd wear a wedding ring proudly.

But a boyfriend . . . that could be possible. Would her boyfriend share? A threesome maybe. He was a demon of lust; a threesome was mild experimentation compared to some things he'd done in his past.

But he instantly found himself dismissing the idea. He didn't want to share Peaches. Even with her boyfriend. If she had a boyfriend.

Only one way to find out. He headed down a short hallway, glancing into the first door he got to, even though it was dark. The bathroom.

Then he heard Georgia's voice, heavy with worry, sounding even huskier than usual.

"Oh, my gosh, are you okay?"

He heard another voice, female, respond, but he couldn't quite make out the words, although he got the impression of someone soft-spoken, maybe a little disoriented.

He could tell which room the voices came from, and he headed in the same direction.

At the doorway, he paused, taking in the sight before him. Georgia was helping a frail, white-haired lady in a long nightgown back into a bed. Georgia got her settled back onto the mattress, making sure the old woman was comfortable before straightening.

"Are you sure you are okay?" Georgia asked again, fiddling once more with the covers.

"Fine," the woman said, although Tristan could see confusion in her dark eyes. "I just lost my balance."

She shook her head. "But I don't recall how."

"You have to use your cane, Grammy," Georgia explained, showing her the four-footed cane standing beside the nightstand. "Your balance isn't what it once was."

The old woman shook her head again, clearly not recalling any of it. But instead of growing more confused and panicked, she smiled sweetly. "Maybe I bumped my head, too."

"Maybe," Georgia agreed with a smile of her own. "But right now you have to rest."

She arranged pillows behind the woman's head.

"Here is your book." Georgia handed her what looked like a dog-eared mystery novel. "And I'll bring you a cup of tea."

"Thank you, Marianne," the old woman said. "I would love some tea."

"Grammy, I'm Georgia."

The old woman's already age-creased brow wrinkled further. "Georgia?"

Then she nodded, recognition clear in her eyes. "Yes, of course, Georgia."

"I'll get you some tea, Grammy." Georgia straightened from fussing over the woman, but her grandmother's next comment stopped her.

"And who is the gentleman in the doorway?"

Georgia slowly looked over her shoulder to see Tristan standing there. Their eyes locked for a moment, and before Georgia could say who he was, her grandmother spoke.

"Georgia, this is your beau, isn't it? I knew you had one."

Georgia shot a surprised look at her grandmother.

"No, Grammy, this is—" she started, but for some reason Tristan couldn't explain himself, he cut her off.

"Hello," he said politely, stepping into the room. "I'm Tristan."

"Tristan." Grammy smiled, clearly liking his name. He wondered why. Her next words gave him his answer.

"My first love was named Tristan."

Georgia frowned at her grandmother. "Grampy wasn't your first love?"

Grammy smiled and patted her granddaughter's hand. "Your grandfather was my true love. Tristan Howe was my first love."

The old woman returned her attention to Tristan. "How long have you been seeing my sweet Georgia?"

"Grammy, he's not—"

Again, Tristan interrupted Georgia. "Only for a little while."

The old woman nodded.

"I'm sorry to meet you in this state," Grammy said, suddenly realizing she was in bed. "But it seems I'm not quite myself today."

"No need to apologize," Tristan assured her. "I don't want to interrupt your rest, but I did want to check on you and Georgia, of course."

"Okay," Georgia said, her voice a little louder and more determined, as if she had decided to take control of this conversation. "Mister— Tristan is right, you do need your rest."

Grammy looked as if she might argue, but then she touched a small, knotted hand to her forehead, suddenly seeming confused again.

"Yes, maybe I do need to rest."

Georgia tucked the quilt around her once more, and then turned to Tristan, hesitating before she walked toward him.

"It was wonderful to meet you, Tristan."

"It's nice to meet you too, ma'am."

"Call me Grace," the old woman said with a sweet smile.

Tristan smiled back. "Okay, Grace."

Georgia stopped, still a foot or so away from him, her own expression nearly as confused as her grandmother's had been. She looked from him to her grammy and back to him.

Finally, she moved closer to him, silently ushering him

out the door. He obeyed, waving to the old woman as he left the doorway, but then pausing in the hallway.

"He is very handsome," her grandmother said.

"Yes, he is," Georgia agreed, although Tristan couldn't really read her tone. "I'll be right back with your tea. Rest."

Her grandmother agreed, and Georgia left the room, shutting the door to leave only a crack. Again she hesitated, seeing Tristan in the hallway. But then she forged ahead, twisting her body to slip past him, although her back still brushed against his in the narrow passageway.

Tristan actually caught his breath at the brief touch. His body, which was already pretty damned aware, jumped to complete attention.

This mortal turned him on more than he could recall anyone ever doing. He didn't understand why, and at this moment, he didn't feel the need to question the enormity of his lust. He just wanted her.

But she didn't seem to be having the same reaction to him. At least, not if anyone was to watch her actions. She quickly left him standing in the hallway, disappearing into the other room.

But fortunately, Tristan wasn't just anyone, and he didn't have to just watch her actions. He could sense her reaction, smell it. Hell, if he concentrated enough, he felt as if he could taste it.

Would she taste as sweet and ripe and ready as her scent? Mmm, he knew she would, his delicious Peaches.

His cock pulsed painfully in his trousers. Damn, he wanted her.

He followed her, strolling along behind, unhurried, like some killer in a slasher film. Just like the horror movie killer, he had no reason to rush. He'd get his victim no matter how far or fast she ran.

For the first time this evening, he actually felt calm and in control. He was going to have her. No need to fret.

He walked into her tiny kitchen just as she was reaching inside the cupboard to get a mug. She clearly was trying to ignore him as she filled it with water, and then put the mug in the microwave.

"So you live with your grandmother?" he finally said. That certainly put a damper on his plans for the night, but a grandmother was far better than a boyfriend.

Tristan didn't contemplate his relief over that realization. Mainly because a sick grandmother meant something else. Georgia needed money. Good money if she was doing in-home care, which she had to be. Grace clearly couldn't be left alone while Georgia was at work.

Georgia paused in the midst of lifting the lid off a canister on the countertop. Then she nodded.

"Yes," she finally said. "She has Alzheimer's and so she's had to live with me for a year or so now."

Tristan nodded, the wheels in his devious mind turning.

"It must be expensive to care for her."

Georgia turned to him, leaning against the counter as if she was very tired and not really up to trying to read his thoughts. Or being "messed with," as she called it.

She did look exhausted and he almost felt guilty for what he intended to do. Almost.

"I can't lose my job," she said instead of answering his question.

Lose her job? He frowned. Why would she think she was going to lose her job? He'd been stupidly bereft without her for just one evening.

"Your job isn't at risk," he told her. "Why would you think that?"

"Why else would you be here?" she asked.

To fuck you senseless. Yeah, he couldn't say that.

Instead, he walked up to her until he was only an inch or so away, effectively caging her against the counter with his height and size, but still not touching her.

"I came here to tell you I need you to work extra late tomorrow night. In fact, very, very late."

She frowned, clearly confused and curious.

"I have a gala to attend tomorrow night. And I need you to go as my date."

"Your date?" She was truly puzzled now. "Surely you have other women who are dying to go with you. Women who are better suited for such an event."

"But I want you to go with me. You are my personal assistant and this is just as much a work function as a social one."

She still looked bewildered, but he wasn't going to give her a chance to argue further.

He pulled his wallet out of his back pocket and plucked up several hundred-dollar bills.

"I want you to go buy a dress and get your hair done. Something sexy, please."

She stared at the money as if it would jump forward and bite her.

"And I will, of course, pay you overtime. This is a work event after all."

She stopped staring at the cash to look at him. She nibbled her lower lip, and he wondered why she was hesitating. She clearly needed money to care for her grandmother.

And he clearly needed to get her somewhere away from the office and away from her apartment.

After another moment, she tentatively reached for the cash.

He smiled.

"So I will see you tomorrow. Take your time getting to work. Shop before you come, so I can approve the dress."

She nodded, still unable to speak.

"Good night, Peaches," he said, then reached out to brush a tendril of pink hair away from her cheek. "I'm looking forward to a night on the town with you."

He leaned forward and just fleetingly brushed his closed lips against hers. He didn't look back as he left her apartment, but he was certain she was still leaning against the counter looking dazed.

He smiled to himself, and once the door was soundly closed behind him, he pulled out his cell phone.

He pressed a few buttons.

"Hello. Yes, this is Tristan McIntyre. I need to book your best suite for tomorrow night. Excellent."

He punched his phone off. Georgia Sullivan was about to get the seduction of her life. And he was about to get himself refocused.

Chapter Nine

G eorgia was having a *Pretty Woman* moment, and it wasn't climbing down a fire escape to be whisked away by the unlikely love of her life in a limousine.

No, of course, she wasn't getting *that Pretty Woman* moment. Georgia was getting the moment where Julia Roberts was being snubbed by exclusive boutique employees as she tried to find an evening gown.

But in Georgia's case it wasn't her obvious lack of money or questionable career choice that was garnering her disdainful looks. . . . It was her size that was prompting the disapproving looks as she browsed the racks of Chez Renee.

She pulled out a dress in granite gray chiffon. The floor-length gown had Grecian styling with a draped bodice and one asymmetrical strap.

Not her style, but maybe she could find her inner goddess and pull off the look. Was gray as slimming as black? Maybe. Hopefully.

She managed to catch the attention of one of the saleswomen, who looked like she'd rather go to the dentist and get a root canal than help Georgia.

But Georgia ignored the woman's pained look, and asked as pleasantly as she could, "Excuse me, do you have this in a size fourteen? Or maybe a sixteen?"

Generally, formal dress sizes did run smaller. She'd learned that after multiple fittings for her cousin's wedding. Now talk about wearing something she wouldn't normally wear. That yellow bridesmaid gown made her look like a giant pineapple.

"I'm sorry," the saleswoman said, although she didn't sound regretful at all. "We don't carry plus sizes here. Perhaps you could try a store that caters to larger women."

Georgia stared at her for a moment, and then nodded. She placed the dress back on the rack.

"Thank you for your help," Georgia said, although she didn't sound as affable as before. She didn't look at any of the other women working there. But she was sure they were all sniggering once she stepped out to the street.

The poor fat girl wants to dress up like a princess. But everyone knew princesses weren't chunky. That wasn't allowed.

She paused on the sidewalk, trying to decide what to do next. None of the other designer shops were going to have her size either.

That was another thing that bothered her about the fashion industry. Designers always bandied around terms like "perfect for the average woman" or "wearable for real women." But Georgia didn't ever see couture that was designed for the average or real woman. At least, not her reality, which included some ample hips and big boobs.

Why did she have to do this anyway? Find an evening gown? A designer gown that would likely make her look like sausage stuffed into a ridiculously expensive and uncomfortable casing?

But the biggest question was why Tristan had insisted she accompany him to a gala in the first place. Georgia knew exactly what this event was, since she handled his business and social calendar. And this gala was a little of both, a huge fund raiser where all the biggest names in the fashion industry would make an appearance. Not to mention actors, actresses, and lots of other famous people.

Tristan was not a man who lacked dates, especially to an event like this one. So why her?

Somehow she felt like the butt of some private joke, which wasn't actually unusual when dealing with Tristan. But now she feared that she wouldn't just be the punch line of one of Tristan's private jokes, but a very public one. Tristan was going to make the society pages, probably a few magazines, and even some celebrity news shows. He couldn't really be excited to be seen at such a significant event with his chubby personal assistant on his arm.

So why had he asked her? And offered her big money as well to go with him?

She just couldn't understand what was motivating him. Hell, he could probably call any woman, even with just a few minutes' notice, and she'd drop everything to attend with him. Actually, no probably about it. Georgia had seen him do just that many times before.

Sometimes she was the one who made the call, only to hear the gorgeous woman—well, she assumed they were gorgeous—eagerly accept his last-minute invite.

Maybe she should just head to the office and suggest he do that. But there was the money, and that wasn't something Georgia could dismiss. Her grandmother's private care was costly and any extra money would make things easier for both Georgia and Grammy.

"So shut up and shop," she muttered to herself, which earned her a strange look from a woman sporting an expensive, size-six designer suit as she passed, swinging her Saks and Bloomingdale's Big Brown bags.

Now there was a woman who clearly didn't need to give herself a pep talk to shop. Unlike Georgia, who still hesitated to brave the next store.

Georgia looked around, trying to decide what to do. She saw a man standing in the entryway of one of the boutiques. He was tall, muscular. He was probably some GQ type of man waiting for his size-two girlfriend or wife to purchase a new dress for a romantic evening out.

This was a nightmare. She wouldn't find anything that would look right without major alterations to fit her curvy figure. And she didn't even want to compare the waiting man's evening with hers. She certainly didn't expect romantic. Although, her wayward heart did thump a little faster at the idea of being romanced by Tristan McIntyre.

She sighed. *Focus, Georgia.*

One thing was certain, she wasn't going to find anything here. But she did know where she would find clothes that fit her, and while they weren't "designer" gowns, one of them was going to have to do. She stepped off the curb and waved for a taxi.

"Oh, yeah, that one is totally you."

Georgia smiled at Chastity, the shop's clerk and a woman she knew well. Georgia hadn't seen the dress yet; the fitting rooms in her favorite vintage shop were nothing more than stalls with psychedelic curtains as doors. But Georgia liked the way the dress fit and the silky swish of satiny material around her calves. Georgia stopped in front of the antique full-length mirror, twisting slightly to get a better view of the sides and back.

"Definitely you," Chastity repeated.

Georgia admired the retro dress again, feeling very feminine, loving the color and style. Flame red, she would call it, in the style of Marilyn Monroe's iconic white halter dress. This would rescue Georgia from all the reviewers' "Worst Dressed" lists, she hoped.

But it wasn't a designer piece, which was probably a huge no-no for an event like this. And she certainly wasn't a size four. She studied her image in the mirror again, and then turned to Chastity.

"I'm going to need a pair of shoes and purse to match."

When Georgia left Chastity's shop, she didn't feel confident that Tristan would like her choice of attire, but at least she would feel comfortable. She looked at her watch. She still had time to go pick up some other things that would help boost her confidence. Some stockings. Maybe a new strapless bra with some lace in a pretty color. Even panties to match.

Purely for herself, she thought, and then chuckled slightly. They certainly wouldn't be for Tristan. He flirted, but she knew that was just a part of his makeup. She certainly couldn't, and wouldn't, take it seriously.

She glanced down the street, trying to decide the best place to buy intimates, when she saw a man lurking inside the doorway of a three-story walkup. Just as she peered at him closer, he leaned back against the wall, so she couldn't see him clearly. She had just a vague image of his height and build. He was very similar to the man she'd seen in that pricey boutique. But it couldn't be. Why would anyone be following her?

Clearly this date with Tristan is stressing you out way too much.

She glanced in the direction of the man one more time. He'd disappeared. Probably into the apartment building, where he probably lived. Mystery solved.

Georgia shook her head at her own crazy thoughts and then she refocused on her task: wrapping up her shopping with a visit to the salon.

"Did you locate Georgia Sullivan?" Eugene asked as soon as Gabriel entered his office.

"Yes, she is shopping,"

Eugene's left eyebrow rose slightly, the only sign he found that news odd. Gabriel knew Georgia Sullivan's routine. She rarely missed work and certainly wouldn't miss it to do something like go on a shopping spree. Gabriel was sure Eugene knew that, too.

Eugene might seem far too calm and unconcerned, but that didn't mean he was unaware.

In his eerie way, Eugene seemed to follow Gabriel's unspoken train of thought.

"Well, we both know that isn't Ms. Sullivan's normal behavior."

"No, it's not," Gabriel agreed.

"I'm sure the shopping spree is somehow related to McIntyre. And I imagine she will be in at some point today. I want you to find out what is going on."

"And what if she doesn't come in?" Gabriel asked.

"I don't think we should be concerned about Ms. Sullivan's absence. In fact, I'm sure she'll be in later. You should be able to talk to her today."

Gabriel nodded, although he still had real doubts about the wisdom of bringing in an average mortal to work as DIA's primary mole. A mortal woman would be spying directly on the most dangerous of this rebellion, the one heading it up. That could backfire so horribly on the DIA. It could lead to dire consequences for Ms. Sullivan, too.

And then there was the very real worry that Georgia Sullivan would tell McIntyre everything. Even telling her that McIntyre was dangerous wouldn't guarantee she wouldn't tell him. And of course telling Ms. Sullivan she was employed by a demon was totally out of the question. Who would believe that? Gabriel sure as hell wouldn't believe it if he hadn't been fighting the damned creatures for years.

"Maybe we should just stick to our old methods. I could act as a mail room clerk and observe what McIntyre is doing."

"And we know how well it went the last time we sent up a slayer to do recognizance," Eugene pointed out.

It hadn't gone well at all. In fact, the mission had led to one of his brethren having to assume a new identity and leave the country. But Gabriel was certain he could be more successful than Michael had been. Not that Michael wasn't a great slayer. He'd just had a few checks against him, coming back into the DIA after being cursed by a demon and frozen into a statue since the late 70s. He didn't have all the new protocol down. But Gabriel knew how the DIA worked. How demons worked, too.

"I feel strongly that Georgia Sullivan is the right person for this task," Eugene said, although his strong feelings weren't evident in his placid tone. "Check the fifteenth floor again this afternoon. I'm sure she will come in at some point."

Gabriel wanted to argue further, but Eugene was as stubborn as he was stoic. So Gabriel simply nodded, but he noticed as he exited the small office that a rare smile curved Eugene's lips, just slightly.

Chapter Ten

"I told her to take her time, but this is ridiculous." Tristan checked his TAG Heuer watch for the fifth time in so many minutes.

Dippy lifted his head from the edge of his doggy bed. "Obsessed. Truly obsessed."

Tristan didn't bother to respond since the damned dog had already said that several times over the course of the last hour. He looked at his watch again.

"You need to stop this," the mutt stated. "I told you that Finola is up to something down there in the mail room. That should have you far more concerned than a late assistant."

Tristan glanced out of his glass-walled office into the catacomb of glass hallways. No sign of Georgia.

He sighed, turning back to Dippy. As much as he hated to admit it, the dog was right. Finola's actions were much more worrisome than his curvy, sexy as hell assistant's tardiness.

"What do you think she's up to?"

Dippy sighed, a sign of annoyance that translated perfectly even in his dog form. "We are talking about Finola, right? Because frankly, I don't care what your personal assistant is doing."

"Yes." Tristan's irritation grew. "Finola."

"I already told you, I think she's working on gathering souls. She's reading the people who work down there, figuring out what they desire most. What would convince them to sell their souls."

Finola could be very good at that. She might be flighty and self-obsessed, but she was damned good at gathering souls when she put herself to the task.

"That hardly sounds like a problem," Tristan said, giving the animal a wry look. "We are here to gather souls, after all. She's just finally doing the work she should have done all along as the leader of this rebellion."

Dippy gave him a look that stated quite eloquently he thought Tristan was utterly dense. "If Finola's busy collecting souls, and you are just chasing after your assistant, don't you think Satan will reconsider his decision to appoint a demon of lust as the head of this rebellion?"

Like a demon of greed had been a much better choice. Finola's greed had never motivated her to focus on the task Satan wanted her to perform. Until now.

"I'm growing tired of talking about my assistant," Tristan stated.

"You could have fooled me," Dippy growled.

"You know what I mean," Tristan stated. "Georgia isn't an issue. And after tonight, she'll be less than an issue. She'll be a non-issue, if you will."

Dippy looked dubious.

"You were the one who suggested that I manage my little focus problem by getting rid of my perpetual hard-on for the woman. So tonight, I plan to seduce her and spend the entire night making sure my hard-on is well sated."

"I believe I suggested using your hand, not Peaches' hoo-ha."

Tristan grinned, just imagining Peaches' hoo-ha. All

plump and pink and glistening with her juices. Then his juices.

He looked at his watch again.

Dippy growled. "Seriously, pumping her hoo-ha is not going to get you refocused."

Tristan grinned wider. "Who said I was going to pump just her hoo-ha?"

Dippy rolled his eyes, and muttered something about demons of lust being ruled by, well, lust as he got up, turned several tight circles, then flung himself back down onto his dog bed, facing away from Tristan.

For Tristan, the hound's action was more of a relief than a snub. He was so sick of that mutt's judging stares and dismayed puppy sighs. But Tristan still needed a break from both Dippy and Finola. Surely, Satan wouldn't expect him to work with all these backseat demons evaluating his every move, every decision.

Time to find Georgia. Maybe she was at her desk and had just gotten to work without checking in with him. He left his office without another word to the demon dog.

Dippy might think demons of lust did nothing but fixate on satisfying their libidos, but Tristan knew what he was doing. One good, sweaty, orgasm-filled night with Peaches, and he'd be more than ready for world domination.

After all, he was only so obsessed with this particular woman because he'd been denying himself. Once he had her, it would be like every other conquest in his long, long existence. He would get his fill of her and then quickly want to move on to his next acquisition.

But he had to admit, he was relieved to see the current object of his desire bustling toward her desk, her arms weighed down with bags.

"I'm sorry I'm so late," she said, her voice breathy and so sexy.

He instantly imagined her in bed, under him, begging him in that same breathy voice. His cock hardened just as instantly. Of course, that was nothing new around his Peaches.

"I—I had to go to a few places to find a dress that would . . ." She pursed her lips. "The right dress."

"And you got your hair done."

Georgia hesitated, fighting the urge to touch her hair self-consciously. Of course, the multiple bags she carried made that impossible anyway. Instead, she just tried to read Tristan's expression. Had she gone too far? Truthfully, her newly dyed black locks striped with chunky, bright red highlights were rather tame for her. She had replaced her hot pink highlights with the red. To match her dress, of course.

"I love the red," he stated. Then to her surprise, he stepped forward to rub one of the flaming red locks between his thumb and forefinger.

"Oh," she said, feeling as if the air was being sucked from her lungs at his closeness. "Good."

She realized that was a lame response, but she couldn't be expected to think straight with him so near. His body seemed to overwhelm her, and his gaze held hers. Vivid green locked with dark brown. His woodsy, spicy scent filled her nostrils, and she desperately wished her hair had nerve endings so she could feel his fingers stroking her.

He touched her hair a moment longer, then seemed to realize what he was doing, and dropped the strand. He stepped back, and she pulled in a shuddering breath. Their eyes held for moment longer, but then the look in Tristan's eyes, an almost dazed look, returned to his usual irreverent, sardonic expression.

Of course, she had to have been imagining that bemused

gaze. Why would he be staring at her that way? She had to be projecting her own overwhelmed feelings onto him. That was the only answer that made sense to her.

"So do I get to see the dress?" His green gaze flicked to the bags she held.

"Isn't it bad luck to see the dress before the big event?" She instantly wanted to groan. Dear God, had she really just made a wedding reference to this man? Her cheeks burned and she knew they probably matched the streaks in her hair.

Tristan grinned, and she had no doubt he noticed her embarrassment.

"I think you are referring to a different kind of event. Plus, we couldn't possibly have bad luck tonight. It's not allowed."

Georgia appreciated his not making more of the stupid comment. Although he probably thought it was pretty presumptuous to imply a man like Tristan McIntyre would marry a woman like her. As always, visions of supermodels danced in her head. Okay, he probably thought it was downright delusional.

But she wasn't going to make any more of her foolish comment. Tristan hadn't, so neither would she.

But she still hesitated, not wanting to see the inevitable disappointment on his gorgeous face when he viewed her dress. Of course, he was going to see it eventually, so what the hell. She wrestled the bundle of bags onto her desk and pulled out the bright red halter, holding it by the shoulder straps in front of her.

Tristan didn't react for a moment, and some of her bravado wavered. She started to lower the dress, but his words stopped her.

"You are going to be the sexiest woman in the room."

She gaped at him. Was he being sarcastic? He didn't appear to be. If anything, that sort of dazed look was back.

She slowly lowered the gown. Her cheeks burned again,

and she wondered if her complexion was going to match her dress all night.

"Thank you." That response was perfectly appropriate, but she still felt as if it wasn't the right one.

Their eyes held again for a moment; then Tristan looked away. He cleared his throat as if surprised, maybe even a little flustered, by his behavior.

"What else did you buy?" He started to reach for one of the bags, but her hand shot out to stop him.

"Just . . . incidentals."

Tristan's smile curled, looking utterly devious. "Incidentals? What kind of incidentals?" He reached for the bags again, and she yanked them away.

"Shoes," she said quickly.

"That's a lot of bags for just a pair of shoes."

"And a purse," she added, still holding his wrist even as she slid the bags closer to her.

"And . . ."

"And other stuff."

His smile widened, and he looked stunningly beautiful and totally naughty. "I like other stuff. I like other stuff a lot."

"Well, too bad you won't get to see it," she said with a flippant smile of her own.

She snatched the bags up and placed them behind her desk. She was surprised at her own cheekiness, but she didn't have time to regret it, because he laughed, the tone deep and rich and decadent like the most delicious salted caramel.

"I guess we'll have to wait and see about that one," he said. "I'll be at your place at eight p.m. Have your incidentals ready to go."

He shot her another wide grin and waggled his dark brows before disappearing through the double doors to his office.

Georgia collapsed into her desk chair, literally. Was he really implying he might possibly seduce her? He couldn't be. Not seriously.

She stared at the now closed door a moment longer, and then straightened up in her seat. Just his usual flirting. Just like always. That was his thing. He probably wasn't any more aware of it than he was his own breathing. It was second nature to him, and she had to remember that and not take him seriously.

But even as she scolded herself, she lifted her legal pad and fanned her flushed skin. Damn, he had way too much effect on her.

After a couple more waves, she noticed a tall man standing just outside the alcove of her reception area. He didn't seem to be aware of her, but was instead busy with the cart in front of him.

A clerk from the mail room, she realized.

She didn't recognize him. An elderly black gentleman named Elton was the one who usually picked up and delivered her mail, but the mail room did have a lot of employees.

Had he witnessed her very inappropriate interaction with her boss? She shot him another covert look. He was still shuffling around his letters and packages.

She studied the man, sure she'd never seen him before. At least not in the *HOT!* offices. But there was something familiar about him. She couldn't place what it was. Truthfully, it was amazing she was even aware of the man given how flustered she was by her conversation with Tristan.

She waved the pad of paper again, and a small rush of air cooled her heated skin just a little.

She dropped the pad, determined to get to work. She turned on her computer, and it hummed to life, grumbling and taking its time to get started. As she waited for it to boot up, Georgia had that strange sensation of being watched.

She glanced back toward the man, but he wasn't looking at her. She watched him a moment longer, trying to figure out why he seemed strangely familiar. But she couldn't place where she might have seen him before. And frankly, her mind was determined to stray back to Tristan McIntyre.

Damn, it was going to be a long afternoon.

Chapter Eleven

Georgia Sullivan was back. And there was no denying, McIntyre was interested in her. Even from a distance, Gabriel couldn't miss the fact that the demon was flirting. But Tristan McIntyre was a demon of lust. It was his nature to flirt with everyone.

Gabriel just couldn't fathom how Elton could be so confident this woman had any more ability to get close to McIntyre than anyone else. Maybe the demon wanted her, but did that mean he'd also trust her? What if McIntyre got suspicious? Using a regular mortal just didn't sit right with Gabriel.

And then there was the look on Georgia Sullivan's face as McIntyre had flirted with her. She liked the guy. That was clear from a distance, too. Gabriel had seen longing in her eyes. Even her funky glasses and heavy eye makeup couldn't hide that.

That made Gabriel think her allegiance was definitely going to lie with McIntyre, and not with some total stranger who told her that her boss, the boss she had the hots for, was dangerous.

Gabriel pretended to focus on sorting the contents of his mail cart, only glancing at the woman when he was certain she wasn't looking in his direction. She'd noticed him watching her earlier, and he hadn't missed her deepening blush. The blush of a woman who knew her desire was obvious. Could they really trust her to be loyal to them when she clearly wanted McIntyre?

"She just looks like a disaster, doesn't she?"

Gabriel started, shooting a look over his shoulder to find Finola White standing behind him. Clearly, he wasn't tuned in like he should be. No one should be able to sneak up behind him, even a demon. Especially a demon.

But he quickly guarded himself, not allowing the she-demon see his surprise, or guess that he was doing anything other than sorting mail.

"I'm sorry," he said, keeping his voice impassive. "Who?" He turned his attention back to his sorting.

"You're always the gentleman, aren't you?" Finola said. "No need to answer that. I know you are."

Gabriel didn't like the way she said that, as if she knew all his secrets. But again, he did nothing but shoot her a glance.

"I was referring to Tristan McIntyre's assistant," Finola said, not keeping the emotion out of her voice. She was disgusted. Probably with the assistant and McIntyre.

"I hadn't noticed." Gabriel continued to organize letters into piles.

Finola moved closer to him, making his body prickle with awareness like unpleasant little snaps of high voltage up his spine. He held himself rigid, trying to ignore the feeling. Trying to remain unaffected.

"I never would have kept her on," Finola continued, apparently oblivious to his reaction. But he didn't trust that she really was—she could be up to something.

"Her hair. Her clothing. And her makeup . . ." She shuddered. "Not an appropriate representation of *HOT!* Not at all. Not appropriate as an employee of this magazine."

Gabriel just nodded. Why was Finola even talking to him? Much less about McIntyre's assistant. It seemed a little too coincidental. Way too coincidental, in fact. What was she up to?

"I'm sorry," Finola said suddenly, her voice turning to that persuasive purr that was far more dangerous than her vitriol. "Were you getting ready to talk with her?"

The prickling along his spine spread to his skin. Oh, she knew something. She had to.

"No," he said instantly. Had she overheard their intention of recruiting Georgia Sullivan to spy on McIntyre? Finola now worked right in the midst of the DIA, and in his opinion, Eugene wasn't treating her presence with the seriousness it deserved. She might have overheard something. No matter how flighty and harmless Finola could appear, she still had been the head of Satan's rebellion until just a few weeks ago. She was very dangerous.

"Are you sure?" she asked again. "You seem to be hovering here like you want to talk to her."

Gabriel looked at her, meeting the demon's pale eyes directly. He was a slayer, dammit. He didn't cower under the leading questions of a filthy hell spawn.

"Actually, I was just getting myself organized for the rest of my afternoon mail pickup. Nothing more," he stated, then offered her a bland smile. "Why aren't you in the mail room attending to your work?"

Her coy smile slipped, but then she turned the half-grin into a full-fledged one. Her white teeth looked villainous against her blood red lips.

But she didn't answer. Instead, she said sweetly, "I guess I should let you get back to work. I wouldn't want to bungle the productivity of the mail room."

He held her gaze, trying to read its pale iciness.

"Carry on," she said with a wave of her hand as if she were still the head of this company. "You know, I have realized the importance of the mail room in just the short time I've been down there."

Oh, she definitely knew something.

He didn't answer, his mind abuzz as he considered what to do next. Approaching Georgia Sullivan was very important to the DIA's work, but he also knew he had to report this conversation to Eugene.

Plus, Gabriel now realized he couldn't talk to Georgia Sullivan here. The walls had ears. He had to talk to her away from *HOT!* He should have realized that all along. He should have approached her while she was shopping, but he'd been afraid he'd just scare her, coming off as some crazy person.

"Well, please excuse me, Gabriel," Finola said, drawing his attention back to her. "It is Gabriel, isn't it?"

"Yes, it is." Even the fact she remembered his name suggested she had more knowledge of the mail room than was safe. Knowledge about the DIA.

"Well, do excuse me, Gabriel, but I need to talk to Tristan."

Gabriel nodded again, itching to know what she was going to discuss with McIntyre. He wished he could follow, under the guise of delivering something. But that would only rouse more suspicion. Not to mention, he'd never get into McIntyre's offices anyway. Georgia Sullivan was as much a sentry as a personal assistant. There was a certain irony to that; that the DIA wanted to recruit the very person who kept its operatives away from McIntyre.

Gabriel remained rooted to the spot, watching as Finola spoke brusquely to Georgia, and then glided through the glass double doors leading to McIntyre's office. Georgia didn't even have time to acknowledge her ex-boss's intent. And from Georgia's wincing expression, she wouldn't have considered stopping the female demon anyway.

Apparently, some mail room employees could wander

right on back there. This was all very interesting. He needed
to talk to Eugene again.

"Hello, my love."

Tristan looked up from choosing pictures for the "Win-
ter Wonderland" fashion layout for the January issue of
HOT! And now he was being interrupted by the demon ice
princess herself.

As always, Finola was clad from head to toe in white: a
tailored, white cotton blazer with a white silk T-shirt and
silk scarf underneath, white skinny jeans, and strappy white
heels. For her, this was a dressed-down look, although Tristan knew the "casual" outfit probably cost more than most
women's seasonal clothing allowance. Still, Finola had clearly
made concessions to her new position as a mail room employee. Which brought him to his first question.

"What are you doing here, Finola? You are supposed to
be down in the mail room, keeping an eye on the employees there."

"Oh, don't worry, darling," she cooed. "I'm only making
a brief visit, just to check in."

She glanced around at Tristan's new office furniture and
décor. "I see you've decided to redecorate. What's the mo-
tif? Early medieval castle? Or is this some kind of homage
to your goth assistant?"

Tristan looked around the— *his* office, making sure not
to reveal how accurate her assessment had been.

"Thanks," he said, even though her raised eyebrow and
the haughty angle of her lips stated she didn't approve of
it, which made him like his decorating choices even more.

Finola wrinkled her nose slightly, before settling into one
of the ornately carved, high back chairs that looked more
like a king's throne than a piece of office furniture.

She regarded him silently. Tristan moved away from
his worktable and leaned against his mahogany, equally

extravagantly carved desk. He crossed his arms over his chest.

"So check in," he prompted.

Finola smiled, offering him a warm grin that he knew was anything but. "I don't think you have much to worry about down there. Just a bunch of dull little worker bees, buzzing around with no realization of the power they work for."

Tristan didn't even pretend to think she was referring to him. She might be referring to their true boss, Satan. Or she might be referring to herself. If he had to guess, it was herself. He had no doubt she still considered herself as the head of this endeavor. She was very wrong.

Behind him, he heard Dippy moving around in his doggy bed. Listening as always.

"Excellent," Tristan said, refusing to react to Finola's little jibes. "And no signs of other slayers or rebels?"

She shook her head. "Not a one."

"But then you have only been down there for two days," Tristan said, just in case she had any hope of not returning to the mail room. "I need you to stay down there, just to be absolutely certain."

"Of course," Finola said readily. Far too readily. But then Dippy had already made Tristan aware of the fact that Finola wasn't down there languishing in a sea of dullards, demeaning tasks, and fashion faux pas. She was busy working on a plan for payback. Tristan didn't doubt that for one moment.

"I will admit," she said, "that when you first suggested I work . . . in the mail room, I was a tad offended."

A tad? When had Finola become the master of understatement?

"But I now see that it is a part of the company that could be very easily overlooked and could be an easy entrance for other demon fighters and rebels."

What was she up to?

"Well, I'm glad you can see the importance of being placed down there," he said, nodding his approval as if he was taking her comments at face value. He wasn't.

Dippy was clearly right; Finola saw the mail room workers as miserable humans ripe to sell their souls for something better, and maybe they were. And maybe Finola would bargain the whole mail room out of their souls. Tristan would take credit.

Didn't Finola see how easy that would be? Let her gather one soul contract after another down there, and then he would simply say, "Why, Satan, my beloved Prince of Darkness, that's exactly why I placed her there. To make sure she did her fair share of the work. You know how dear Finola gets off track, caught up in her own greedy desires."

Satan would believe that without hesitation, and Tristan would get the pat on the back, not only for the new souls, but also for knowing how to manage his unruly staff.

He smiled broadly at the idea.

"You look quite pleased," Finola observed. "What has you looking like the cat that got the cream?"

Or the demon who got all the praise and power, Tristan amended in his head.

"I'm just in a good mood," Tristan said, moving to collapse into his own throne, appropriately larger and more ornate than the one Finola sat on. "Tonight is Rocco Von Furstenmaur's fund raiser. It will be the social gathering of the season. You know how hideously rich, ridiculously over-dressed mortals love to raise money for the impoverished and fashion-deprived masses."

Finola nodded, and Tristan knew she was schooling her features into a mask of bland boredom. He also knew she was writhing inside. This event promised just the kind of excess Finola loved.

And being a demon of greed, she couldn't contain her desire to attend. It promised wealth and decadence and desperate souls who always wanted more, who were ripe to make a deal with the Devil.

"And do you have an appropriately beautiful and extravagant date?" she asked, unable to stop herself.

Tristan's smiled broadened. Oh, how she wanted Tristan to ask her to attend with him. She missed these lavish events as much if not more than the power of running *HOT!* It must be killing her not to be on the scene. Not getting the greediest souls herself.

But was she truly crazy enough to think he'd even consider asking her? Apparently so, and that made revealing his actual date all the more delightful.

His smile turned crooked and smug. "Indeed, I do. I will be attending with the delightfully quirky and voluptuous"—quirky and voluptuous both being traits Finola would not find appealing in the least—"Georgia Sullivan."

Finola didn't react for a moment. Then she couldn't contain her outrage, her perfect masklike face distorting into something ugly. "Your assistant?"

"Yes." Damn, he was loving this.

Finola looked as if she might take demon form right then and there.

"That . . . that woman is not a proper representation of what this magazine stands for, what *we* stand for."

"And what do we stand for, Fin?"

Her eyes narrowed, taking on their natural reptilian shape.

"We are demons. . . . We value beauty and wealth and power and excess. We *are* those things. We acquire those things. Aside from an excess of eye makeup and weight and bad taste, that mortal doesn't even factor into our world. She's nothing more than a human who would readily sell us her soul to be just like us. You should be snapping up her pathetic soul, not taking her out to a gala and parading her around like an equal."

Tristan would have agreed with her about any other mortal. But in this instance, he didn't. Nothing about Georgia struck him as pathetic. He actually felt offended for Georgia. Odd that.

This was all part of his strange obsession with her. And once he took her in every way possible he could physically, he'd also take her soul. He'd hardly gone soft on that front.

"What is wrong with you?" Finola asked, some of her ire replaced by concern. Feigned concern, he knew.

"There is nothing wrong with me," Tristan assured her. "I intend to enjoy myself with Miss Georgia Sullivan, thoroughly, and then I will do just as you have said, snap up her soul."

But tonight, he planned to think about nothing but his and Peaches' pleasure. And maybe the fact that Finola was writhing in agony at being left behind like some demonic Cinderella.

"I hope so," Finola said, standing. Her features were back to their perfect, emotionless beauty. "You were one of the evilest demons I ever knew. I'd hate to think an odd, rather homely mortal somehow weakened you."

"Hardly," Tristan stated. He was still evil and driven to do Satan's misdeeds. But he was also a demon of lust. And he was lusting hard for Georgia Sullivan, whom he found neither odd nor homely.

"It's not like it hasn't happened before," she pointed out.

Tristan sighed. "I know it has, but not to a demon of lust and certainly not to me. We don't feel . . . that particular emotion. I only feel lust, need, and the drive for gratification."

"Again, I hope so." She didn't say or react anymore, simply exiting his office.

"I hope so, too," Dippy growled in a whisper as he followed his "owner."

Tristan watched them leave, feeling that he'd just gone from thoroughly enjoying his position of power to losing it completely. But that feeling wouldn't last. He knew what he was doing.

Chapter Twelve

Was it possible to feel both relief and dread at the same time? Georgia gathered up her shopping bags and headed out of the *HOT!* offices, debating that very question. She was so relieved to be done with work, which had been torture. She hadn't been able to focus on her job or get a single thing done. But she was also dreading the fact that the end of the workday meant she was minutes closer to her date with Tristan.

"It's not a date," she muttered to herself as she stepped out onto the busy Manhattan street. She was just going as his . . . companion. Did they hire people to be seat fillers at the awards ceremonies like the Academy Awards and the Grammys? That was all she was, a seat filler.

She still couldn't comprehend why Tristan McIntyre would need a seat filler though. Whatever the answer, that was how she was going to look at the night. To consider anything else was silly—and frankly too nerve-wrecking.

Still, even with the endless pep talks, her nerves were frayed.

She contemplated flagging down a cab, but decided to walk. The crisp spring air cooled her flushed skin and she hoped it would clear her head as well. The street bustled with pedestrians and traffic; rush hour was in full swing.

The noise served as a good distraction. And she remembered why she had wanted to move here. She loved the city. The action, all the different types of people, the thrill of being in one of the most exciting cities in the world.

And she was attending an exclusive gala with the most handsome man she'd ever met. She should be feeling like a princess about to attend her very first ball. Instead of being nervous and second guessing every single thing, she should be enjoying every moment of this.

She loved her dress. She loved her shoes and stockings. Her jewelry, while paste, was funky and flashy and made her feel like a million bucks.

"Just have fun," she murmured to herself. "Just enjoy the experience."

She noticed a passerby gave her an absent look, noting she was talking to herself, but not particularly surprised by it. That was another interesting fact of living in a big city. She could talk to herself and barely raise an eyebrow.

She chuckled, feeling lighter than she had since Tristan had first asked her to join him. Maybe it was the fresh air, or just that her pep talk was finally working, but she would enjoy her night. Georgia loved new experiences and this one was a doozy.

She smiled to herself as she hurried the last blocks to her apartment building, walking up the concrete steps as quickly as her open-toed platform heels would take her.

"Georgia."

Georgia didn't quite register the person saying her name over the honk of a waiting taxi in front of her building. But when the elderly couple from apartment 1B trundled past her in the lobby, she just assumed it had been one of them speaking to her. She smiled and called hello in reply, then continued on to the mailboxes that lined the wall next to the elevator.

"Georgia Sullivan?"

This time there was no mistaking the voice calling her name. She spun around, looking for the person who was speaking to her. At first she didn't see the man, until he stepped out from the alcove that led to the downstairs apartments.

Her first thought was of the men she'd noticed lurking in the doorways earlier today. As he moved closer, two realizations hit her at once. This guy was the mail room clerk she thought had been watching her earlier, and he *was* the same guy she'd noticed while shopping, too. He hadn't been two different men. He'd been just the one, this one, and he had to have been following her. And now he'd followed her home.

Georgia looked around warily, wishing the old couple had not left to catch their cab. Not that she was sure what Cecil and Adele Goldstein were going to do to protect her. At least Cecil had a cane and Adele always carried a large purse. That was better than what she was armed with . . . unless she could get to her new high heels. A six-inch heel to the side of the head would probably do some serious damage. If she could reach the side of his head. This guy was huge, much bigger than he looked from a distance.

Still she risked a glance away to try to figure out which bag the shoes were in, only to decide that would take too much time. She decided to use her own purse, which wasn't as substantial as Adele Goldstein's, but would have to do.

She dropped her shopping bags and raised her small satchel style purse, wishing it looked a little more threatening. The small embroidered Hello Kitty heads dotting the leather didn't add to the intimidation factor.

But to her surprise, the hulk of a man immediately lifted his hands in a sign of surrender.

"Georgia," he said in a low, soothingly deep voice. "I'm not here to hurt you. Quite the opposite."

She frowned, not lowering her killer Hello Kitty purse. Didn't psychos always say they weren't going to hurt you right before they did horrible things?

"Who are you?" she demanded, taking a step back, forcing herself not to break her stare even as she heard a crinkle from stepping on one of her shopping bags.

"My name is Gabriel. I work at *HOT!*, too."

"In the mail room."

He nodded.

"You've been following me today, haven't you?"

The large man's eyes widened slightly, but then he nodded. "Yes, but I really don't mean you any harm. I just need to talk to you."

"You were standing only several feet from my desk today. You could have talked to me there."

"I couldn't talk to you there. It isn't safe." He lowered his hands and took another step toward her.

"Stop right there," Georgia said, although the order sounded shaky, even to her. "I have pepper spray."

Like he'd believe that, but he did raise his hands again.

"Honestly, Georgia, I'm not here to hurt you. I'm here to tell you that you could be in danger and to ask that you help me."

She stared at him. What the hell was this lunatic talking about?

"I know you have no reason to believe me, but I'm telling you the truth."

She couldn't believe she was listening to this, but she was. Maybe she was as crazy as he.

"Why am I possibly in danger?"

This was probably the point where he laughed evilly and lunged for her, showing her exactly how she was in danger.

Instead, he kept his hands up and simply said, "You could be in danger from Tristan McIntyre."

Gabriel hadn't expected Georgia to listen to him even this long. After all, he was just a stranger approaching her in her own apartment building. And then she was already aware he'd been following her today.

Clearly, he was losing his touch at going unnoticed.

"Tristan?" she said, her brows drawing together over the tortoiseshell rims of her glasses. "I mean, Mr. McIntyre? How am I in danger from him?"

Gabriel caught her initial familiarity with her boss. Again his gut tightened, wondering if this plan would really work. If Georgia really trusted McIntyre, then it was pretty damned likely she'd tell him about this encounter. Gabriel had to make his warning sound believable, yet also not scare her away from helping. A fine line, to be sure.

"I work for a company that is investigating Mr. McIntyre. We have reason to believe he's involved in some . . . underworld activities."

Underworld, that wasn't even a lie.

"Okay," she said slowly, clearly not seeing how she fit into this issue.

"We need someone, someone who already works closely with him, to give us some feedback on his interactions with . . . his associates."

"Why can't someone from your company just follow him?"

"Well, we're clearly not that great at following people, are we?" Gabriel hadn't expected to make a joke, and from her stunned expression, Georgia hadn't expected one either.

But she slowly shook her head. "No, you are pretty terrible at being covert."

He smiled sheepishly. Maybe his years in the office had dulled his slayer skills, too. And here he'd been so quick to comment on his fellow slayer who had gotten noticed just a little while ago.

He clearly owed Michael an apology next time they talked.

But right now he had to get this job done, and done right. "The reason we are asking for your help is because you work so closely with him. You already have access to his meetings and appointments. He trusts and counts on you."

Gabriel hoped McIntyre trusted her. Georgia would be in very real danger if McIntyre perceived her as a threat.

She's in real danger now, he reminded himself. That was why it was worth the risk of asking for her help.

Georgia considered his words, her ruby red lips pursed in thought.

"So Tristan— Mr. McIntyre is mixed up in illegal activities? Or at least you think so?"

Gabriel nodded. "We believe he is working with a whole legion of underworld . . . henchmen. And what we need to know is who he is working with. Names. Places. So we can figure out our best strategy to bring them all down."

She fell silent again, still thinking about what she'd just heard. That actually made Gabriel feel better about this woman. She wasn't impulsive. She looked like she should be with her crazy hair and clothing, but she clearly thought things out. That made her more trustworthy in Gabriel's book.

"So I'd be a spy?" she finally asked.

"Yes."

She nodded, digesting that idea.

"Is—is he potentially deadly?"

It was Gabriel's turn to think out his answer. He wanted to make her understand how much they needed her help, but he didn't want to frighten her away either. After a moment, he decided to go with the truth. His gut told him Georgia Sullivan respected the truth, even if it wasn't what she wanted to hear.

"We believe he could be."

Georgia's skin paled, making her black eye makeup look even starker behind her glasses.

"But I will be at *HOT!* keeping an eye on you. You won't be alone. My team will be there to protect you."

Georgia didn't look convinced or even mildly reassured. Given what she'd seen of his work thus far, he didn't blame her.

"I— I can't answer you now."

Gabriel wasn't surprised by that response. What he'd told her was a lot to take in. And he also knew she was attracted to McIntyre. That was going to make this even harder to comprehend. No one liked the idea of the person they liked being less than what they thought.

"I totally understand. I will let you think it over, and if you have any other questions"—he took a step toward her, closing the gap between them just enough to lean forward and hand her his card—"this is my cell. I will answer any time, day or night. Also I will be in the mail room, very close by. Please don't hesitate to contact me."

She accepted the small, plain white rectangle, but didn't look at it. He wasn't sure if that was a good or bad sign.

"Again, I'm sorry to have scared you."

She nodded, watching him as he walked past her. The heel of her shoe was stuck on the handle of one of the plastic shopping bags, which moved with her as she turned, but she didn't seem to notice. She was too busy scrutinizing him to even be aware of the clinging bag.

He paused at the front door of the building. "Again, you

don't have anything to worry about from me or the company I work for. We are the good guys. And whatever you decide, please be cautious around McIntyre. He's definitely not one of the good guys."

Chapter Thirteen

Georgia stared at the large man who called himself Gabriel, not looking away until the door clicked shut, locking behind him.

How had he gotten in here anyway? Not that it was terribly hard to enter any locked apartment building. He just had to wait until someone entered or exited and go inside with them. But he'd also had her address. How had he gotten that?

He worked for *HOT!* so it probably wasn't too hard to track down her address. But then, there was the story he'd told her. Tristan was a mob kingpin—or something like that. She'd been working for Finola and then Tristan for several months, nearly a year, and she hadn't noticed anything odd going on. Well, not odd in an illegal, gangster sort of way.

"And aside from *Good Fellas* and *Casino,* what would you know about mob activity?" she mumbled to herself. Hell, she hadn't even seen the *Godfather* movies. It had seemed like too much of a time commitment, and she was more of a *Buffy the Vampire Slayer* and *Underworld* kinda gal.

Underworld. There was an irony there, given Gabriel had used that word, but certainly not in a vampire, werewolf, paranormal creature sort of way.

Now that might have intrigued her.

Really, was she standing here, honestly contemplating all of this? Clearly, this Gabriel was a loon.

She glanced down at his card. The cardstock was plain with just his name, Gabriel Evans, and a number. No company logo, no position title, no nothing. This man had to be nuts.

Damn, talk about a series of strange events. First Tristan asked her to attend a posh gala, then some odd stranger with huge biceps and an inability to tail a person unnoticed told her that she was working for a high-ranking mob boss. Her life couldn't get any weirder.

"Maybe you shouldn't risk that," she told herself. "And maybe you should stop talking to yourself, too."

Georgia looked at the clock on her nightstand. Seven-thirty. Crap.

Her mind was a swirl of crazy thoughts and concerns. What if she did make some worst dressed list in some magazine—probably in *HOT!* with her luck. And what did Tristan expect from this night? Was he just taking his assistant because it was easy? He didn't have to wine or dine her. It was just a simple business arrangement. Maybe that was why he had asked her in the first place.

Then there was the problem of wacky Gabriel and his outlandish story. She couldn't decide how to handle him. One part of her thought she should probably just tell Tristan he had a nutty, conspiracy theorist working in his mail room. Clearly that was what Gabriel had to be. Tristan a mobster—that was silly. And frankly, Gabriel's whole approach—following her and showing up at her apartment building—was all a bit too *True Lies* for her.

You will be helping your country and the whole free world by spying on your boss, the editor-in-chief of a fashion magazine.

The only crime Tristan was committing was helping to convince women all over the world that they were lacking if they weren't a size four with toned bodies, flawless skin, and boobs that only happened naturally on a size-sixteen woman.

She looked at herself in the mirror, turning to the side to get a partial view of her dress from the back. Well, she had the size-sixteen boobs. Unfortunately, she had the butt, hips, and waist to match.

She made a face at herself in the mirror, and then moved in closer to touch up her makeup.

It seemed so obvious what she should do. She needed to tell Tristan about his deluded employee. Even though she ultimately didn't feel threatened by Gabriel, that didn't mean he couldn't be dangerous later on. And he did know where she lived. That was unnerving.

Yet, she still wasn't sure. Maybe she should wait and see. Maybe watch Tristan's communications and activities a little closer. It couldn't hurt for a couple of days. After all, what if Gabriel was telling the truth?

"You're as nutty as he is," she said, pausing in her application of mascara to address herself. And all this talking to herself would only confirm that to the rest of the world.

She finished her makeup and fixed her hair, then pulled in a deep breath. Gabriel's wild accusations were forgotten for the time being. Instead, her stomach fluttered with nervous energy and doubts began to niggle at her again.

She couldn't do this. A gala with all the beautiful people, and she would be on the arm of one of the most beautiful. She felt more like the beast than the princess.

Don't get yourself worked up. Don't get yourself worked up.

At least she wasn't talking aloud to herself, she thought as she headed down the hallway to the living room. That was a start in getting herself composed.

Maybe.

★   ★   ★

"Oh, darling, you look beautiful."

Georgia smiled at her grandmother, who sat on the over-sized aubergine velvet sofa, her frail form nearly swallowed up by the plush cushions. She worked on a scarf for Georgia, her knitting needles clacking away even as she admired her granddaughter.

"Thank you, Grammy." But instead of the reassuring effect the compliment should have had, Georgia's stomach quivered more.

She appreciated her grandmother's compliment, but Grace Sullivan wasn't a fashion expert. She wasn't looking at the exact fit of the satin around Georgia's too thick arms. Or the fact that Georgia probably was showing dreaded back fat, made worse by her strapless bra. Or the fact that her dress was off the rack, a vintage number of unknown origin.

But the number one thing Grammy didn't understand was that Georgia was a nobody about to go out on a date, or whatever she was supposed to call it, with one of fashion's most powerful—and desired—men.

Everyone at the gala would see all of those things. They would see every flaw, and more.

Georgia's stomach roiled at the thought. God, she was going to be sick. But it was far better to do that here than at the gala. Puking on the red carpet was sure to get gossip rag attention—as well as airtime on *TMZ*.

"Your Tristan is going to be speechless," Grammy said, clearly oblivious to Georgia's rapidly developing shade of green.

Hopefully not speechless in a bad way, Georgia thought. But she didn't make her worries known. Instead, she forced a smile and then told her grandmother that she was going to give Marnie a call to make sure she remembered she had agreed to come over for the evening.

"I don't need anyone to stay with me." Grammy sniffed indignantly, her knitting needles clacking once more, maybe a little louder.

"Marnie said she didn't have anything to do, and she'd like the company tonight," Georgia assured Grammy, knowing the older woman didn't like the idea of essentially having a babysitter. And who could blame her?

"Well, okay," Grammy said. "I guess a little company would be nice."

Georgia smiled and headed to her bedroom to retrieve her cell phone. Alzheimer's was a funny disease, in a very not funny way. Sometimes Grammy knew exactly what was going on. Other times, she was completely confused, having no recollection of anything they'd talked about, even moments before.

But tonight, she seemed to be doing well. She certainly remembered Tristan and his fib that they were a couple. Georgia supposed that would be pretty memorable. Tristan was memorable all on his own, without his cockamamie lie.

She scrolled through her saved contacts to find Marnie's number. Marnie lived in the same apartment building, three floors up, and was Georgia's only good friend in the city besides Grammy. Marnie often came down to sit with Grammy when Georgia was running late at work, which was a lifesaver. Georgia always gave her friend something for staying with her grandmother, but it wasn't a fraction of the cost of the home care nurse. And Marnie appreciated the arrangement, too, since she was a struggling artist. Georgia knew when Grammy got worse, she wouldn't be able to rely on Marnie as much, but right now it benefited everyone.

Marnie's number simply rang and rang.

"Great." Maybe in her whirlwind to get ready for tonight, she'd forgotten to contact Marnie. She thought she had, but after this crazy day, who could remember?

Georgia looked at the alarm clock again. Tristan would be here any moment.

Just then a knock sounded at the apartment door. He was here. Tristan had a weird habit of doing that—materializing as soon as she thought of him.

"I'll get it," Grammy called, but Georgia rushed out of her room, racing past the living room as fast as her new, strappy, bright red high heels would carry her.

"Relax, Gram, I got it."

She paused at the door, touching her hair and smoothing down the skirt of her dress. She pulled in a deep breath, wishing she had taken a shot of tequila or maybe a horse tranquilizer. Something to calm her frenzied nerves.

It's just Tristan.

She snorted at that line of thought. Just Tristan. Like he wasn't unnerving enough without fashion bigwigs, Hollywood elite, and paparazzi all around them.

And possibly hired henchmen, she added, then pushed that thought aside.

Did she have any tequila in the house? Maybe she had time for a swig or two.

Another knock echoed through the small hallway.

Or not.

She pulled in one more deep breath and opened the door, bracing herself.

"Damn, girl, don't you look like a sexy fifties' pinup bomb. That dress is smokin'. I love it."

"Marnie." Georgia literally sagged with relief.

"Were you that worried I wouldn't show? I told you I would be here."

"It's not that," Georgia said, although she had been a little worried about whether her friend would show. "I'm just a nervous wreck."

Marnie was a pixie of a woman with super-short hair that

made her big brown eyes look even bigger and her full lips look even fuller. She wore her usual baggy jeans and paint-splotched flannel shirt with a tank top underneath. Georgia was always amazed that her hair and clothes and lack of makeup only managed to make her look all the more feminine. She was stunning.

A niggle of regret and envy tightened Georgia's chest. Would she look like Miss Piggy with a retro flare standing beside small, adorable Marnie? Maybe that wasn't such a bad thing. Maybe Tristan would see the mistake he'd made by asking Georgia to attend this gala with him. Maybe he'd decide she didn't need to go with him after all.

So if it wasn't such a bad thing, why did the idea make her feel so miserable?

Apparently, her misery was written on her face.

"Okay, the dress and the shoes," Marnie waved a hand downward from Georgia's head to her toes, "the whole look screams fabulous night out. But your expression—you look more than stressed, sweetie. What's got my usually fierce friend looking so shaken?"

Georgia laughed despite her frazzled nerves. "Fierce? I hardly think that describes me."

"Oh, I'd say that describes you to a tee."

Both women turned to see Tristan leaning against the doorframe, his broad shoulders encased in a perfectly fitted black suit that was probably made specifically for him and specifically for this evening's event.

Neither woman spoke until Tristan shifted and raised an eyebrow, clearly waiting for an invitation inside.

"Oh," Georgia said, stepping back, "please come in."

"Thank you," he said with another of his crooked and utterly breathtaking smiles.

Again, Georgia's mind seemed to blank. She'd seen Tristan dressed for special occasions many times, but tonight he seemed more amazingly handsome than she ever remembered. Maybe because he was going to be with her all evening.

With her. Oh, dear, she was starting to feel ill again.

"Hello," Tristan said after another moment of awkward silence as he watched Georgia panic and change colors. Red to green to a deeper green. He held out his hand to Marnie. "I'm Tristan McIntyre."

"Mr. McIntyre is my boss," Georgia explained, then realized that Marnie didn't need the extra clarification. "Of course, I've told you about him before."

Georgia felt her cheeks heat. And go back to red.

"Talking to your friends about me, huh?" Tristan said, shooting Georgia a teasing look.

"Only good things," Marnie assured him, accepting his extended hand.

"Well, Georgia is an excellent employee." He glanced in Georgia's direction again. "Definitely the best."

Was there an underlying implication there? Georgia was probably just reading too much into his words. He was being his usual flirty self. Although, the smile he gave Marnie was nothing but polite. No naughty twist to his lips, or devilish twinkle in his impossibly green eyes.

"Georgia, is your handsome man here?" Grammy called out from the living room.

Georgia winced, but before she could answer, Tristan beat her to it.

"Grace." He immediately headed to the living room.

"Wow," Marnie whispered when he was far enough out of earshot, "you didn't tell me he was *that* good looking."

"Would mere words really have done him justice?"

Marnie chuckled and shook her head. "No, you definitely need to see him to believe it."

"And that's why I feel like I'm going to be ill."

Marnie chuckled and patted her friend's arm, clearly not taking Georgia seriously.

Tristan was already settled onto the overstuffed sofa, chatting easily with her grandmother when they stepped into the room. Grammy glowed under his attention.

"Isn't your boy looking handsome?" Grammy said, the twinkle in her eyes and the grin on her face making her look like a young woman.

"Grammy, he's not my—"

"Grace, you are the one looking lovely tonight. Did you get your hair done today?"

She had, and Georgia didn't think Tristan was just throwing compliments out there in hopes one might stick. She genuinely got the impression that he'd noticed, which made her heart race even faster in her chest. There was something so appealing about a man who noticed small things like that.

Grace preened, again looking like a young schoolgirl. "Just a little rinse and set."

"Well, it looks smashing. And what are you working on here?" he asked.

Grammy told him about the scarf she was making for Georgia, and Tristan listened to the trials and tribulations of pearling and double stitching as if it was the most fascinating thing he'd heard in ages. And Georgia and Marnie watched him as if he were the most fascinating thing they'd encountered in ages, too.

Once Grammy was done with the adventures in knitting, Tristan reached out to pat the woman's gnarled hand.

"I wish I could stay and chat longer," Tristan told her. "But Georgia and I must get to Lincoln Center to make our appearances and make sure the paparazzi get as many photos of my stunning Georgia as possible."

Lincoln Center . . . paparazzi . . . stunning . . . his Georgia.

Oh, God, Georgia felt woozy. She couldn't do this.

"Lincoln Center," Marnie said, impressed. "This must be one swank affair."

"A very swank affair, indeed." Tristan's gaze met Georgia's, but she couldn't decide what to make of the look or his comment. Why did she get the feeling he was emphasizing affair rather than swank?

Because you are losing your mind.

"We certainly don't want to make you late," Grammy said.

"No, definitely not," Marnie agreed.

Apprehension tightened Georgia's stomach again. "Let me just go grab my wrap and my purse."

She left the room, not rushing this time.

Calm down. Calm down. Stop being such a twit. She'd never make it through this night if she didn't get a handle on herself.

She paused inside her cluttered room, trying to compose herself and remember exactly what the heck she'd come in here to get.

"Pull it together, Georgia," she muttered to herself.

Great, she was back to talking aloud to herself. She snatched up her pashmina and searched in her jumble of clothing and other clutter for her clutch purse.

"Girl, you really need to calm down." Marnie walked into her room. "You are a mess."

"Thanks for sugarcoating it."

Marnie made a pained face. "I don't think you have time for me to sugarcoat it. You are getting ready to go out for a night of stars and fashion and opulence with the most beautiful man I've ever seen."

"You're not helping."

Georgia tossed aside a pair of flannel pajama bottoms, growing more agitated by the moment.

"Georgia, stop."

Georgia shot her friend a desperate look. "I have to find my purse."

"This one?" Marnie held up the clutch Georgia had been

ripping the room apart to find. It was a fifties' vintage piece in black and red patent leather.

"Yes," Georgia said with a sigh of relief. She reached for it, but Marnie pulled it back before she grabbed it.

Georgia gave her a puzzled look, her hand still held out for the purse.

Marnie ignored her impatient wave. "Georgia, you really have no clue how stunning and amazing you are, do you?"

Georgia wasn't sure she could handle a pep talk—even though she knew she needed one.

"I'm serious, chickie," Marnie said with a wide and fond smile. "You are amazing and beautiful and when you walk into a room, you just shine. Don't second guess yourself and your style. You know yourself, and I'm positive that is one thing most of those Hollywood stars and critics and even the designers themselves can't say. Don't . . . doubt . . . you."

Georgia focused on her friend's words. She shouldn't doubt herself. So she was curvy with big boobs and an apple bottom. So she loved everything retro. And she loved hair dye and makeup. She always had—since she was a teenager. Though she'd refined her look since those days.

She caught her image in the mirror. Marnie was right. Georgia did know herself. And she did like herself. Either Tristan would dig her look, too, or this would be her one and only grand outing with the man. It probably was anyway, so she'd just chill and enjoy it.

"You're right," Georgia said, turning to her friend to hug her. "I just need to enjoy every moment of this fabulous, once-in-a-lifetime evening. Who cares what anyone else thinks?"

Marnie squeezed her back. "Exactly. But I can tell you now, people are going to be blown away."

Chapter Fourteen

"What is this?"

Tristan looked at Georgia's profile, not that he'd been able to take his eyes off her for more than a few seconds at a time. The way the satin of her dress draped over her full hips. That low-cut neckline, which was now hidden by her wrap, beautifully displayed her round breasts and the deep valley of cleavage between them. His mouth literally watered even just in memory.

How the hell was he going to stay at the gala long enough to talk with his newest recruits, and not just whisk her away to the suite he had reserved? Just getting to the gala, period, was going to be an astronomical feat.

Then his gaze moved up to her face and saw the expression on it was filled with surprise. He realized she'd asked him a question, although she didn't seem to notice he hadn't answered her. Her eyes were locked on the shiny, black stretch limo parked in front of her building.

He blinked, making himself shove aside the haze of lust blurring his thoughts. Even her look of wonder, like a child's on Christmas morning—not that he was personally familiar with children or Christmas morning—but still that awestruck look of hers still managed to drive him wild.

She dragged her gaze away from the limousine to him. "A limo?"

Tristan raised an eyebrow. "You hardly expected me to drive, now did you?"

She made a gesture somewhere between a shake of her head and a shrug. "Well, it's not exactly like you have a shabby car, but I guess I should have realized you would use the limo service for an event like this. I mean you are expected to, right?"

"You know my life. A slave to appearance," he said wryly.

Her expression of amazement faded slightly, but Tristan didn't have time to ponder why as his driver came around the front of the vehicle.

"Good evening—" William hesitated when he saw Georgia. "Georgia?"

Georgia's already flushed cheeks reddened even more. "William. Hi."

Was she embarrassed to be seen with him? That idea didn't sit well with Tristan. No one was embarrassed to be seen with him. But his dismay over Georgia's reaction was quickly replaced by the driver's.

The hulking driver's dark gaze roamed over Georgia, appreciation clear on his face. He smiled, a wide grin that revealed deep dimples and made his teeth gleam against his dark complexion.

"Dam—" William caught himself, realizing his boss was right there. "Don't you look gorgeous tonight, Miss Georgia."

Georgia laughed, her cheeks a pretty pink, her expression more relaxed than Tristan had seen it since he'd asked her to join him tonight.

" 'Miss Georgia'? Really? But thank you, William," she said with a natural easiness that made Tristan's gut wrench with some emotion he didn't understand. He just knew she never spoke so easily with him.

"You hardly expected to see me attending one of these chichi events, did you? Neither did I."

William chuckled, the sound low and rumbling as if they were sharing some private joke.

Tristan wasn't amused.

"Well, you look the part," William said, and nodded with more appreciation.

Lust wafted off the large man, so thick Tristan was surprised even Georgia couldn't smell it.

Tristan really wasn't amused.

Tristan placed a hand on the small of Georgia's back. She started at the touch, but didn't move away. Her familiar scent surrounded him, blocking out William's just a bit. Enough for Tristan's tension to relax, a little anyway. She still wanted Tristan.

As if there was any doubt.

"William," Tristan said, his tone more curt than he intended, "we don't want to be late."

The driver immediately nodded, realizing his behavior was unprofessional. He bowed slightly, his black jacket straining against his broad shoulders and bulging biceps.

"Yes, Mr. McIntyre." He hurried to open the door for them.

Tristan frowned as Georgia offered the large man another smile and thanked him. Tristan placed himself between the man and Georgia, helping usher her into the back. For a moment, he struggled to describe the foreign feeling, but his pondering was replaced by the appreciation of her nice derriere as she leaned forward, trying to figure out the most ladylike way to crawl into the vehicle.

That appreciation was quickly marred when he noticed William's gaze admiring her actions, too.

After a second, she opted to turn, sit and slide across the bench seat. Tristan was sad to see the lovely view disappear, but not disappointed that William was no longer admiring it along with him.

Still, Tristan couldn't help shooting the man a warning

look, which William had the sense to heed. William glanced down, waiting for Tristan to follow her into the limo. Which he did, sliding across the seat, until his shoulder, hip, and leg were pressed against Georgia.

More of that strange feeling swelled inside Tristan, but he ignored it, gesturing for William to close the door.

Once they were alone, Tristan turned toward her, his leg pressing tighter against hers.

"So you know William."

Georgia shot him a glance; then her gaze dropped to where they touched. "Of course. He's your usual driver, so I talk to him quite often. He sometimes comes up to the reception area when he's waiting for you."

Tristan nodded. That made sense, and why was he even asking? More importantly, why did he even care? So the man was attracted to her. Usually that just ramped up his own lust. He fed just as easily off of other people's lust for each other as he did off lust directed toward him. In fact, he'd normally be considering a threesome. After all, the more desire, the better. Lust fed him. Made him stronger, more powerful.

But tonight, he didn't feel that usual drive or satisfaction. Tonight, William's lust for Georgia hadn't aroused him. It had . . . pissed him off. Tristan was only interested in one human's lust and she was seated right beside him.

But singling out one, when he could clearly have double the lust . . . that was very strange.

Up front, William got into the limo and started to pull into traffic. Georgia turned her attention to the passing scenery.

The air wasn't filled with desire, but awkwardness. Not at all what Tristan wanted for this night.

So why was he focused on another man's desire for Peaches, when he should be working on his own seduction? Clearly, he desperately needed to seduce her so he could get back to feeling like his normal insatiable self, rather than having the highly pedestrian feeling of being ready to fight for the attention of just one woman.

He intended to rectify that right now.

Except instead of saying something suave or flirty, he said, "William is attracted to you."

Why the hell had he said that?

Georgia shot him a surprised look; then she laughed. "That's silly. He is not."

Then he realized why he'd told her. Not to make her aware of the other man's interest, but to see how she reacted. And aside from her obvious amusement, and maybe a touch of bewilderment, she didn't react at all. No flare of that lust he sensed and smelled when he flirted with her. None.

Tristan's usual smugness returned. She wasn't interested in the large, muscular man. Not in the least.

"Well, I can hardly blame him. You are stunning."

Whoosh. And just like that, the whole back of the limousine was heavy with the rich, luscious scent of her desire.

He smiled, feeling much more like himself. He shifted, pressing closer to her. More desire.

He didn't need to speculate on his earlier odd feelings. All he needed to focus on was this intense desire of hers, his own lust, and his plans of seduction.

"Let's have some music and a drink."

"Okay," Georgia agreed guardedly, her voice a little breathy. None of the ease of talking to William, but Tristan would rectify that, too.

Tristan reached over his head and pressed a button and the back compartment of the vehicle filled with music. Not overtly romantic music, but the beat was fun and somewhat sensual.

"The Cure?" she said, casting him another surprised look.

"Am I right to peg you as an eighties alternative girl?"

She smiled then. "Totally."

Damn, her smile was gorgeous. Tristan wanted to kiss her right then and there, but he knew he couldn't rush. Seducing his Peaches was going to take time and finesse. And that was part of the fun.

"How about a little champagne?"

"Yes. Please."

He slid forward to retrieve a bottle of Dom Perignon 1966 from the ice bucket readied for them. A pop echoed over the music as he deftly uncorked it and poured her a glass.

"Thank you," she said, that slightly bemused look back on her face as she accepted the champagne flute from him.

He poured himself a glass and settled back beside her. Both sipped silently for a few moments as The Cure's "Love Song" filled the air around them.

She polished off her champagne in record time, and she didn't refuse when he took the glass and refilled it.

When that glass was nearly empty, he asked, "Good, isn't it?"

She paused, her glass partway to her lips, shooting him a sheepish look.

"It's very good."

He nodded and took a deep swallow of his own. He could already feel her body relaxing beside his. Champagne was rather miraculous that way, going straight to mortals' heads.

"And what do you think of the limo?"

She didn't answer right away. Then to his surprise, she giggled. "I feel like we should be picking up our friends and heading to the prom."

Tristan stared at her for a moment, and then laughed himself. "What?" he said, confused.

"I feel like we should be on the way to the prom."

"Well, I'm not terribly familiar with proms, so explain this reasoning to me," he said, honestly interested.

"Yeah, right," she said dubiously. "Like you weren't the prom king or something."

He shook his head, finding himself watching her and grinning. He liked this more relaxed side of her. Loved it, in fact.

Because it promised lots of fun in bed, he told himself, even as he felt the strangest twinge in his chest at her adorable smile.

"Honestly," he said, "we didn't have proms where I'm from."

"No proms—where would that wonderful world be?" She sighed as if he were telling her he came from over the rainbow. Apparently, proms were not something she had enjoyed.

"I had a pretty austere upbringing. Proms would have been considered far too frivolous for my world."

"Did you grow up in that town in *Footloose*?"

He frowned, growing more confused by the moment. "I'm not sure what town you are referring to. And I have no idea what 'footloose' is aside from being paired with 'fancy-free.' "

Georgia laughed. A genuine laugh that thrilled Tristan to the marrow.

"I'm sure you know the term 'footloose and fancy-free' very, very well." She laughed again.

He didn't deny that, but continued on with this fascinating conversation. "So explain what happens at a prom."

"Well," she said slowly, "it's a high school ritual where the girls wait and pray that some sweaty, pimply teenage boys will ask them to be their date. Then the girls wear gowns that they later wonder why the heck they ever thought they looked good in. And the parents take tons of embarrassing pictures that will be used as blackmail at a later date, and when everyone finally gets to the dance, they just stand around, not dancing, wondering why they desperately wanted to attend."

"That sounds"—Tristan made a pained face—"really awful."

"I think for most, it pretty much is." She giggled again and took another sip of her champagne.

He took a sip, too, pleased that she was actually at ease with him. He'd seen moments of this lighthearted side of her, but not as much as he'd liked. And he did like it. A lot.

"So wait," he said, "I still don't connect how a limo goes with this prom thing."

She shifted slightly toward him. "Oh, well. That's one of the things kids feel they need to make that special night extra-special."

"A limo? To attend a high school dance while wearing unfortunate fashion choices where you don't actually dance?"

She nodded. "Yep." Then she added, "To be fair, I suppose some kids dance. I did."

"And did you attend with the sweaty, pimply teenage boy of your dreams?"

"No, I went with my gay best friend. That's why I danced."

He chuckled, shaking his head. "I'm still not sure I understand proms."

She laughed, that lovely, throaty tone filling the back of the limo. "It's probably best to leave that one of life's mysteries anyway."

He nodded, smiling widely.

★   ★   ★

Georgia covertly studied him, loving that smile still lingering on his lips. And wondering how the heck she'd told him all of that. Proms, really.

Surely, it was the champagne, which had readily spread warmth and a wonderful sense of cheerful calm through her. Did he think she was ridiculous?

She cast another sidelong glance in his direction. He looked very content and happy, too.

She decided not to worry about it. She worried far too much: about her grandmother, her job, money, and her inappropriate attraction to her boss. She *should* really be worrying about that last one tonight, but she couldn't bring herself to bother at this moment.

Sure, she was in a limo, her side pressed against his, going to a posh gala with him. If there was a time to worry about her reaction to him, it was now, but she just wasn't.

And then there was that guy—her champagne-clouded brain couldn't even recall his name. Gabriel. That was it. There was his crazy story, and stalking, that should be worrying her, but she just couldn't muster up the energy to do so. She'd decide what to do about that tomorrow.

Instead, she took another sip of her champagne and sneaked another look at Tristan. This time, he was looking back.

She felt her cheeks heat, but it wasn't with the usual embarrassment. This time, it was with awareness. Did she see real desire in his eyes?

Okay, the champagne really was going to her head. Still, she considered what she'd do if her boss made a move tonight. The way she was feeling right now, all warm and tingly and happy, she might just go for it.

Such a bad idea. Bad, bad idea.

"Did I mention how beautiful you look?" he said, and his face seemed to move closer to hers. Maybe it was just the limo jostling slightly. Maybe it was an effect of the bubbly.

But whatever the reason, she didn't shift away. She leaned toward those beautiful sculpted lips. And just as she closed her eyes and waited for them to press against hers, the limo door opened.

Chapter Fifteen

Georgia's eyes snapped open and she clutched the edge of the seat to pull herself away from Tristan and to get her bearings. William's large frame blocked the bright lights of Lincoln Center behind him. But the cool air and the sound of cars and a crowd were enough to ruin the magical moment between her and Tristan in their private, warm, bubbly, and Cure-filled cocoon.

She blinked again, some of her usual anxiety returning. Had she really been about to kiss Tristan—Mr. McIntyre—her boss? No matter how wonderful and safe the back of that limo had seemed, kissing her boss was a terrible idea. Maybe all her worries had finally caused her to lose her mind.

But it was more likely the champagne. She never could hold her liquor.

"Sorry to startle you, sir," William said, giving them both an awkward look, reinforcing the realization that she'd just been moments from doing something colossally stupid. "But we are here."

"Thank you," Tristan said, his rich, chocolaty voice clipped.

Was that tone because Tristan was disappointed to have the moment interrupted? Or was it because he was uncomfortable with the idea that William might have seen it? Or just uncomfortable in general?

The answer didn't really matter. It was just a good thing the moment had been stopped. Of course, her aroused body didn't agree in the least.

William stepped aside and Tristan slid forward, extending his long legs out the door to stand. He turned and offered his hand to her. She hesitated for only a second before slipping her hand into his. He helped her out, and continued to hold her fingers as they stepped away from the limousine.

Reality hit with blinding force. Large lights illuminated the carpeted walkway up the steps of Lincoln Center, and seas of people crowded the rope barriers on either side of the carpet, creating an undulating wall caging them in. Cameras flashed and people yelled.

"This way!"

"Mr. McIntyre!"

"Over here!"

Georgia didn't know where to look first, and the pleasant feeling the champagne had created while seated in the back of the limo now became discomfort in all the pandemonium. Her head swam and she had a hard time focusing her eyes.

"Are you okay?" Tristan squeezed her hand and pulled her closer to his side.

"This is . . . a lot."

He chuckled, although Georgia couldn't figure out what was amusing. She made a slight noise of dismay as he released her hand. She didn't want to lose that connection. She couldn't make her entrance without him to anchor her. Without his hand locked around hers, she felt as if she'd been set adrift. And although realistically, the mob couldn't get any closer to them because of the barricades and the security, she felt as if their sheer energy would drag her away.

Just when she would have flung out a hand to catch Tristan's again, his arm slipped around her waist, holding her tight to his side.

"Don't be nervous," he said, his voice close to her ear, deep and calm. "Just stay close to me and smile. You look amazing. We look amazing."

If she wasn't so overwhelmed, she might have laughed at his arrogance, but right now she needed that confidence.

Tristan began to walk. He raised his free hand and waved, and Georgia was blinded by more flashes and shouts.

Stay calm, she told herself. And just follow Tristan's lead. She didn't wave, but she did manage to plaster a smile on her face. She also managed to get her swirling head calmed so she could take in what was going on around her. The crowd swarming the barricades was large, but they just jostled to get a look at the celebrities, not to physically reach out to them. Between that realization and Tristan's secure hold, she calmed even more. And maybe it was the champagne again.

Tristan paused, which confused Georgia for a moment; then she realized he was stopping to give photographers a chance to snap shots. He waved and smiled.

"Have fun, Georgia," Tristan murmured, his voice close to her ear again.

Maybe it was Tristan. Or maybe her subconscious had taken on the voice of Tristan. The side of her subconscious that urged her to be audacious and decadent and wild.

It made sense that the devilish side of her psyche would sound like the man she knew was all of those things. Her angelic side remained silent.

Georgia smiled and raised a hand to wave, too. Who cared if the paparazzi didn't really care about her? She would take advantage of this pretty darned amazing moment.

She was walking a red carpet with Tristan McIntyre, the

editor-in-chief of *HOT!* magazine. And he was one gorgeous man. Why not enjoy this?

Tristan hugged her closer. "What do you think, beautiful?"

She smiled up at him, back to how she'd been in the limo, letting herself enjoy this moment. This Cinderella at the ball moment. It would be over in the harsh light of tomorrow, but tonight, why not just enjoy?

"The carpet isn't red," she said, a fact she'd noticed right away. It was gold. Literally glistening like polished precious metal under her heeled feet.

Tristan laughed that full, spontaneous laugh of his.

He shook his head, his wide smile gorgeous. "You never say what I expect you will. You always surprise me."

"Is that a good thing?" she asked.

"Very," he said. "Since I'm not easy to surprise."

But it was his turn to surprise her. His head came down, his lips capturing hers. She froze, for just a moment, then made a slight whimper and kissed him back. Bright lights flashed behind her closed lids, but she only barely registered them. She was too lost in the feel and taste of this man. His lips moved over hers, strong and velvety soft at the same time.

His tongue teased the seam of her lips, but when she would have parted hers to allow him in, to taste his full heady flavor, he lifted his head.

Their eyes held for a moment, and then she heard cheers and more flashes of light and remembered exactly where they were.

How did he do that? Steal her inhibitions. Make her forget where she was. In front of hundreds of curious lookyloos.

"I'm sorry," he said, although she got no sense that he felt the least bit of remorse. "I just couldn't resist those rosebud lips of yours."

She nodded slightly, because she didn't know what else to do.

"Come on," he said, nudging her into movement. "I think the paparazzi got more photo ops than they expected."

Boy, did they. She fell into step alongside him, her legs as wobbly as jelly, or at least they felt that way. But she managed to walk up the steps and into the massive building without incident.

"Are you okay?" Tristan asked once they were away from the madness outside.

She nodded, still not able to find her voice, or even sure what to say if she did.

"Are you sure? You look pale."

She did? Probably because she knew she was going to regret her behavior in spades come tomorrow morning. But right now, honestly, she just wished he'd kiss her again.

"Come on," he said, apparently realizing she wasn't going to say anything. "Let's get another drink."

Tristan directed Georgia toward the ballroom and directly toward the bar set up in one corner of the enormous room. He hadn't intended to kiss her. Not in such a public forum. A *hugely* public forum.

It was probably not a wise choice. If Dippy and Finola got wind of his public display of affection toward Georgia, they would likely see it as weakness on his part. A distraction from his purpose here. And they would both get the idea that they could wheedle their way into the position of leader of the rebellion.

What they wouldn't understand was that the kiss wasn't a display of affection, but a display of lust. A lust that would be quenched tonight.

He looked back at Georgia. She stood to the side of the large room, wide-eyed as she took in her opulent surroundings. Absently, she touched her fingers to her glossed, rosy lips, and his body reacted instantly. She was remembering their kiss. So was he.

"Good evening, sir," the bartender greeted him. "What can I get you?"

Tristan ordered two more champagnes. Not the quality of what they'd been drinking earlier, but good enough. Good enough to hopefully calm his raging need and keep Georgia relaxed. Although he didn't think he'd need liquid lubrication to get her back to the suite with him. She was ripe for his seduction.

He let his gaze slide down her body as he approached her. He wouldn't need any sort of lubricant tonight. He could smell how ready she was for him.

"Here you go." He held out the champagne flute.

She accepted, giving him a teasing smile. "I think you are trying to get me drunk."

"Maybe," he agreed.

"Shame on you," she said, but then took a sip of the golden liquid.

"Well, Peaches, you know I'm very determined when it comes to getting what I want."

She nodded, and for the first time, he saw some of the wariness that she usually kept wrapped around her. He didn't want that. He loved the relaxed woman who had appeared in the limo, who had allowed his kiss, even with photographers and journalists watching every moment of the embrace.

He also realized he didn't want to be at this event any longer than necessary. He wanted to be alone with Peaches—as soon as possible.

That meant he had to get his act together and do the work that was needed for the takeover. He casually took a sip of his own drink, casting a gaze around the room. He easily spotted the men he needed to see tonight: Garwood Higgins and Frank Barrington.

Higgins was the editor of *Grace,* a highly popular rival magazine, and Barrington was one of the most famous fashion photographers in the industry. And both men were greedy and highly ambitious.

Both had been ridiculously easy to recruit. They were humans who wanted the ability and strength of demons. They'd been more than willing to sell their souls for more power. And tonight was the time for them to pay up on having their deepest desires granted. They hadn't just sold Tristan their souls. They'd sold him their loyalty and influence.

"I hate to have to do this," he said to Georgia, being honest, "but I have to handle a little business before we enjoy our night. I just want to get it out of the way."

"Of course," Georgia said readily. "I know these events are just as much about work as fun."

She did know that. As his personal assistant, she knew a lot about his work. But not all of it, that was for sure.

For a moment, he studied her as she looked around the room, her face so pretty and cherubic. What would Peaches think about the fact that she worked for one of Satan's minions? He didn't think she'd understand. He didn't think he could buy her soul either.

Maybe that was part of why he found her so intriguing and so beautiful. She wouldn't sell her soul for some selfish desire. He didn't know how he knew that fact, but he did.

But others were more than willing to do so, and right now, he had to deal with them.

"Okay, I'll be right back. Don't disappear on me."

"Skip out on *the* Tristan McIntyre. I wouldn't dare."

"Yeah, right," he said, enjoying her teasing, but he wasn't going to risk her leaving for any reason. Tonight was really about her, even if it should be about recruiting more humans to aid Satan's plan for world domination.

"Don't go anywhere," he ordered, although his tone was teasing, too.

"Yes, sir."

He chuckled to himself as he left her to cross the room to where Higgins and Barrington stood talking, cohorts in their greed. And stupidity.

Tristan realized he shouldn't disparage humans like these men for the ridiculous ease with which they parted with their souls. After all, it did make his job so much easier, but he sometimes wondered why any human would be foolish enough to believe material gain, power, or even carnal satisfaction was worth damning his eternal soul.

He frowned at his own train of thought. That was all far too philosophical for a demon. Far too moral, too.

Shit, if Dippy could hear his thoughts, he'd think Tristan was going soft.

"Hardly," he muttered to himself, then pasted on a suave smile as he approached his targets of the evening. Well, his demonic targets. His real target waited behind him in a sexy red dress and silk stockings.

"Hello, gentlemen," he said, forcing himself to deal with the task at hand. "We need to talk."

Chapter Sixteen

"Yes, No Doubt is working on a new CD."

Georgia lingered, listening, although she tried to look like she was fascinated with an ornate floral arrangement decorating one of the tables nearby. She was less than five feet away from Gwen Stefani.

Gwen Stefani!

Of course, the room was brimming with the rich and famous, just as she'd known it would be. She'd seen several celebrated designers. Stella McCartney. Tommy Hilfiger. And P. Diddy, or whatever name he was going by now. Then there were the celebrities. Brad Pitt and Angelina Jolie. $$$ and $$$.

Georgia struggled not to take her cellphone from her purse and try to covertly take some pictures of all of them. But she was supposed to be here as an equal, not an awestruck fan.

"Excuse me."

Georgia turned to find herself face to face with Gwen. Crap, she must have realized that Georgia couldn't be that inordinately fascinated with a flower arrangement for so long.

"I just have to tell you I love your dress. The color is awesome." Gwen smiled, and randomly Georgia noted she was wearing her signature ruby red lipstick.

Georgia blinked, and then managed a smile of her own. "Thank you. Thank you so much."

Gwen nodded, then moved on to mingle with $$$ and $$$.

Oh. My. God. Gwen Stefani had just complimented her dress. Of course, she would be the most likely in the room to appreciate her rockabilly style. Still, Georgia couldn't believe it. A compliment from a famous rocker chick and designer. And a kiss from Tristan McIntyre. This was definitely a Cinderella sort of night.

Not for the first time, the rich and famous faded from Georgia's thoughts and she returned to that kiss. Her toes curled in her designer knockoffs, also not for the first time since it had happened.

She'd had no doubt Tristan McIntyre was a good kisser. He exuded far too much sex appeal not to be, but the reality was amazing. Breathtaking. Unbelievable.

And despite the champagne—she was now working on her fourth glass (but it was okay, they were small)—she was attempting to be pragmatic about it. Tristan was a flirt. He loved attention. And he liked making the celebrity gossip rags. So she knew the kiss was nothing but a combination of all those things and she'd do best not to even make any comment about it. Tristan would probably forget it completely in a day or two.

She, on the other hand, would not. But that didn't mean she had to make a big deal out of it. Just enjoy the kiss for what it was—a bit of fun.

She wandered around the room, pausing here and there to listen to conversations. Some were as pretentious as one would expect at a gathering like this, but many were just normal chats. How are the kids? I heard your mother was in the hospital? She even heard Ellen Degeneres telling a story about her basement flooding. It was, of course, a humorous story, but still a story about a shoddy hot water heater, water damage, and the woes of dealing with home-owner's insurance. Normal stuff.

That realization comforted Georgia. Not that she was stressed. Okay, she could admit that maybe the kiss was niggling her a bit. She couldn't let it affect her job. She needed the money her job as personal assistant paid. And she also couldn't allow the memory of it to consume her, or cause her to have romantic notions about Tristan.

She would admit, to herself anyway, she had a crush on her boss. But crushes were harmless and she would not let her feelings get away from her.

Lifting her champagne glass to her lips, she realized it was empty. She debated getting another, but decided she'd had enough. Another glass might make her too loose lipped. If she wasn't careful, she'd end up telling Tristan she had a crush on him, but not to worry, it wouldn't affect her job. Or admitting something even stupider like she'd had a crush on him all along, and it hadn't hindered her ability to get work done. Or maybe she'd tell him she certainly wouldn't make more of their kiss than she should. Although, she'd really liked the kiss.

She sighed dreamily. The kiss.

Making a slight noise of dismay, she looked down at the empty glass. No, another glass was not an option. In fact, she was starting to think maybe four had been too many.

She placed the empty glass on the tray of a waiter passing by, and then looked around for the restroom. She needed to go freshen up and pull herself together.

To her right, she spotted a hallway. That seemed like a likely place to find restrooms. She walked in that direction, realizing her gait was a little unsteady.

Yeah, four glasses was definitely too many.

She stepped out into the hallway, relieved to see it was empty. Using the wall to steady herself, she teetered toward where she thought the ladies' room might be. The lighting was lower in the hallway, more ambient than direct. She walked slowly, her head swimming again.

Ahead of her, she saw a little sitting area, furnished with antique wingback chairs with a small table between them. The hallway continued to the right, but she decided to sit for a moment until her vertigo passed. She sat down and rested her head on the chair back, letting her eyes drift shut just for a moment.

Damn, she had to get it together. She didn't want Tristan to return to find her tipsy and a mess. And she didn't want to say anything stupid. Like talking about their kiss.

Stop thinking about the damned kiss. Oh, yeah, she needed to get herself together.

She breathed in slowly through her nose, willing the dizziness away, repeating to herself she didn't want to say something stupid to Tristan.

As soon as she thought his name, she could have sworn she heard him talking.

"Listen, gentlemen, a deal is a deal."

She frowned. Why would she imagine him saying that? Crap, she really was drunk. Then she heard another voice.

"We did sign the contracts, but it didn't say anything about working for . . ." The other man's voice dropped to almost a whisper, and Georgia couldn't hear the rest of what he said.

She opened her eyes and straightened in her seat. She leaned forward, looking around the wingback of the chair and down the hallway that jutted off the main one she'd just come down. At the end of the hallway, she saw shadows. They looked like the shadows of three men.

"Well, you can't believe that once you make a deal with the Devil you don't have to pay."

That voice was definitely Tristan's. Even as serious and stern as he sounded, she would recognize his anywhere.

A deal with the Devil? Was he talking about himself? What did he expect from the other men?

"It's not as if you aren't getting exactly what you want," Tristan added. "Can you deny it? Haven't you been getting all the things you wanted, just like I said you would?"

The first voice said, "Yes."

"And if anything, what I'm asking will only profit you more. More money, more power," Tristan told them. "Isn't that what you want?"

Two voices agreed.

"So do what I ask, and you will only know more success," Tristan said.

"I'm in," a voice she didn't recognize said.

"Excellent, Higgins," Tristan said, and Georgia could hear the smile in his voice. That smug smile she knew . . . and had often found attractive.

Higgins? Did she recognize that name? Was it someone Tristan had worked with at the magazine? Had she seen Higgins in his appointment books? She wasn't sure.

She stood, not understanding why she suddenly felt that she needed to get out of there. But something told her she needed to leave. To not be seen.

This time when she hurried down the hall, her footing was sure, no weaving, no lightheadedness. But her mind whirred. Who were those men and what had they been discussing?

Instantly, that strange guy—Gabriel—came to mind, and all the things he'd told her. Did Tristan have underworld affiliations as Gabriel had said? Was he a criminal? Was he dangerous?

He was clearly holding those men to some sort of contract. He was asking them to do something they hesitated to do.

She paused outside the ballroom, leaning against the wall,

feeling oddly breathless. She couldn't think clearly amidst all those people, and she needed to replay the dialogue she'd heard.

She had to be reading too much into it. After all, Tristan had told her that he had to go talk business, and it wasn't as if she'd heard him say anything that clearly stated he expected these men to do something illegal. Nor had she heard him make any actual threats. The men had signed some sort of contract and Tristan expected them to uphold that contract.

She'd worked for Tristan for months. She knew he had contracts with lots of people: photographers, writers, even designers. That had to be the kind of contract he was talking about.

Still, one line kept echoing in her head. *When you make a deal with the Devil.* That didn't sound good. But it also could simply be a turn of phrase. People used it all the time. It didn't truly imply that Tristan was dangerous, or threatening.

She touched a hand to her temple. She'd had too much to drink. That much she did know. And her overactive mind was getting away from her.

She dropped her hand and straightened away from the wall as two men appeared in the hallway and walked in her direction. Were those the men who'd been talking to Tristan? She didn't know.

Both men nodded at her as they returned to the ballroom. She should go back in, too, but before she could follow, her purse vibrated. It took her a moment to realize what was causing the insistent tremor.

Her cellphone, she finally realized, scolding herself for being so frazzled. She flipped open the purse and pulled out her phone.

Marnie's name lit up the touch screen. Concern tightened her chest. Marnie wouldn't call unless it was really necessary.

"Hello," she said, all the worry she'd been determined to suppress that night bubbling to the surface.

"Georgia, I'm headed to the hospital with your grandmother."

"Oh, my God, what's wrong?"

"It's nothing life-threatening," Marnie quickly assured her. "Your grandmother fell and hurt her ankle. I wasn't sure how bad it was, so I decided I'd better call an ambulance rather than try to move her myself. The EMTs checked her over and felt that she might have broken her ankle."

"Oh, no," Georgia said, guilt filling her chest. She should have been with her grandmother tonight. "Which hospital are you going to?"

"Beth Israel."

"Okay, I'll be right there. Please tell Grammy that I'll be there as soon as I can."

"I will," Marnie said. "Please don't panic. She's doing okay, just in some pain."

Georgia nodded, even though Marnie couldn't see that. "I'll be right there."

"Georgia," Tristan said, at her side when she hung up her phone. "What's wrong?"

A wave of relief flooded Georgia, making her weak. "I have to go. Grammy fell and she's on her way to Beth Israel Hospital. I need to get to her."

"Of course," Tristan said, taking her hand and hurrying her through the ballroom and toward the front entrance. His own cell was in his hand, and Georgia was vaguely aware that Tristan was calling William, telling him they needed the limo, right away.

They walked down the golden carpet to where they'd

been dropped off. Paparazzi still lingered, waiting for more photo opportunities. Cameras clicked and flashes blazed, but Tristan didn't slow down, instead pulling her tightly to his side as if to protect her from their unwanted attention.

Somehow William got the limo through the crush of traffic in a much shorter time than Georgia would have thought possible, although every minute felt like hours to her. Tristan quickly ushered her to the car and helped her in, telling William where they needed to go, and pronto. Then he crawled in behind her, again pulling Georgia close, wrapping his arm around her.

"We'll be there in just a few minutes," Tristan assured her. Then he kissed the top of her head, murmuring more words of reassurance.

Georgia leaned against his chest, allowing his comfort, thankful he was there.

Chapter Seventeen

"I'm so sorry," Marnie said.

Georgia collapsed onto the sofa where her grandmother had been when they'd left earlier that night.

"Please don't apologize," Georgia told her friend, and Tristan had to agree. It was at least the tenth time the woman had apologized. Frankly, Tristan didn't see the point of doing it over and over.

"I know this isn't how you expected your special night to go," Marnie said, leaning in the doorway of the living room, looking upset.

It sure as hell wasn't how he'd expected the night to go. By this time, he had planned to have had Georgia under him, on top of him, and bent over for him. But instead he'd spent his night in a hospital, and the only one who got taken to a bed and poked and prodded was an elderly woman with a broken ankle and a bump on her head.

"It's fine," Georgia reassured Marnie again. "I'm just glad you were here and that Grammy didn't get hurt worse when she fell. This is another reason I just can't leave her alone. Even for a few moments."

Tristan moved to sit beside Georgia. "I think it's a good thing they kept her overnight. Just to watch her and make sure nothing else is wrong."

Georgia nodded.

"Well, I'm going to go. Please call me in the morning and let me know how she is feeling," Marnie said, heading to the apartment door. Tristan rose to follow her.

"Are you going to stay with Georgia?" Marnie whispered when they were out of earshot.

"If she wants me to."

"I think you should. She's pretty shaken and looks really exhausted. I think it would be good for her to have someone here if she needs something. I can stay, if you want."

Tristan shook his head. "No, I'll stay."

Marnie smiled. "Good." She said her good-byes and left.

Finally, Tristan thought as he locked the apartment door. Tonight hadn't gone as he'd imagined, but that didn't mean he couldn't salvage a little of it.

Taking a woman who was preoccupied and stressed wasn't his method of seduction, but when it came to Georgia, he found himself willing to have her any way he could.

He walked back into the living room to find her with her eyes closed and her head resting against the back of the sofa. Her usually rosy cheeks were pale and her full rosebud mouth was drawn into a thin line, its pinkness gone.

She cracked an eye open when she heard him, forcing her head upright. "It's my turn to say I'm sorry. I know that gala was a big event for you and the magazine. I should have insisted you stay. It wasn't as if you needed to waste your night sitting in a hospital watching a parade of open-backed johnnies when you could have been with some of the world's most famous designers."

"It wasn't a big deal," he said, sitting beside her, "and truthfully, the johnnies were more fashionable than some of the spring fashions I've seen."

Georgia laughed, and he could hear the exhaustion in it.

"What can I do to help you?" he asked, and for a moment he considered saying something flirty like "help you to bed?" Or "get you out of that dress," but he found him-

self more concerned about her pallor and fatigue than his
libido.

Only because you've waited this long for her, he told
himself. You wouldn't want anything less than a full performance.

"You look totally drained. Why don't you go get into
some pajamas and I'll fix you a drink," he said, doing something he didn't believe he'd ever done in his whole existence. He gave her knee a reassuring pat. No rub, no sliding
up her thigh. Not even a squeeze.

"No more drinks," she groaned. "I definitely cannot do
more alcohol. But a cup of Earl Grey would be wonderful."

"You got it," he said, surprised that he meant it. He held
out a hand to help her up, which she readily accepted. As
she stood, she stumbled a little, bumping against him. He
caught her against his chest to steady her, and then held her
there, looking down at her wan, but still adorable face.

Again, to his utter surprise, he placed a kiss on the tip of
her upturned nose, and then directed her past him.

"Okay, go change and I'll get that tea for you."

She nodded, a strangely bemused look on her face. Then
she stepped past him to head down the hallway.

Tristan remained rooted to the spot. What the hell was
he doing? He was a demon of lust not a damned nursemaid.
He seduced women . . . sometimes men, for his satisfaction.
For his personal gain. And more often than not just because
it was fun. And now he was patting knees and kissing the
tips of noses like some demonic version of a doting father.

Check that, even during those sweet and nonsexual interactions with Georgia, what he felt was not fatherly. Not
in the least. But he did feel something different for her.
Something kind and gentle and caring.

Affection. Could that be it? He'd denied that particular
emotion earlier, but now he was thinking maybe he did feel
affection for her.

Well, wasn't that disturbing? Thoroughly and utterly disturbing.

He wandered into the kitchen and looked through the cabinets to find teabags and a mug. Then he filled the kettle on the stove and turned on the burner. Crossing his arms over his chest, he considered this new strange sensation.

He supposed affection wasn't completely foreign to him. At one time he'd cared about Finola. Kinda. Sorta. Not really. And Dippy.

He made a noise of contempt. That beast plucked his last nerve. What about other women he'd been mad to have? He liked them fine. He'd even seen several women over an extended period of time. He hesitated to call it "dating" or "a relationship," but he must have felt something for them. He pondered it, trying to recall. He'd . . . liked them. That was about all he could say.

This was so strange. It couldn't be the first time he'd ever experienced this feeling. Yet, try as he might, he couldn't think of one past lover who had affected him so readily. So intensely.

"Oh, I feel so much better already." Georgia padded into the room wearing fleece pajama bottoms, red with white polka dots, and a red camisole that showed glimpses of her cleavage and revealed fully that she no longer wore a bra and her breasts were all natural and very perky.

Some of the pinkness returned to her cheeks as she noticed where he was looking. And her nipples hardened in reaction, too. She had big, pointed nipples that Tristan would have sold his soul to the Devil to taste, if he had a soul and he didn't already belong to Satan.

"Maybe I should go put on a T-shirt," Georgia said, the comment revealing more than anything how tired she was. If she were thinking clearly, she wouldn't have actually said something to reveal she knew where he was looking. She would have normally pretended she didn't notice.

But she did notice. And he was still noticing her. He stepped forward and caught her around the waist, pulling her against him.

"Do you have any idea how much I want you?" he growled, knowing this wasn't the optimal time to tell her. But everything was out of whack with him tonight. His emotions, his timing. Only one thing seemed to be working with its unfailing consistency and that was his cock, which currently pressed against Georgia's belly, hard and thick and ready.

"Tristan," she said, his name breathy and sexy in his ears. "I'm not sure— That is I don't know if this is a good idea."

"I think it's the best idea I've had all night."

She looked up at him, her eyes dark and wide. There was a vulnerability there, behind her funky glasses frames, made more pronounced by the smudges of purple under her lower lashes.

More of that odd feeling filled him. And it wasn't just affection; it seemed to be mixed with something else. Something just as foreign to him. It was like he wanted to take care of her.

Protectiveness maybe. Although, even as he thought it, it seemed like a dirty word in his mind. *Protective.*

No, ignore those bizarre feelings and take her, his lustful side urged. She will give herself to you. She wants you.

He lowered his lips to hers, capturing them. She surrendered willingly, her lips soft and pliant under his. And unlike their earlier kiss in public at Lincoln Center, now he didn't need to temper his hunger for her. He could taste her, his tongue sliding between those eager lips, their tongues dancing around each other. The movements were as sensual as he could ever recall a kiss to be.

He groaned deep in his throat, pulling her tighter to him, his hands tangling in her hair, holding the back of her head. He felt her hands gripping his shoulders, her fingertips digging into him through his jacket and shirt. He wanted to feel them digging into his skin.

He groaned again, kissing her deeper.

She moaned in response.

Vaguely, Tristan registered that he'd never felt this way before. This desperation. This out-of-control feeling that urged him on.

Suddenly the room was filled with a loud whistling that somehow managed to penetrate his lust-filled brain. He lifted his head, looking around him, trying to figure out what caused the noise. Large billows of steam rolled over the stove and into the kitchen, and he finally realized it was the teakettle.

He looked back at Georgia, who met his gaze, her eyes filled with desire and that same drained vulnerability he'd seen earlier.

Her lips were parted and red and swollen from his kiss. Her breathing was uneven, broken. She was the picture of longing and surrender, and he wanted her.

But again, that surge of protectiveness filled him. She was overwhelmed, tired, maybe still under the influence of the champagne she'd had. He didn't want her that way. A surrender based on anything less than giving in to her desire wouldn't satisfy him.

He didn't understand why, but he knew it was the truth. He studied her a moment longer, wishing he could ignore these strange, new, and oddly proper motivations. But he couldn't.

"I know you've had a stressful night and you are exhausted. Go into the living room and relax. I'll fix your tea and bring it in to you."

She nibbled her lip, looking as confused as he felt, but then she nodded. "Okay, thank you."

She padded out of the room as he turned to the stove, flipping off the burner. Steam moistened his skin, making his denied need almost unbearable. He wanted to be buried in her moistened flesh, feeling her wet heat all around his aching cock.

But rather than following her and doing just that, he poured hot water over the teabag in the mug. The teabag soaked in the water, swelling, releasing its essence into the brew.

His thoughts went back to being deep inside her, swelling until he came, his essence mingling with hers.

He growled, low and frustrated. When making tea became as graphic and arousing as any sexual act, he knew he needed to assuage his lust, and soon.

Instead, he forced himself to calmly call to Georgia. "What do you take in your tea?"

Georgia didn't answer for a moment, and he couldn't help hoping she was struggling with sexual need as much as he was.

He could still smell her desire in the air. His ripe Peach. *So go take her, damn it!*

But something still kept him in the kitchen, dunking a teabag up and down in the cup, awaiting her direction.

"Just a little milk, please."

He went to the fridge, retrieved the milk, and finished making her tea. Then, after several shuddering breaths, he took the cup into the living room. Georgia sat up from her reclined position as he entered the room.

She reached out to take the mug, and he could see her hands were shaking.

This was insane. They were both so desperate for each other, they were literally shaking with it. But neither made a further move. Georgia took a sip of her tea and Tristan took a seat in the oversized chair next to the sofa, stretching out his long legs, not caring if she saw his erection jutting up against the fly of his trousers.

If she did, she didn't reveal it. She kept her attention focused on her tea.

Finally, when the air was just a little less thick with desire, she said, "You don't have to stay, you know."

"I know," he said. "But I don't think you should really be alone tonight. Just in case."

She didn't ask just in case of what. She simply nodded and leaned back against the couch cushions. Again, he could see how tired she was.

He watched her for a moment, and then spotted the television remote on the coffee table. "Why don't we see if we can find a movie or something?"

"Okay," she agreed, but he couldn't tell if there was disappointment or relief in her voice. And he refused to ponder it, pressing the button to bring the TV to life.

All he knew was that he had never given up the opportunity to spend the night fucking a willing, sexy-as-hell woman to watch reruns of *Frasier*.

Something wasn't right, and it worried him. A lot.

Chapter Eighteen

Georgia wasn't sure when she dozed off, but when she woke up, the television was still on. An infomercial about some contraption of a workout machine was on with an overly excited spokesman telling a studio audience this was the easiest way to build ab muscles and lose weight that he'd ever encountered.

Georgia blinked, trying to clear her sleep-clouded brain, looking around to see Tristan asleep in the chair near her, his head bent at a strange angle and his expensive black suit coat serving as a blanket.

She watched him for a moment, taking in the steady rise and fall of his chest. The beauty of his face relaxed in sleep. He looked almost too handsome to be real. He looked like a fallen angel, too perfect for this world.

He shifted slightly in his sleep, obviously trying to find a more comfortable position, but he didn't open his eyes, allowing her to continue her perusal.

Even in her own sleepy haze, her body reacted to him. She wanted him. She had wanted him desperately earlier, during their second kiss. It had taken every bit of her willpower to stay in here while he finished making her tea. She'd wanted to go back into the kitchen and have sex with him right there on the kitchen counter. Or the floor. Or both.

Only the fact that he was her boss stopped her, and looking at him now, she again struggled to care about that detail. She'd never known a need like the one coursing through her. It was clouding her thoughts and making it impossible to remember all the reasons she should not want him.

So she lay there, repeating them all over and over in her head. He's your boss. He's nothing but a player. He's too good looking for his own, or your own, good. She couldn't risk her job, especially with Grammy hurt. He might be a member of the mob.

That last one she dismissed instantly, deciding then and there, that odd Gabriel person was a nutter. The only way Tristan McIntyre was dangerous was to her heart. She could easily fall for him. Especially when he took care of her the way he had last night. She found that so appealing, because she was used to being the one who took care of things. She did so at the job and she did so at home. So having him stick around last night while Grammy was examined and moved from the ER into a hospital room, then coming home with her and staying to look after her, well, it was a rare delight. That made him all the more appealing, if such a thing was possible.

But it was possible. She found him damned near irresistible, which had been obvious from her reaction to his kiss in the kitchen. If the teakettle hadn't whistled, and if Tristan hadn't ended their embrace right then, Georgia knew she wouldn't have.

She gazed at him a moment longer, then reached out to touch his hand, which dangled over the arm of the chair. He had beautiful hands with broad palms and long, tapered fingers. They were hands that managed to look masculine and elegant at the same time. Talented hands.

She imagined how talented they would be touching her body, bringing her to arousal. She ran a fingertip over his palm, tracing the lines there, moving out to graze over the length of each finger.

Her attention was so focused on her fleeting touch, she didn't immediately notice the change in Tristan, not until his fingers curled loosely around hers.

Her eyes shot up to find Tristan awake, watching her.

"Hi," he said, his voice raspy from sleep.

"Hi," she said back.

Neither pulled their hand away from the other; they just remained still in the flickering light of the television, studying each other.

"Are you okay?" he finally asked, his thumb caressing the side of the hand he held.

No, no, she wasn't. She wanted him so desperately it was almost painful. But she didn't say that. How could she say such a thing to him? Her boss. The most beautiful man she'd ever seen.

After a moment, when it was clear she wasn't going to answer, because she couldn't, he straightened, although he didn't release his hold on her hand.

He did flex his muscles, stretching his neck and back.

"Maybe I should go," he said, although again he made no move to release her. "It's got to be almost morning and I should go back to my place to get ready for another workday."

She nodded, but still his thumb stroked over the skin of her palm.

"Don't come in today," he said, his voice low and gentle, at odds with the businesslike things he was saying. "Get your grandmother home and settled. I should be able to make it one day without you. But only one."

She knew he referred to doing without her only as his personal assistant, but still her heart leapt at his words.

She still didn't speak though. He regarded her a moment

longer, then stood. Their hands remained connected, fingers intertwined.

"I should go," he repeated and started to slowly extract his hold from hers. But her own fingers tightened, refusing to let go.

Inside, she struggled to find the words she wanted to say, that she'd wanted to say since their very first kiss. She couldn't let this moment go.

She was clearly losing her mind. Everything about what she wanted to ask, to tell him, was wrong. It could put her whole life and her heart at jeopardy, but she felt this might be her only opportunity to do something like this. Something so wanton and outrageous.

"Don't go," she whispered, her voice sounding husky and foreign even to herself.

"Georgia," Tristan said, his tone uncertain. That uncertainty should have been enough to make her doubt what she was thinking. But it didn't. Something deep inside pushed her forward.

She tugged his hand, urging him to come closer to her. He did.

"I want you to stay," she told him, only hesitating for a moment before adding, "I want you."

He studied her for a heartbeat, and then made a noise low in his throat. A desperate, hungry sound like a man who'd been denied food and now found himself in front of a buffet.

He stepped forward, his movements odd, almost as if he was being drawn to her, not against his will, but helpless to do anything else.

She rose up on the sofa, looking at him, feeling very much the same way. Despite all the reasons she knew she shouldn't do this, even consider it, she was unable to do anything else.

He stood before her, and she rose up farther until she was

on her knees, her face level with his chest. He looked down at her, his eyes smoldering, his breath coming in short little gasps. He was as affected as she was, as desperate and filled with need. That realization gave her courage.

She reached up and touched his face, pressing her hand to his cheek. She could feel the hint of stubble there, the slight roughness exciting.

He turned his head, kissing her palm, a kiss that hinted at the way he planned to kiss her whole body. Openmouthed kisses, nipping and with a small lick here and there. With that one kiss to her palm, he seemed to make a silent promise that he was going to explore her whole body with his mouth.

The idea made her moan, and she felt his smile against her open hand.

He met her gaze again, just a hint of the smile curving his perfectly sculpted lips. That smug little smile she found so utterly masculine, so sexy.

She rose up farther, so as he looked down at her, her upturned head was just below his, her lips just inches away from that smile.

The smile faded, replaced by a smoldering look of pure desire. It was her turn to smile, her own self-satisfied little grin.

Desire flared in Tristan's eyes.

That look spurred Georgia on, making her bolder. Her fingers moved to his shirt, working the buttons open, starting at his throat and going downward, exposing more and more of his hard, muscular chest with each button undone.

She slid her hands inside the fine fabric, feeling his smooth skin and rippling muscles. He stood still, letting her hands explore him, then her mouth as she kissed his chest. Her lips found his puckered nipple, licking it, and then gently sucking.

Tristan made that desperate growling noise again, and she

could feel his body quiver as if it was taking all his willpower to remain motionless. But he didn't move, allowing her to touch him, allowing her to set the pace.

She teased his nipples a little longer, until she swore she could feel and hear his heart thumping wildly in his chest. The idea that he was so turned on made her almost wild with need herself.

Her hands moved to his pants, struggling with the belt. As if mirroring her own frantic desire, he pushed her hands away and undid it himself, pulling the whole thing out of his pants and tossing it on the floor.

She smiled up at him, so pleased by his frenzied reaction. He wanted her just as much as she wanted him. What an amazing and heady feeling.

Her fingers returned to his pants to make short work of the button and zipper. She eased the designer pants down over his narrow hips to reveal the designer boxer briefs underneath. But it was his erection under that, hard and heavy, that drew her attention. She pushed the boxers down and his cock bobbed free.

Her eyes widened, and she gaped up at him. He was huge.

A moment of reality sneaked in. What was she doing? She couldn't handle this man, and not just his huge penis; she couldn't handle anything about him.

But Tristan smiled that smug smile of his, which contradicted his pleading tone as he said, "Please touch me. Damn, please."

She felt that surge of control again—of power. He wanted her. He'd beg to have her. Nothing had ever turned her on more than the idea of this man begging her to have sex with him.

She took his cock into her hand, amazed at the girth and the weight. She'd never seen anything like it. Not that she was exactly an expert when it came to this department, but she was hardly a virgin either.

But she couldn't take her eyes off of it, as if she'd never seen one before. Never touched one. She stroked her fingers up and down the long length, testing where he liked to be touched best. One place would make him gasp. Another, moan. Circling the head made him say, "Oh, shit," in a deep, guttural tone. She liked that one best.

And she got even more of that response as she leaned forward and licked the head. She moaned, too, loving the warm, slightly salty taste of him. It was earthy and seductive and made her want more, but he only allowed a few full-mouth tastes before he caught her shoulders and gently nudged her away.

"You've gotten to play," he said, his voice husky and raw, the richness gone, blocked out by pure need. "Now I want to explore you."

Again, reality returned. She wanted him to touch her and taste her, but she also knew she wasn't some tiny model. She had hips and boobs and a belly. And she couldn't bear to see his desire replaced by displeasure or worse, disgust.

But his eyes still burned with hunger as he reached for the hem of her camisole top and lifted it up over her head. His smoldering eyes, like emerald fire, locked on her bare breasts.

He groaned. "I can't tell you how many times I imagined baring you like this." He cupped a breast in each hand, their size filling his palms; then he ran his thumbs over the sensitive nipples that puckered and pouted under his touch.

She gasped as he pinched and rolled the nipple between his forefinger and thumb. The delicious sensation, somewhere between delight and a deep ache, spread through her body, going straight to the throbbing heat between her thighs.

"I imagined doing this," he said, leaning forward to suck one of her distended nipples deep between his lips, drawing on the sensitive flesh to make her whole body react.

Her head fell back as he suckled her, first one breast, and then the other.

He continued to suck and nip and tease her, even as he caught her under her arms and pulled her to her feet in front of him. He pushed at her pajama bottoms until they pooled around her feet in a puddle of fuzzy fleece. He shifted back to get a better view of her. She was naked except for the red lace boy shorts she'd bought to match the dress.

He didn't speak for a moment, and more doubts niggled at her. Then he pulled in an unsteady breath, his eyes filled with something akin to awe.

"You are so much more beautiful than I even imagined you." He then offered her a crooked smile. "And believe me, I've imagined you a lot."

That smile, that look of reverence, blotted out all her fears. She smiled, moving closer to him, pressing her breasts against his chest and her hips into his.

"Show me what else you imagined."

He growled, and pulled her fully against him.

"Oh, darling, you do not need to ask that twice."

He kissed her, his mouth frenzied against hers. Then he grabbed her hand and led her into the center of the room.

To her surprise, he kneeled in front of her. He hooked his fingers around the waistband of her panties, and slowly eased them down over her full hips. He untangled them from around her feet and cast them aside. He raised his head, his face level with the apex of her thighs.

His gaze was again worshipful as he looked at her close-shaved mons.

"So beautiful," he murmured, reaching out to run a finger between the full lips down there. His finger glistened with her desire and he licked the juices from it.

They both moaned.

"You taste like heaven," he said, his voice rich again, stroking over her skin like another hand. "Not that I have any idea what heaven tastes like. Not that I've even wondered until this moment."

She wasn't sure what he was talking about, but it didn't matter. His fingers now parted her, exposing the wet pink flesh of her sex. Then he delved his tongue into her, finding the hard bud of her clitoris, licking and sucking until she had to grasp his shoulders to keep herself upright.

He continued to eat her, alternating between exquisite roughness and extreme gentleness, going on as orgasm after orgasm washed over her, each one more intense than the one before.

She began to groan and cry out incoherently, the intensity of what he was doing to her almost too much.

"Please," she begged, "please, Tristan, I need you inside me." And she did. Even with all of the release she'd found, she didn't feel that she could really be satisfied until he was inside her. Deep inside her.

He lifted his mouth away from her, his beautiful lips wet with her come.

"Lie down for me," he whispered, his expression dazed as if he'd experienced each of her orgasms himself. She did as he asked, lying down before him on the carpet. He moved over her, bracing his weight on his arms, the muscles of his biceps bulging. He positioned himself between her thighs, and leaned down to kiss her. She could taste herself on his lips and feel his hard, thick cock nudging at her desperately sensitive sex.

He reached down to angle his cock to enter her. Her hands clutched the hard muscles of his back, waiting for the stretch of his entrance.

And she did stretch, his girth filling her, slowly. He took his time, going in tiny increments that made Georgia wild for him and for release all over again.

"That's it, darling," he said against her ear. "Let me in. Take all of me. Every inch."

She gasped, wanting nothing more. And when he was buried deep inside her, she finally felt she'd gotten exactly what she had been so hungry for.

Then he began to thrust his hips and she was lost. She writhed under him, mindless except for the feeling of him pounding into her and her own building desire.

His thrusts grew more powerful, more demanding until they both shouted out their release. And he collapsed on top of her.

Georgia lay there, surrounded by Tristan, her body weak and spent, her breathing rapid and raspy. She'd never experienced anything like that before. Even the air seemed to be charged with their sexual release. She could feel it and taste it. Smell it like the most heady of perfumes. She closed her eyes, basking in the whole sensation.

Could sexual tension and release be a living thing? she thought, her mind vague and sleepy.

She didn't know, but she was sure their lovemaking was more amazing than anything she could have imagined.

"Heaven," she heard Tristan murmur, before she fell into an exhausted and sated sleep.

Chapter Nineteen

Early morning light, gray and shadowy, filtered through the shades of Georgia's living room window. Tristan lay on his side, his muscles weak and heavy, still sapped from his encounter with Georgia. She slept beside him, sprawled on her back, her round, firm breasts, pale pink nipples, and full hips like a carnal smorgasbord laid out in front of him. His cock jutted, hard and throbbing, against his stomach, but he didn't touch her. He didn't play with those plump lips between her thighs. Or lean forward to suck her sweet, taut nipples.

He didn't dare.

What the hell had happened to him?

He'd fucked many mortal women. Hundreds, maybe hundreds upon hundreds. Sex was necessary to his existence. Yet no human female had affected him like Georgia.

As always, he'd experienced each of her orgasms as if they were his own. That was normal for him. Her release became his, and his strength grew with each rush of his partner's sexual release. But not tonight. Each of her orgasms rippled through him, powerful and stunningly wonderful. An intense ecstasy he'd never felt before, but instead of taking energy and strength from her orgasms, he'd been left drained, weak.

He didn't understand it. The sex had been the best he

could remember; her reaction to him, her orgasms, all perfection. He should feel like a damned superhero. He did feel utterly satisfied, blissful, and wonderfully content in a way sex never left him, but none of the usual vitality coursed through his veins.

What had this woman done to him?

He lifted his hand, wanting to touch her soft, smooth skin. But before his fingertips connected with her warm flesh, he dropped his hand back to the floor, digging his fingers into the pile of the carpet. Something akin to . . . fear stopped him.

What the hell was wrong with him?

Georgia made a little noise in her sleep, a sound somewhere between a sigh and a whimper. Tristan watched her breast move up and down with her deep, even breathing.

God, he wanted to touch her. To play with those beautiful breasts. To run his tongue over her warm, pale skin. To bury his face again between her thighs. Then bury his cock there, too.

But instead he levered himself upright and carefully moved to gather all his scattered clothing. He had to leave. He needed space to think. When he was near her, his brain was cloudy, his thoughts focused on nothing but her. And he needed to think. He had to figure out why he was feeling this way. He had to figure out what kind of power she had over him.

Garments in hand, he quietly rose and strode naked to the kitchen.

Not normal. Not normal. That was all his hazy brain could manage to comprehend. Never had he experienced this sensation. Never had he crept away to dress in private, nor had he ever sneaked out of a one-night stand. He'd never had any qualms about just telling his conquest that he was leaving. That he'd gotten what he wanted, and he was done.

But this was not a normal situation, and Georgia was not his usual conquest. And he hated to admit it, but he was shaken. Shaken to his core.

He tugged on his clothes, his movements jerky and awkward as if he couldn't get his limbs to cooperate. Twice, he had to attempt to get his foot into his boxers, losing his balance, his equilibrium shot.

What the hell was wrong with him?

He sure as shit couldn't figure that out here. He needed to get away from this apartment, and the heady, mind-boggling scent of Georgia. Even with the space between them, he could still smell her as if she was standing in the same room.

He paused, his pants halfway up his legs. He shot a look over his shoulder, half-expecting to see her standing there, but the room was empty. The apartment was silent.

He jerked his pants up, not bothering to finish fastening them. He pulled on his shirt, leaving that open as well. He doubted his shaky hands could manage the small buttons anyway.

He hurried from the kitchen toward the front door, only to stop at the living room doorway. Georgia hadn't moved; their sexual encounter clearly had exhausted her, too. But that was normal.

The light from the window illuminated her pale skin, and she looked like some voluptuous goddess splayed out for him. Only him.

His cock hardened instantly, but he moved back away from her. He wanted her—as desperately as he had before they had had sex, but instead he headed to the door.

Slowly, he turned the handle and stepped out into the hallway. He pulled in a deep breath, but his body still quivered with exhaustion. His brain still whirred.

He didn't allow himself to consider his reaction any longer. He just needed to leave.

* ★ ★

A shrill noise penetrated Georgia's sleep-hazed brain. She groaned.

God, her back hurt.

She rolled over, trying to find a more comfortable position, but as she did, her eyes snapped open.

Where was she?

She moved her hand, realizing her fingers weren't stroking the soft sheets of her bed, but rather the rough weave of a carpet. Then her memory returned. She'd had sex with Tristan on her living room floor. She sat up, realizing she was still there. She was naked in the middle of her living room.

She made a noise, pushing herself upright, looking around her. The living room was empty. Tristan was gone. His clothes were gone, too.

She struggled to her feet, muscles she didn't even know she had aching. Spotting her camisole on the arm of the sofa, she snatched it up and tugged it over her head. Then she found her panties and quickly donned those.

"Tristan," she called, her voice husky and hesitant. Her feeble cry was met with silence. "Tristan?"

She walked into the hallway and was met with more quiet. He wasn't here. A mixture of disappointment and humiliation tightened her chest, and she found it hard to pull in a deep breath.

She'd had sex with him and then he'd left. She closed her eyes, willing away the tears that threatened to fill them.

God, what had she been thinking?

"You weren't thinking," she muttered to herself, angry at her own stupidity. And she couldn't even claim that she'd just let the moment get away from her. She'd initiated that moment.

She dropped her head into her hands and groaned. This was awful. So awful.

Again, a shrill ring echoed through the apartment, and she gathered her thoughts enough to realize it must have been the phone that had woken her up.

Then she remembered her grandmother at the hospital. What if they'd been trying to call and she'd slept through it, because she was passed out on the floor after seducing her boss?

"Oh, God," she groaned, amazed that she could be even more ashamed. She rushed into the kitchen and grabbed the cordless phone from its cradle on the wall.

"Hello?"

"Georgia."

She recognized Tristan's voice immediately, and both relief and apprehension swirled in the pit of her stomach. She was glad to know he didn't intend to avoid her. But she also worried that he might be calling to tell her something awful, like she was out of a job, and who could blame him? What she'd done was totally unprofessional.

But he hadn't stopped it either. In fact, he'd told her how he'd imagined having sex with her. So could she really be totally at fault?

"How are you?" he asked, his voice low. She almost thought she heard uncertainty there as if he was nervous to call her.

"I'm fine."

"Good," he said; then he was silent for a moment. "I just wanted to check on you and to tell you not to come in to work."

Her heart sank and she leaned heavily against the wall. He was going to fire her.

"I know I told you that last night, too, but just wanted to be sure you knew it was fine. I know picking up your grandmother at the hospital and getting her settled in at your place will take some time. So please take today—and tomorrow if you need it."

"Oh, right," she said, relieved. "T—thank you."

He was silent again, and she wondered if he was waiting for her to address what had happened last night, but she couldn't find the words to even begin that conversation. She was too embarrassed, and if she was being honest, too concerned that he regretted what they'd done.

One thing was for sure. He wasn't his usual charming, glib self. Georgia didn't think that was a good sign.

"Okay," he finally said, probably realizing she wasn't going to speak. "Just keep me posted and please give Grace my regards."

His regards. He was being more formal with her than he'd ever been. Surely that wasn't a good sign.

"I will," she told him.

"And again, take whatever time you need."

"I will," she said again, wishing she could find the courage to say something about what had happened between them. But the words didn't come.

Again, he hesitated, and then said, "Okay. Good-bye then."

"Good-bye."

Georgia hung up the phone. Well, that hadn't done anything to reassure her that everything would be fine between the two of them. But could she really expect it to be? She'd banged her boss in her living room.

"You idiot," she muttered. You stupid, stupid idiot.

And while her poor grandmother was in the hospital to boot. What had she been thinking?

She looked at the clock on the microwave. It was only a little after nine. At least she hadn't continued to sleep away on the carpet, passed out in a post-coital oblivion while poor Grammy waited for her.

She groaned again. This was a nightmare. And the worst part of it was it was a nightmare of her own making. Tristan had even tried to rebuff her, to keep things professional. She was the one who'd pushed for what had happened.

She was going to have to say something to him, but clearly she didn't need to do that today.

Just concentrate on Grammy and getting her home and situated comfortably, she told herself as she headed to her bedroom. She could figure out what to say to Tristan later. And maybe they'd both just act like nothing had happened. Maybe that was the safest course of action anyway. What could either of them really say?

Georgia had known going into it, that he would offer no more than a fling—a one-night stand, really. And she knew that if she went there with him, she'd have to accept that fact. So why bother to say anything? They both knew the score.

She grabbed her robe off the end of her bed and headed to the bathroom. She shoved back the shower curtain and turned on the water.

She then went to the mirror and looked at her pale, drawn face, her tangled hair, and kiss-swollen lips.

Of course, knowing the score didn't make her feel any less like a fool. Or any less like crying.

Tristan stared at the phone, wanting to pick it up and re-dial Georgia's number.

And say what? He didn't know. He'd only called her about not coming in to work as an excuse to hear her voice. To know she was all right.

What could he call her about a second time?

Well, if you hadn't suddenly lost your damned balls somewhere, you could call her and actually talk about what happened between you.

Except he wasn't any closer to knowing exactly what that was now than when he'd fled her apartment. And that was precisely what he'd done. Fled. Like some damned coward.

Truth be told, he still didn't understand the effect she had on him. How could he, when it had never happened before in his long, long existence? He just knew something was very different about Georgia Sullivan. And he also knew his plan that a one-night stand would end his obsession with her had not worked. Not in the least. He was more fixated on her than ever. And he wanted to be back in her arms. Back inside her. To the point that he almost felt a little mad with desire.

"My God, you look like hell."

Tristan started, completely unaware Finola was there until she spoke. Which also wasn't normal. Even when in the most desperate need of sex, he was usually aware of everything around him. His lust never consumed him to the point of total distraction.

At least not until now.

"What do you want now, Finola?" he said, knowing he sounded weary, which she would surely take glee in, probably thinking the job was too much for him.

Finola walked over to one of his throne chairs and took a seat. She leaned forward and set Dippy, who had been riding in her tote, on the floor.

Dippy gave Tristan a look as if to say he agreed with Finola's assessment of how he looked; then the white, fluffy, *judgmental* pain in the ass trotted over to his dog bed to circle three times and flop down with a sigh.

Well, if they both thought he looked like hell, they should experience how he felt.

But instead of saying anything of the kind, he asked again, "Why are you here?"

Finola gave him another look that said she was less than impressed with him.

"I came to find out how last night went. Did you make the connections you needed to make?"

Tristan bristled at her question. He already felt out of sorts enough without being micromanaged by his former boss. But he was not going to let her see how agitated he was. She was always looking for chinks in his armor. He would not show her he was frazzled.

"Everything went perfectly. Not that it is any of your business anymore," he couldn't resist adding.

"And your awful assistant? How did that go?"

Immediately Tristan's ire began to rise. He didn't want to talk about Georgia with her. And he especially didn't want to hear Finola's catty insults.

"Again, that is none of your business," he stated, his tone hard and final.

Finola wasn't intimidated. "I couldn't help noticing she wasn't at her desk. Did she need a day to recover? Poor pudgy dear with her silly hair and horrid fashion sense. She had to realize she was out of her league last night."

Tristan gritted his teeth, anger roiling inside him like a tsunami rising under a calm sea.

"Or did you finally do what I intended before my early retirement as head of *HOT!*? Get the pathetic wretch to sign a soul contract promising her she'd be thin and pretty and fit into this world, only to cast her straight to hell? Tell me, Tristan, did you make another one of your runs to the Jersey Shore to drop off her soulless body amid the other unfortunates there? No one would even notice a fashion faux pas like her there."

Tristan shot out of his seat. "Get out!"

He pointed at the door. "Get. The. Fuck. Out."

Finola's pale gray eyes widened, and she rose instantly. He wasn't sure which frightened her more, his furious tone, or the fact that his human form was slipping, revealing the demon within him. He could feel the horns poking out of his head and his muscles bulging.

Some satisfaction calmed his anger and frayed nerves as he watched her scurry to the door. Maybe this was the way to handle her. Clearly, trying to play it cool hadn't worked.

"Nice," came a voice from the other side of the room.

Dippy watched him, looking unimpressed. "Do you think Satan would be pleased if he knew you were having random Incredible Hulk moments? The horns and bulging muscles kind of tip off mortals that something isn't quite right with you."

Tristan sighed, wishing Finola had taken her chatty, opinionated canine with her.

"She was irritating me."

"She irritates everyone," Dippy growled. "And you gave her exactly what she wanted. She wanted you to get worked up. She's trying to get under your skin. The more you lose your cool, the better a story she has for Satan."

Tristan knew the annoying little mutt was right. But what was that old saying? "Even a broken clock is right twice a day." He hoped the fleabag wasn't going to be right again.

"And she did have a valid point," Dippy added. "You do look like hell. What exactly happened last night? Did Project Pork Personal Assistant not go as planned?"

Tristan struggled to suppress a sigh. No, it did not go as planned. He still didn't even understand how it went. But when he'd decided to seduce Georgia and get her out of his system, he never saw her taking the initiative. He never saw his bizarre reaction to the sex. And he definitely didn't see his obsession with her becoming more intense rather than lessening.

But he was not going to tell Dippy the Dog any of that. No one liked to hear "I told you so," especially from the family pet.

But Tristan decided to tell him a partial truth. "No, things didn't go as planned. Her grandmother ended up in the hospital, so that sort of put a damper on the evening's activities."

Sort of.

Dippy's dark, beady gaze roamed over him; then he

bobbed his furry head. "Maybe that's a good thing. Maybe you shouldn't go there with your assistant. Clearly, you need to focus on the takeover, because for once, Finola seems to be."

Tristan couldn't deny that. Finola was far more interested in the takeover now than when she was running it. Of course, that was a common reaction, even for demons. You always wanted back the one thing you lost.

"All the more reason I need you to be her shadow."

Dippy hesitated, reluctance on his fuzzy features. He obviously thought Tristan needed just as much watching as Finola.

Maybe he's right. Maybe I'm losing control.

Tristan pushed the thought aside. Okay, he was having a very strange reaction to Georgia, but it wasn't something he couldn't sort out and then forget. Maybe he just needed more of the voluptuous, amazingly responsive woman.

Just at the thought of being with her again, his dick sprang to life.

But as much as Tristan hated to admit it, and damn if that old clock adage wasn't true, Dippy was right again. He had to focus on work right now. Finola was definitely plotting and planning. He needed to make sure none of her tactics worked. And there was the added job of getting his newest recruits, Higgins and Barrington, to work.

He didn't have time to think about boning Georgia. Not to mention, she was going to be busy with her grandmother. Maybe he would consider a repeat performance with her, but right now, he had work to do.

Chapter Twenty

Gabriel pushed the mail cart past the reception area of McIntyre's office for the fifth time that day. Probably the other *HOT!* employees thought he was the most confused mail room employee ever, or the most hardworking, making rounds every hour or so.

Georgia wasn't at work again. And unlike yesterday, he hadn't followed her to see what she was doing. But he should have, because she didn't appear to be coming in at all today.

He glanced at his watch. It was after four. It seemed highly unlikely that she'd bother to come in now. And there was, of course, the concern that something might have happened to her. Employees did disappear from *HOT!* Not as much as they had even a year ago, but they did disappear, and Ms. Sullivan had spent the evening with a very dangerous demon.

What if she had confronted McIntyre with the things Gabriel had told her? Would McIntyre decide it was just easier to get rid of the woman rather than tell her lies to cover himself?

Unease prickled over Gabriel's skin. Maybe he should go to Ms. Sullivan's residence again, but he knew he had to check in with Eugene first. His boss had been annoyed that Gabriel had gone to her apartment building.

"It makes you look too much like some potentially un-balanced coworker. Like you could be the dangerous one."

Eugene's tone had been calm as usual, almost blasé, but Gabriel knew his boss was not pleased with him.

Gabriel couldn't disagree. It might not have been his best decision. But now, he felt he had to go to her apartment to check on her. What if she was in danger? Or McIntyre had already hurt her? The only way to be sure she was okay was to see if she was home. Maybe he could just call. He could get her number. Just a quick call to hear her voice and then he could hang up.

Not a great plan either, since she would see his number on her cell, or be able to *69 it on her landline. Sometimes technology didn't make things easier. At least not when you were trying to be covert.

He would go to her place. Then he could physically see if she was okay, and he could also talk to her again. Maybe she had seen something last night that had convinced her McIntyre was not what he seemed.

Maybe.

Damn, this was all such a long shot.

He wheeled the cart back to the elevator and pressed the button for the basement level of the building. When he stepped into the mail room, the large room was bustling as always. As was now his habit, he scanned the place for Fi-nola White. She wasn't at her station, but then she hardly ever was.

But he saw no flashes of her signature white blond hair and white clothing. Where was she? And what was she up to?

Gabriel really wished he wasn't the only one who seemed to care.

He sighed, and then strode toward Eugene's office, which was little more than a particle-board box in the center of the room. Not the most private office, and as if to validate his thoughts, he heard voices as he got closer.

"Oh, Eugene, you are such a delight."

Gabriel heard Eugene laugh. Or at least he assumed it was Eugene. He couldn't recall ever hearing Eugene laugh, so maybe some other male was in the office, too.

"I could say the same thing about you, Ms. White."

It was Eugene. And he seemed to be . . . flirting? Flirting with Finola White?

"So, Eugene, what does a handsome man like you do outside of managing a mail room?"

Handsome? She was laying it on thick. But then, she was clearly after something.

"My life is very dull, I'm afraid."

"I don't believe that."

Gabriel just bet she didn't. Surely Eugene had to know she was fishing. He couldn't be the head of the DIA and be that clueless.

"It's true," Eugene said. "I'd like to tell you otherwise, but all I do is work."

"All work and no play makes Eugene a dull boy," Finola purred, and Gabriel could just imagine her draped over Eugene's small desk, ruffling his tidy, brown hair.

"That is also true," Eugene said with another laugh. The sound was short and rusty, but definitely a laugh.

"Maybe you need to do something fun. Maybe you should do something fun with me."

Gabriel waited. Eugene would never agree to that. Being with her, alone, was a risky move, especially if she knew something. But even if she didn't, Gabriel didn't believe for a moment her suggestion was because she was genuinely concerned about Eugene's boring life. She was up to something, just like she had been with everyone in the mail room.

"I would like that."

Gabriel's breath actually caught. No. No. Eugene wouldn't be so stupid.

Gabriel's muscles, which he hadn't even realized were coiled as if ready to attack, relaxed. Eugene had to have a plan. He wouldn't fall under Finola's spell, even though she was a very powerful demon.

"Well, think of something you'd like to do," she said, her voice deceptively sweet, "and ask me."

"I will," Eugene said readily.

Gabriel saw Finola's shadow on the floor, moving toward the doorway. He backed away, not wanting her to realize he'd been listening.

She reached the doorway, and then stopped to turn back to Eugene.

"And please don't make me wait too long." She wagged her fingers at Eugene, and then stepped out of the office.

Right away, she noticed Gabriel, who strolled in her direction. He hoped she would think he was just arriving there. But the slight smirk on her lips and the calculating look in her gray eyes made it hard to tell what she was thinking.

"Hello, Gabriel," she said, her tone congenial, but he doubted very much that she was really feeling friendly.

He nodded.

She sauntered past him, her arm brushing his as she passed.

Another flirting move? Or a subtle gesture of challenge? Gabriel wasn't sure. He didn't trust a single thing about her.

He watched her as she headed back to her sorting station. She talked to several of the other employees, the DIA staff. Most of them seemed comfortable with her comments, responding and smiling as if she was an old friend.

Was all the DIA falling under her charm? Gabriel hated to believe the well-trained staff was so easily enchanted by her beauty and charisma. But Gabriel didn't feel confident.

He didn't feel confident about much the DIA was doing when it came to bringing down this demonic rebellion.

Which brought him back to what he considered another bad idea, Georgia Sullivan and recruiting her. But right now he was more concerned with being sure she was safe.

Gabriel rapped on the doorframe of Eugene's office.

Eugene looked up, his expression deadpan as usual. No sign that he'd just been flirting and laughing with a demon.

"Gabriel, I've been hoping you would stop by. Please come in and close the door."

Gabriel did, glad that Eugene seemed to be somewhat aware that it was far too easy to eavesdrop on this makeshift office.

"Georgia Sullivan didn't come in again today, did she?" Eugene said before Gabriel could tell him.

Gabriel wasn't sure how he knew, but he simply nodded. "I'm worried about her."

"Did Tristan McIntyre work today?"

"Yes," Gabriel said, "although, I didn't see much of him. He mainly stayed in his office. I think I should go check on Ms. Sullivan, just to be safe. And if she is there, I could also ask her if she had time to think about what I said."

"I'm sure she's thought about what you said. After all, you did tell her a pretty crazy story."

Gabriel didn't say anything, although he did feel a little annoyed. Hadn't he been making that argument ever since Eugene suggested this plan?

"I know you still have doubts about this," Eugene said. "But I think she will eventually agree to help us. And she does have access to the names of everyone Tristan McIntyre meets and where and when. She also has his trust. She could get him to reveal his plans."

Gabriel wasn't sure about any of that, but he *was* worried about her.

"I'm going to check on her. I know you don't think it's

a good idea to go to her apartment, but I'm really concerned."

Eugene was silent for a moment, then nodded. "That is fine."

Gabriel started to the door. At least his boss was being reasonable about this. He might be flirting with evil, literally, but he was being cautious about Georgia. Gabriel appreciated it.

"Gabriel."

He stopped, turning back to his boss.

"I know you don't always understand or agree with how I handle things," Eugene said, his voice even, almost emotionless, "but you have to trust I know what I'm doing."

Gabriel stared at him for a moment. His boss did have an uncanny way of addressing the very concerns that were going through his head. In this case, he wasn't sure if Eugene was referring to his worries about Georgia Sullivan or Finola White, but given that the man didn't even know Gabriel had overheard the exchange with Finola, he had to assume it was a reference to Ms. Sullivan.

But all Gabriel did was nod. He hoped Eugene knew what he was doing—with both females.

"Are you comfortable?" Georgia asked, arranging a pillow behind her grandmother's back.

"I am, but I feel terrible that you are having to wait on me hand and foot." Grammy sighed, frustration clear on her lined face. "Damned clumsy fool."

She said the last disparaging remark to herself.

Georgia reached for her grandmother's hand, squeezing it gently. She knew Grammy was very upset. The older woman rarely swore, and that alone showed how distressed she was.

"Don't worry about it. It could just as easily have happened to me. You know what a klutz I am."

Grammy squeezed back, her gnarled hand feeling so small and fragile in Georgia's. Considering how thin and frail the old woman was, it was a miracle only her ankle had been injured. And in truth, she'd only fallen because she'd already twisted it. Of course, a break would take some time to heal. But a broken ankle was far better than a broken hip. Georgia didn't even want to think about how that would have affected her grandmother. At least with a broken ankle, Georgia could still keep Grammy here in the apartment with her.

Her grandmother managed a smile, and then slipped her hand out of Georgia's to pat her cheek. "You have never been a klutz, Marianne."

Georgia smiled, albeit sadly. Unfortunately, the trauma of the fall and the hospital stay seemed to have brought on a bout of confusion. Grammy hadn't been fully aware of exactly what had happened, and she'd thought Georgia was her long dead daughter all day.

The doctor told Georgia that her grandmother's disorientation wasn't unusual, but he did remind her that the Alzheimer's would only get worse and eventually Georgia would have to make some tough decisions about her grandmother's care. But she couldn't do that right now.

And right now, Georgia could take care of her.

"I'm going to make some soup. Would you like some? Maybe a nice bowl of tomato. And a grilled cheese?"

Grammy smiled. "That sounds delicious."

"And want me to turn on your TV?"

The old woman nodded. "I'd like to watch the news."

Georgia walked around the bed to get the remote from the top of the dresser. She pressed a button and the small flat-screen switched on. She handed her grandmother the remote.

"I'll be right back," Georgia told her. "Just call for me if you need anything."

"You are so good to me, Marianne."

Georgia just nodded.

Once in the kitchen, Georgia took a moment to pull in a few calming breaths. Her eyes burned from the tears she'd managed to keep at bay so far.

Getting her grandmother checked out of the hospital and situated in the apartment had taken most of the day. Which in some ways had been good for Georgia, but she hated the stress it had put on Grammy.

But it had kept her from thinking about Tristan—for the most part. She'd still managed to find moments to fixate on what had happened last night, but overall, she'd managed to stay focused on what had to be done with her grandmother and not panic about what would happen when she saw Tristan again.

Unfortunately, now she did have time to think. And that wasn't a good thing. What would she even say to him the next time she saw him? Maybe neither of them would say anything.

But how would she react if he told her it had been a horrible mistake? Her rational mind had to agree with that, but her emotional side knew she'd be devastated to hear him say it.

"What does it really matter?" Georgia muttered to herself. It wasn't as if it would ever happen again. But even as she thought that, her chest tightened.

"Stop being so stupid," she told herself. "Of course, it wouldn't happen again, and you don't want it to happen again. What would be the point?"

It wasn't like she was going to have a relationship with the man. That had never been a possibility. She knew that. But ninny that she was, that didn't stop her from wanting it to be a possibility.

"Just be happy you have a damned job," she said. What would she do if he'd decided that he couldn't work with her? She stopped buttering a slice of bread as the thought hit her.

He still could decide that.

Just then a knock sounded at the apartment door. She shot a look over her shoulder. What if that was Tristan right now? To tell her that very news?

She set down the bread and knife and wiped her hands on a dish towel. Nervously, she headed to the door, starting when the person on the other side knocked again.

It's probably just Marnie, she told herself. But she still took a deep breath and hesitantly reached for the knob.

Bracing herself for the worst, she pulled it open.

She gaped. "Gabriel."

The large man looked about as pleased to be there as she was to see him.

"Hello, Ms. Sullivan. Could I speak with you again?"

Chapter Twenty-one

Georgia's first thought was to say no, and quickly shut the door in the man's face. She didn't think she could handle any more stress today. Standing face to face with, at best, a delusional coworker, and at worst, a psychotic stalker wasn't going to calm her in any way. But she suspected simply closing the door wasn't going to get rid of him.

However, she really couldn't deal with his craziness. Not now, and frankly, not ever.

"This really isn't a good time," she said, starting to close the door, but his large hand shot out to keep it open. A small, alarmed squeak escaped her, but he instantly raised his hands in the air just as he had the night before.

"Ms. Sullivan, I promise you I'm not here to hurt you or frighten you, although I know it's kind of late for that last one."

She stared at him for a moment. He didn't look like he intended to hurt her. Of course, by all accounts, Ted Bundy hadn't looked dangerous either—until it was too late.

"I don't have anything to discuss with you."

Gabriel nodded. "I understand, Ms. Sullivan. And I know what I told you sounded crazy. But I assure you, I'm telling you the truth about Tristan McIntyre."

She was still trying to process the fact that she'd slept with Tristan; she couldn't hear more about how dangerous he was. She knew he was dangerous—to her emotional well-being anyway.

"I'm really not even here to pressure you about that," Gabriel added. "I just got concerned when you didn't come into work that maybe something bad had happened to you."

"That Tristan had done something bad to me, you mean."

Gabriel nodded again. "I know you don't think he's a threat, but he truly is, Ms. Sullivan."

Oh, Tristan was a threat all right. To her peace of mind. To her rational thought processes. To her heart. But she didn't believe he'd hurt her. Not in a physical way.

"Last night . . ." Just saying those words brought her right back to what she'd done with Tristan.

"Last night," she repeated, "Tristan was nothing but a gentleman."

After all, she'd been the one to initiate the sex, not him.

"Are you sure?" Gabriel asked, his gaze roaming her face. "Because honestly, you look rather shaken."

Oh, she was shaken, all right, but not for any reason she was going to share with this man. A lunatic stranger.

Still, she heard herself saying, "I am a little frazzled, but not because of Tristan McIntyre."

He regarded her for a moment, and must have decided he wasn't going to get anywhere with her. "I just wanted to be sure you were okay."

Georgia didn't know what to say. Thanking him, or offering any sort of gratitude didn't seem right since she hadn't asked for, and didn't want, his concern. She didn't even know him. And she certainly didn't want to encourage this behavior from him.

"I'm fine," she finally said, realizing she had to say something, or he was apparently going to continue to stand there.

"Okay," he said, and she had a faint hope that he was satisfied and would just leave. Unfortunately, that hope didn't last long.

"Are you sure you didn't notice anything strange last night?" he asked. "Anything that seemed odd to you? Maybe something about McIntyre's behavior that seemed . . . off to you?"

Only her own behavior.

Then she recalled the conversation she'd overheard in the hallway. *A deal with the devil.* That turn of phrase echoed in her head again. She had to admit that had sounded odd to her. Almost a little too overdramatic if Tristan was just discussing something to do with the magazine. But then again, what did Georgia really know about the situation? Tristan had said the men had a contract with him, so maybe they had reneged on the contract. Perhaps Tristan was feeling that he had to make the situation sound extreme, so the men in question knew Tristan expected the terms of the contract to be met. She honestly didn't know, but she didn't believe that conversation showed Tristan was dangerous, or that he was involved in some kind of mob activity.

"We attended the gala, but the evening was cut short. I had a family emergency," Georgia told him, her tone clipped. She didn't really want to be telling him any of this, but she didn't think he'd leave until he was certain she wasn't going to listen to any more of his nonsense.

"He left early with me and actually stayed with me until the problem was sorted out." He'd stayed longer than that, too, but she absolutely wasn't sharing that information.

"Marianne? Marianne, are you there?"

Georgia shot a look over her shoulder. "I'll be right there, Grammy. Just one second."

She turned back to Gabriel. "I have to go. Please don't come here anymore."

She expected him to argue, to continue to try to persuade her. But all he did was say, "Promise me you will come to me if something happens. I'm here for you."

She didn't answer, except to say an abrupt good-bye. Once the door was securely closed and locked, she hurried down the hall, afraid her grandmother might try to get out of bed.

But when she rushed into the room, her grandmother was still propped up amongst her pillows, watching television.

"Are you okay? Did you need something?"

Grammy's wrinkled brow creased more as she considered Georgia's words. "I heard you talking. Is that your father? Is he home early from work?"

Grammy still didn't know who Georgia was, and she must have thought the male voice was her long-dead husband, Georgia's grandfather.

"No," Georgia assured her calmly. "That was someone from my office. I'm Georgia, Grammy. Your granddaughter."

Grammy looked confused and a little scared. "Georgia?"

"Yes, Grammy." She walked over to her grandmother and touched her hand. "Don't worry, you are fine. I'm going to make you that soup now."

Grammy looked small and frail and frightened. She looked around the room as if trying to remember. Finally, she nodded. "Okay, Georgia."

Georgia wasn't sure if Grammy was remembering, but she forced a reassuring smile and left the room.

This was all too much. But Georgia had to hold herself together. Her grandmother needed her. She had to stay focused on that. And on keeping her job, and pushing this Gabriel person's weird behavior out of her mind.

If Gabriel approached her again, she would have to tell Tristan that there was a nutter working in the mail room.

After all, it seemed far more likely Gabriel was the one who was a threat, who was a real danger.

Not that he'd done anything to really intimidate her. Aside from coming to her apartment building—twice. That alone was scary.

Although both times, he'd made sure his stance and demeanor were reassuring. He held his hands in the air, keeping plenty of space between them. But that could have changed at any moment. Georgia watched enough true-crime shows to know that. Maybe she should tell Tristan as soon as she saw him again.

Maybe that would be a better conversation than the one she didn't want to have—about sex on the living room floor.

Once back in the kitchen, she put the kettle on to make Grammy some of her favorite tea.

Take care of your grandmother, she ordered herself, and don't think about anything else. It was too much.

She returned to buttering the bread for sandwiches.

Grilled cheese and tomato soup. Good comfort food. That was all she and Grammy needed right now.

The piercing whistle of the kettle filled the small kitchen, and all thoughts of comfort food vanished like the billow of steam pouring out of the kettle spout.

That sound had stopped their kiss. Why hadn't she left it at that? Why hadn't she used her damned head?

Then she wouldn't be dealing with all this. All these memories of the best sex of her life. With the most gorgeous man she'd even met.

She gathered herself and turned off the kettle. The whistling stopped. If only the memories would.

She had just shifted the kettle to a cool burner when another sharp rap at the door resounded through the apartment.

Georgia closed her eyes and let her head fall back in utter misery and frustration. Gabriel. He had to be back with more questions. She couldn't cope with him again. Not when she felt like doing nothing more than crawling into bed, covering her head with her quilt, and wallowing in her humiliation and shame.

But that wasn't an option.

It was, however, an option to tell this loony-toon to leave her alone, or she would be forced to call the police. And tell Tristan all the nonsense he'd said to her.

This time, she had no hesitation as she went to the door and gripped the knob.

"Listen, Gabriel," she said as she whipped it open, only to let the words to die on her lips. "Oh, hi."

Chapter Twenty-two

"Hmm, forgotten my name already," Tristan said, managing to sound appropriately sardonic.

"I'm sorry," Georgia said, brushing her hair away from her face, looking more than a little flustered. "I—I thought you were someone else."

"I noticed." He smiled, even as he wondered who Gabriel was. And was she flustered to see him? Or flustered because she was expecting this Gabriel person?

Of course, the bigger question was why he was at all concerned who Gabriel was. As if he should care. But then, he'd spent an entire day thinking about her. He didn't like the idea that she might have been thinking about someone else.

Stop, damn it. He needed to get control of all these new, weird and very unnerving feelings. He didn't care for any of them. Not in the least.

"I'm sorry if I'm interrupting something," he said, pleased that his voice sounded normal.

"You— you're not." Still she didn't back up to let him in. Nor did she say anything more.

"Can I come in?" he finally asked.

She seemed to snap out of her rattled daze, and quickly stepped aside. "Of course, I'm sorry."

"No more apologizing," he said moving past her, making

sure he didn't touch her. He didn't dare. His whole body, which didn't even feel like his own anymore, was aware of her. Wanted to touch her, but he didn't trust himself to risk even the briefest contact.

Which was as insane as the way he'd been unable to think of anything but her all day. Just because he was a demon of lust didn't mean he had no self-control. Hell, self-control was as much a part of his makeup as giving up control.

Once inside and a few feet away from her, he stopped. "I came to see Grace. How is she?"

Georgia blinked, and again he got the feeling she was trying to shake off the anxiousness that darkened her pretty eyes to near black. "Oh, um, she's a little confused today, and the ankle is pretty sore, but she seems to be resting okay now."

"That's good."

She nodded, and fell silent again.

This wasn't going well. She clearly felt uncomfortable with him, which wasn't a total surprise, but it still bothered him. Sex hadn't helped things in any way. It certainly hadn't helped his issues.

"Do you think it would upset her, if I said hello?" he asked after a moment. He didn't want to leave, but he didn't want to stand in the foyer, staring awkwardly at Georgia either.

"Oh, yeah," she said. "Sure."

This time she squeezed past him, clearly not wanting to touch him either.

Tristan wasn't sure how he'd expected this meeting to go, but not like this.

She led him down the hall, and despite his own agitation at his almost insane attraction to her, he found his eyes drifting down to the sway of her hips and the nice, round curve of her rear end.

He wanted to take her from behind next time. He took

a longer stride, bringing him closer to her. Close enough to grab those full hips. He raised his arms, hands poised to catch her. He could bend her over right here, and—

"Grammy, you have a visitor."

Georgia's words pulled him out of his libidinous thoughts, and he dropped his hands.

Shit. Had he really been about to take her in the hallway, with an injured, elderly woman just feet away?

He was losing his mind. Okay, if Georgia enjoyed a little sneaky, "we might get caught action," then he'd be all over it. But Georgia would never do something like that around her dear grandmother, and he hadn't been looking at it as a kinky scenario. He'd been driven by a need far stronger than any he'd felt in his whole existence.

And frankly, this lack of control, or near lack of control, was freaking him out.

"Grammy, Tristan is here," Georgia said when she reached the doorway. "He came by to check on you."

Tristan came up behind her, again not getting too close, but close enough so he could look over Georgia's shoulder.

Grace peered at him, clearly confused, but then she smiled and waved for him to enter the room. Georgia stepped in and he followed.

"Come," Grace said, patting the edge of her bed. "Come sit down."

Tristan hesitated, but then did as she asked.

"My goodness," Grace said, shaking her head. "I haven't seen you in . . . my goodness, it's been years."

Tristan shot Georgia a confused look, which she met with a helpless tilt of her head. She had said her grandmother was confused, and clearly Grace didn't know whom she was talking to. Or rather, she thought she knew whom she was talking to, but it wasn't Tristan.

Grace reached out a gnarled hand, her knuckles large with arthritis and her skin paper thin over bones and veins.

Not pretty hands, not anymore. But her touch was gentle and her skin smooth against his wrist.

"Tristan, it really has been so, so long."

Tristan frowned. Wait, she did know he was Tristan. Perhaps she just couldn't recall that she'd seen him only yesterday.

"Hello, Grace," he said. "How are you feeling?"

She shook her head, her cloudy eyes filled with sympathy. Sympathy Tristan didn't understand. He wasn't the one deserving of her concern. Well, perhaps if she knew how utterly obsessed with her granddaughter he was, he might merit some sympathy.

"Please don't worry about how I am," she said, her tone soft, yet emphatic. She squeezed his fingers in reassurance. "I'm the one who is worried about you."

Tristan glanced at Georgia again. She shrugged, clearly having no idea what her grandmother was talking about either.

"I have always felt so bad I didn't tell you about my marriage in person."

Tristan's frown deepened. "Your marriage?"

Grace sighed. "I know it must have come as such a shock. To come see me at my parents', only to discover I'd married and moved to Bingham."

Tristan didn't respond right away, trying to piece together what would be the correct response to all of this. Then he recalled her mentioning that her first love had been named Tristan.

"It was a shock," he said, although he knew he still sounded a little puzzled.

"Of course it was," she sympathized, her fragile, soft skin stroking his wrist and arm. "And I did plan to wait for you. But . . ."

She shook her head again, looking so pained.

"Tristan, I wasn't sure how long you'd be gone. And well, I met Joseph, and . . ." She sighed. "Well, I won't lie. The flesh is weak."

Tristan paused, and then shot another look at Georgia. Her expression was as wide-eyed, and probably as comical, as his own. Apparently, Grammy was confessing to "Tristan" that she'd run around on him. Wow.

"I—I understand, Grace," he said when he'd finally gotten his expression schooled to one of understanding.

Of course, he did understand. He was dealing with the weakness of the flesh himself. But he wasn't going to make that confession.

"I know I can't really expect forgiveness," Grace said. "But I do hope you will believe that I never meant to hurt you in any way."

Tristan opened his mouth to say he understood totally, but Grace continued, "I just want you to also know it wasn't that I had a roaming eye. I was waiting for you. But Joseph"—her voice got dreamy as she said the other man's name—"he is just so handsome. And so strong. And well, he was such a wonderful kisser, I just fell for him. And his hands." She sighed. "Such talented hands."

As far as apologies went, this wasn't the best he'd ever heard. The real Tristan was probably better off having never gotten it. At least Tristan hoped the poor man never did, although he was finding it all rather entertaining.

Tristan and Georgia exchanged a look. Her eyes were still wide, now in a combination of disbelief and amusement.

"I know I was your first," Grace continued, drawing both his and Georgia's attention right back to her. "And you were, of course, mine."

Wow, they were really finding out the dirt on Grammy today.

"And I know that was enough reason to believe we would marry, but I just couldn't let Joseph go. He's my soul mate."

Tristan glanced at Georgia. Their eyes met, holding for a moment, but Grace's stroking fingers pulled his gaze back to her.

"I hope you understand." Grace smiled sadly, an almost pleading look in her hazy eyes.

He might not be the Tristan this apology was meant for. But he understood her need to be forgiven. How? He couldn't say. Demons were never forgiven. And maybe that's why her odd apology touched him. Or maybe he was going daft. Probably that was it, but he reached out his other hand to cover hers on his wrist.

"I forgive you, Grace. A soul mate is something you can't deny and never want to lose."

Grace instantly looked relieved.

He wished he felt the same way. But his own words, while said to comfort Grace, worried him. What did he know about souls? Aside from bartering for them, making sure that humans lost them for all eternity, he didn't understand souls, or the whole idea of a soul mate. Since he didn't have a soul, how could he ever understand the power of having a soul mate?

He glanced at Georgia. She watched him, a strange longing in her dark eyes. But when she realized he was looking at her, she looked away from him to her grandmother, that longing gone.

And while he didn't understand the look he saw on Georgia's face, he did feel a strange longing of his own. A weird yearning, as if he had a void inside himself and he wanted something, or someone to fill it.

"I'm so glad you understand," Grace said. "I feel better talking to you."

Tristan wished he could say the same thing.

"I'm glad," he said. "And I do forgive you."

Grace smiled, a serene look softening her wrinkled features. She settled back against her pillows, content.

Tristan wished he could feel that contentment.

"Thank you, Tristan."

He nodded. "Well, I'm going to let you rest now."

He rose from the bed, being careful not to jostle her ankle too much.

"I'll come back with your dinner," Georgia said as they headed to the door, and only then did her grandmother seem confused about what was going on.

"Marianne," she said, her tone a tad admonishing. "Did you listen to my talk with my old friend?"

"No," Georgia assured her.

Her grandmother still didn't seem convinced, and Tristan wondered who Grace had thought Georgia was when she'd been standing there the whole time. Or maybe Grace truly hadn't noticed her. But now she thought she was someone named Marianne. And from Georgia's reaction, that was not like the confessions of Grammy's romantic past. Georgia was used to this misidentification.

"Just rest," Georgia said, her tone low and soothing. "I'll be back in a minute. I think *Murder, She Wrote* is on."

That information seemed to distract Grace because she turned her attention to the television on her dresser.

Tristan glanced at the old woman once more, still thinking about what she'd said, then followed Georgia out of the room. Once in the hallway, Georgia made a noise, a low gurgle deep in her chest, and Tristan tensed with alarm.

Oh, God, she wasn't crying, was she? He imagined it was hard to see her beloved grandmother so confused. But when Georgia reached the kitchen and he joined her there, she turned to look at him.

There were tears in her eyes, but not from distress or sadness, but restrained laughter.

She did giggle then, a fit of giggles, in fact.

Tristan found himself grinning with amusement, too.

"I'm sorry," she finally said, "but I did tell you she was confused today."

He nodded his head. "Indeed, she is."

"So how does it feel to be dumped by an eighty-five-year-old woman?"

"No breakup is easy," he said, attempting to look wounded.

She giggled again, and he found himself lost in the sound and the joyous look on her face. Her eyes sparkled and her cheeks were stained a pale, pretty pink. And those bow lips—so rosy and delectable.

"At least it was for a soul mate, though," he said slowly, distracted by how truly beautiful she was.

Her smile faded slightly as she noticed the intent look on his face. He took a step toward her, and though she held her ground, he noticed she looked almost worried. He didn't like that. He wanted her joy back.

He wanted . . .

"Georgia, I have a confession of my own."

Chapter Twenty-three

Funny, Georgia had managed to forget the situation was weird between her and Tristan. That was until he got that oddly serious look and then said he had a confession.

She was willing to bet she didn't want to hear this confession. Would it be that he regretted having sex with her? Or that he didn't think he could work with her now, because of their awkward situation? Or was he just going to go into a long explanation of why it couldn't happen again. She definitely didn't know how to handle any of those confessions.

Just play it cool. If he apologizes for last night, just act like it's no big deal. Or if he says it was fun, but can't happen again, agree. And if he decides he can't work with you, well, tell him . . .

"I really like you."

Georgia's strategy planning stopped.

"What?"

Tristan smiled that crooked, sexy, oh-so-naughty smile of his. "That sounded really stupid, didn't it?"

She didn't respond, trying to switch gears. He liked her? She hadn't thought of a casual comeback for that confession.

"I—I like you, too," she said, her tone sounding befuddled even to her own ears.

He laughed then, and for a moment, she thought his admission must be some sort of joke.

"God, I feel like some tongue-tied teenage boy. Or at least I think I do." He said the latter almost under his breath.

That confused her even further, but he continued. "Last night was pretty damned spectacular."

She nodded.

"And I find that I don't really want to just have a one-night stand with you."

She nodded again, not quite sure where he was going with this.

"And while I don't usually 'date,' I find that I want to date you."

She wasn't sure if she should be flattered or insulted. He was hardly offering her words of adoration—not that she expected them. She expected to get fired. But still, given how charming he could be, this was rather underwhelming.

"And why do you find yourself wanting that?" She was surprised at her own question, but really, she needed more from him than "I like you and I don't know why, but I want to date you."

"Honestly," he said, his expression going from a smile to a rather bemused look, "I can't get you off my mind. I've been thinking about you nonstop all day."

That was a bit more flattering, or it would have been if he didn't look so muddled by the concept.

"I mean, I have had a lot of . . . sexual relations, and"—he shook his head—"you have just affected me more than anyone."

Again, his words could have been complimentary, minus the first part.

She grimaced, not sure what to say.

"That didn't sound right, did it?" he said as soon as he saw her face.

She shook her head.

"I'm sorry," he said immediately. "I have to admit, I'm a little shaken. I have just never . . . felt this way. It's like I'm . . . obsessed with you."

She grimaced a little more.

"That didn't sound any better, did it?"

"No," she said, offering him a pained look. She almost felt sorry for him. He really was shaken. By her. Or rather by feeling the way he did about her.

He moved closer and reached for her hands.

"Okay, let me actually get this right." His thumbs caressed the backs of her hands, and she was shocked how sensitive the skin there was. She felt his touch throughout her whole body.

"I won't deny I've dated a lot. I mean, as my assistant, you know that."

True, and all of those dates, many of which she had arranged for him, had caused her a lot of envy.

"And while I can't explain it, you and our time together have affected me far more than any of them. I'm going to be honest, I don't know what I'm doing, but I just know I want to see you more. I need to see more of you."

Well, that explanation was much better than the others. She didn't even mind his odd desperation and bewilderment. After all, she felt a little bewildered herself. And he was saying she had made more impact on him than all the others. Others who were stunningly beautiful. Amazingly elegant. And decidedly more put together than she was.

Self-consciously, she pulled one of her hands away from his to touch her disheveled hair, pulled into a haphazard ponytail.

He immediately caught her hand again and pressed his lips to her knuckles. Her heart thundered in her chest.

"I know this isn't what I suggested initially," he said, his expression almost . . . pleading. Could this gorgeous man really be pleading with her?

"But I really want to continue seeing you. Beyond our work relationship."

She stared at him, still expecting this to be some sort of joke. But he simply stood waiting, his expression sincere and a little . . . nervous?

God, a part of her wanted to just say yes. Exuberantly say yes. But she was a wise enough woman to know she had to have just a little self-preservation.

"How will this affect my job?"

Instead of looking offended, he smiled, a glint in his vivid green eyes that looked very much like he was impressed.

"I think that's part of what draws me to you," he said.

"What's that?"

"That you are sensible as well as sexy." He kissed her knuckles again, this time his tongue darting out to taste her.

"I don't feel particularly sensible," she said, her voice reedy with her building arousal.

"Oh? How do you feel?"

She met his gaze, although she was sure her eyes were as hooded by lust as his were.

"You know I'm attracted to you," she said, not willing to put herself out there more than that. This strange announcement he'd made was still new and she needed time to process it. Which certainly wasn't easy with him so close, and his lips on her skin, even if it was the back of her hand.

"Your job will be unaffected, not matter how this dating thing plays out. I know you have huge concerns when it comes to your grandmother, and I respect that."

She nodded, watching with dazed eyes as he uncurled her fingers from around his and proceeded to pull one into his mouth, his tongue playing over the sensitive pad of her fingertip.

"And— and how will we behave at work?" she managed, squeezing his other hand which still held hers.

"Like complete professionals."

She nodded, or at least she thought she nodded.

"And how do we end this when our interest and attraction finally play out?" As soon as she asked the question, she held her breath. And not because of his teeth grazing across the knuckle of her index finger. Yet another place she had no idea was so sensitive.

"Well, when that happens, we will again be adult and mature and handle it graciously."

Georgia noticed he said *when* rather than *if.* For a moment, her heart lurched in her chest. But she supposed it was only reasonable to remain pragmatic about this.

And God knows she did want more of him. More of his attention, more of his flirting, more of his mouth, she thought dreamily as she watched him suck her finger.

But she forced herself to focus. Ground rules were good. They would save them both a lot of confusion and pain. Although, she feared the only one truly at risk of pain was she. As if to accentuate that thought, he nipped her fingertip, just lightly.

And not that kind of pain.

"So when either of us decides we are finished with the relationship—"

He smiled around her finger, and then popped it out of his mouth. "I like that word: relationship."

She frowned slightly. As if he'd never had a relationship. Dear God, he was truly acting like this was the only time he'd ever considered seeing just one person for longer than a date or two.

Wait, he *was* considering dating just one person, wasn't he?

First things first.

"When either of us decides to end the relationship, we

will do so before moving on to another . . ." Clearly relationships weren't how he labeled most of his dating. She finally opted on, "Person."

"Absolutely." His tongue moved from her finger to her palm.

"And,"—back to her previous concern—"we will date exclusively until that time."

"Definitely." He pressed a kiss to the inside of her wrist.

"And we will also have safe sex," she added, trying very desperately to stay focused. But this one was a must. She was already kicking herself for her lack of responsibility the night before. Now hearing him say aloud that he'd had many sexual relations, that was definitely a must.

However, this one gave him pause. "Safe sex? I assure you I am totally safe in that regard."

She made a dubious face. "That's what all the boys say."

"They do?" He seemed genuinely surprised by that news.

"Yes," she said, not being swayed by his rather adorable puzzled look. "So condoms from here on out."

"What about last night?" he pointed out as if he'd got her now.

"We were caught up in the heat of the moment. Thankfully, I am on the pill, so we are safe on that count," she assured him. "But we still need to be safe about other things."

"I don't have any other things," he muttered. Clearly some of his ardor had been doused by the idea of a latex raincoat down there.

Too bad, she thought. Although, she did miss his lips on her wrist, and she was curious about where he'd planned to kiss next.

"Okay," he finally said begrudgingly. "What else?"

She could tell from his expression, he was finding her to be a bit of a party-pooper.

"And . . ." She thought for a second. "I guess that's it. For me anyway. Do you have any requests?"

"Yes," he said immediately. "You are not to wear panties to work."

That was his one stipulation?

"No panties?"

"None."

"That doesn't seem very professional," she pointed out, keeping her tone practical, although she could feel her cheeks burning.

"Yes, well, *HOT!* is a fashion magazine. Think of it as a fashion statement," he said. Then he smiled in that crooked way of his that she was sure got him damned near everything he wanted.

"All right," she agreed, albeit hesitantly. She wasn't going to bring up that particular time of the month, but surely that was a loophole. She'd just assume it was.

"So are we agreed?" he asked, his lips moving back to her upturned wrist.

She nodded, and then cleared her throat to find her voice. It was not easy as she watched his lips move over her wrist and up the inside of her arm.

"Yes."

He lifted his head and grinned that smug smile she'd seen dozens of times before. Although, this time, she could swear she saw something that looked like relief in his verdant gaze.

"Marianne, are you there?"

Both of them looked toward the kitchen door like guilty teenagers caught in the act.

"And your grandmother always takes precedence over anything else," Tristan said with a slightly disappointed smile.

But Georgia found that last rule the one that clinched her horrendously enormous crush on him. A dangerous crush to be sure, but she couldn't seem to control it.

"I'm here," Georgia answered. "I'll be right there."

Tristan released her hands and she hurried past him, only to pause in the doorway. "Would you like to stay for dinner? It's nothing gourmet. Just grilled cheese and tomato soup."

Tristan smiled, stealing her breath away. "I'd love to."

She nodded and rushed down the hall.

Holy crap, what had she agreed to now?

Chapter Twenty-four

Tristan finished the last bite of his grilled cheese, and then sighed. "That was delicious. What do you mean 'not gourmet'? What kind of cheese was that?"

Georgia paused in her chewing, and then quickly swallowed. "Velveeta."

"Well, I've never heard of it, but if it isn't gourmet, it clearly should be."

Georgia laughed. "I don't want to sound rude, but I sometimes wonder where you came from."

Tristan's smile faltered, just slightly. Then he said wryly, "Believe me, you wouldn't want to know."

He set his plate on the table and reached for the glass of white wine. It was the one thing she had added to the simple meal to make it a little fancier.

"No dancing. No Velveeta. Clearly not," she said, reaching for her own wine.

"Oh, I didn't say there was no dancing. Just no proms. Dancing is actually accepted. Although, it's usually done naked and around raging fires. More ritualistic than for entertainment."

She paused, the glass halfway to her lips, shocked by his comment. Then he smiled, and she relaxed, shaking her head.

"You had me going for a moment," she laughed.

He smiled, but it didn't seem to reach his eyes. For a second, she wondered again if maybe he'd been telling the truth. Or trying to share something about his past.

"You are so beautiful when you laugh."

She met his gaze, realizing that serious look was desire. Desire for her. Amazing.

"Thank you."

He started to reach for her hand, and then stopped. "Should we check on your grandmother?"

Georgia nodded, although she hated to agree. She wanted that touch. But as he'd stipulated earlier, her grandmother always came first.

"I'll check on her," she said, placing her wineglass back on the table and uncurling from the sofa. "You can just relax. Maybe there's a movie on TV."

She hesitated. "That is if you wanted to stay."

"Oh, I want to stay," he assured her, and she got the feeling it wasn't to watch a movie. Her toes curled into the soft pile of the carpet.

She nodded and headed to her grandmother's room. They had sat with her as she ate, waiting to eat their dinner later. Her grandmother had looked tired and Georgia had just made hers and brought it directly to her.

She eased open the door to see her grandmother's bedside lamp was still on, but Grammy slept, her lips slightly open, her Agatha Christie mystery spread open on her chest. Georgia could hear her even breathing from across the room and the sound comforted her.

She tiptoed to the nightstand and switched off the light. A lit white, opaque figurine of a Victorian couple in a sleigh cast a soft light around the room, just enough so that if Grammy woke in the night, she wouldn't be disoriented. Well, hopefully she wouldn't be disoriented.

Georgia hoped tomorrow would be better for her than

today, but she knew eventually the bad days would be more frequent than the good. The idea depressed her.

Georgia watched her a moment longer, then carefully pulled the door almost shut, wanting to be sure she heard Grammy if she woke up needing something.

As Georgia walked back toward the living room, she heard the water on in the kitchen and the gentle clatter of dishes. She stopped in the kitchen doorway to find Tristan loading the dishwasher. He had a perplexed expression as he tried to find a place for a soup bowl as if he was trying to solve a Rubik's cube in twenty moves or less. Of course, Georgia was positive he'd never loaded a dishwasher before. The fact he was even trying was rather endearing. Or very endearing.

"Can I help?"

He looked up, and then smiled sheepishly. "Is it that obvious I've never done this before?"

"Yeah," she said with a grin, and then strode over to ease the dish out of his hand. "I'll do it."

She bent over to place the bowl on the bottom rack, and Tristan took that opportunity to replace the bowl between his hands with her hips.

"I think I like loading dishwashers. A lot."

She couldn't help herself, and she pressed back against him. His large erection prodded into her lower back.

"Well, it isn't usually quite so exciting," she admitted.

He rubbed tighter against her. "Oh, I bet it is always this exciting with you."

She straightened and turned to face him. His hands stayed on her hips, again pulling her close, and all thoughts of a pithy comeback escaped her. She was far too distracted by his beautiful lips close to hers.

His gaze moved to her lips as well just before he lowered his head to kiss her.

His mouth amazed her, soft and hard all at the same time. Controlling and persuasive. Tangy and sweet.

She made a small noise deep in throat, loving all the contrasts: loving his hard body against her soft one, his fingers digging into the cushion of her hips.

"I've wanted to do that from the moment you opened your door," he murmured against her lips.

"I've wanted you to," she admitted.

She felt his smile against her lips, and he kissed her again, slowly and thoroughly, which just fanned the fire in her, taking it from a slow burn to a roar.

He positioned her so her back was against the sideboard and his legs between hers. She reached behind her, feeling for the countertop to steady herself, even though Tristan still held her hips.

Her hand brushed against one of the dirty plates and it clattered into the sink.

They jumped apart, looking around them guiltily. When the apartment remained quiet, they both laughed.

"We do act a bit like sneaky teenagers," Georgia said.

"Sneaky, horny teenagers," Tristan said, sounding appropriately desperate.

"Is there any other kind?" She leaned in to kiss him again.

"I have no idea," he murmured before he captured her mouth again.

This kiss was more frantic than the last, his tongue parting her lips and tasting her. Hers tasted him back. Her hands moved from the counter to knot in his hair, the short silky waves curling around her fingers as if tugging her back.

"Is your grandmother okay?" he managed to pant against the side of her neck.

She wasn't sure how he had the concentration to consider double-checking, but she nodded.

"Yes, asleep."

"Good," he said and spun her around. She followed his direction readily, leaning back against his chest as his hands came around her waist to find the button of her jeans. He popped them open with a dexterity that she decided to appreciate rather than analyze. Then he wedged his fingers into the waistband to work them down over her hips. She shimmied to help him and he groaned and stopped pushing at them.

He stepped back and she nearly groaned herself at the loss of his body heat and hardness against her.

"Do that again," he said, his tone managing to be somewhere between an order and a plea.

She paused for only a second, then did as he asked, pivoting her hips from side to side as she pulled her jeans down over her hips.

Tristan groaned again. She had the most amazing ass. A waist that flared into full hips, a round, pale rear end with two adorable dimples on either side of her tailbone. All of it was so curved and soft and feminine.

"Damn, you are so sexy," he whispered, his words filled with worship.

She glanced over her shoulder at him, some of her hair coming loose from her ponytail, her glasses slipping down her pert nose. She reminded him of a very, very naughty schoolteacher.

She opened her mouth as if to say something, but instead she just wiggled her derriere at him in invitation. And he didn't need to be invited more than once. He unfastened his own pants and freed his throbbing erection. Then he moved back to press himself against all that pale softness. She made a small noise, somewhere between a hiss and a whimper, and thrust her hips against him.

"Can I take you like this?" he whispered in her ear. "From behind, right here in the kitchen?"

She nodded, making another whimpering noise. He gently bit her ear, tugging the velvety skin of her earlobe. She bucked against him again. But still he didn't bend her over and enter her.

Instead, he slid a hand between her thighs to stroke her desire-dampened lips. He slipped his fingers farther inside her, his thumb entering her hot, tight vagina and his fingers massaging her swollen clit.

He rubbed her and filled her that way, feeling her lust drench his hand, and her breath come in short, sharp gasps.

"Do you want me inside you?" he asked when he'd felt her shudder of release as if it were his own.

"Yes," she said, her voice low and breathy.

"Do you?"

"Yes," she cried this time, her voice cracking with need.

He positioned himself and her, pushing her down against the countertop until her back was arched and her butt was up in the air, offered to him.

Then he filled her. To his utter shock, he almost came right then. But he remained still, gathering himself. Then he began to thrust deep into her. Their labored breath and the sound of their bodies slamming together filled the kitchen. It was the most erotic sound he'd ever heard.

She made a noise deep in her chest as if she was trying to hold in a scream, but her climax rushed over him, around him. He shook with it, the feeling so powerful his knees nearly buckled. But he continued to fill her over and over. She came again, this time crying out, low and keening. And that orgasm was too much for him. Far too intense for him to stop his own. He made a deep growl and thrust to the hilt, his cock pulsing inside her tight vagina.

"Oh, my God," she said, shivering with her own release and weakness.

Oh, my God, was right. God was certainly never a deity

he cried out to, but in this instance, he was more than willing to agree with her. Then he collapsed over her, his body pinning her to the counter, weak and shaking.

Oh, my God.

Chapter Twenty-five

Georgia patted her face dry, trying to decide how she felt about this strange turn of events. She made a muddled expression at herself in the bathroom mirror.

"You're seeing Tristan McIntyre. *The* Tristan McIntyre." She made another face. "Your boss."

She made another face, and then paused. She tilted her head, hearing something outside the bathroom. Was Grammy awake? She listened closer, and then realized it was a male voice. Tristan, of course. Was he talking to her grandmother?

She opened the bathroom door, poking her head out. Tristan was talking, but his voice was coming from the direction of the living room.

She tossed the damp towel she still held into the sink, and then headed in that direction. She paused just outside the door, feeling a moment of guilt for eavesdropping, but her guilt was quickly dismissed as she heard Tristan's words.

"What I'm doing on my time away from the takeover isn't your business. And I sure as hell don't need you telling me how to do my job."

There was a pause.

"Listen"—his voice lowered to nearly a whisper—"the Prince of Darkness isn't going to think Finola is a better choice for the job. I know what I'm doing."

Another pause.

"I'm not distracted. I'm on the job. Believe me. All the newest pawns are in position. This takeover is practically in the bag."

Silence.

"You have nothing to worry about. None of us are going to feel his wrath on anything. And Finola isn't going to work her way back into his good graces either. But if you are so concerned, I'll come in and see what she is doing."

Another moment of silence.

"Okay. Okay. I'll be there. By the way, how did you dial the phone anyway?"

Another few seconds of silence, before Tristan said his abrupt good-bye.

Georgia looked around quickly, debating what she should do. She didn't want to get caught listening. She rushed back to her bedroom door, trying to make it look like she was just stepping out from inside her room.

It must have worked, because when he walked into the hallway and saw her, he simply smiled regretfully.

"I'm sorry. I have to head back to the office. It seems we are having a fashion editorial crisis."

She nodded, although her mind was abuzz with what she'd overheard versus what he was saying.

He strolled up to her and leaned down to steal a kiss, which despite her whirling thoughts, she reciprocated. Before she knew it, she was utterly distracted by the velvety softness of his lips.

"I'd planned to angle my way into spending the night," he murmured against her mouth.

"I'm not sure horny teenagers actually get to spend the night together," she pointed out. "They just run around behind their parents' backs, sneaking sex where they can."

"Hmm, I don't think I like that scenario," he said. "Because I was planning to spend tomorrow night instead."

"Well, I can't stop you from trying," she said airily, even as the idea made her heart rate shoot through the roof.

"Oh, I'm going to put my whole effort into it." He grinned naughtily and leaned down for another lingering kiss.

"Okay, as much as I don't want to go, the *capo dei capi* calls."

Georgia nodded, but the last term brought her thoughts right back to the overheard phone conversation. Who had he been talking to, and about what exactly? It clearly had involved work in some way, or at least Finola was involved in what they had been discussing. But she didn't know if Tristan and whoever was on the other end of the phone had truly been talking about an issue at the magazine. In truth, it didn't sound like it to Georgia. Tristan had mentioned a takeover. And someone that they all seemed to work for. The Prince of Darkness, though? Was that some sort of code name? Or maybe a sarcastic name? It had to be, because obviously they weren't talking about the actual Prince of Darkness.

If such a being even existed.

Tristan paused in the open apartment doorway. "Will I see you at the office tomorrow?"

"Yes, my grandmother's nurse will be here."

He smiled, appearing relieved. "That's good. You are the only one keeping me sane."

Again, Georgia didn't understand exactly what he meant. Just as she didn't understand what he'd been discussing with the person on the other end of his cellphone, but still her body reacted to his words. To his clear desire and need for her.

Whatever he'd been talking about, he still wanted her. And she couldn't lie, that was a heady feeling.

He ducked back into the doorway for one last kiss, as if

he were reading her thoughts and knew how attracted she was to him. Insanely attracted.

"See you tomorrow."

She nodded and then he left. She remained in the foyer, lost in a combination of dazed happiness and mild confusion. Then she decided to focus on only one of those emotions, and turned to head to her bedroom with a silly smile on her face.

The last place Tristan wanted to be was in the office, not when he had a sexy, sweet bombshell waiting in bed for him.

Georgia. Peaches. Damn, this woman was everything . . . everything. She had filled him. Totally. It was such a strange feeling, but one he was getting addicted to. And not just the sex. Sex was always his addiction. It was who he was. His identity. But sex with Georgia was just the very tip of what he felt. He loved everything about her. The simple things. Talking to her. Hearing her laugh. Her sense of humor. Hell, eating Velveeta with her.

This woman was . . .

He strode past her desk, only to stop and give it a second look. A little cluttered but in her own fabulous way. He picked up a pen that lay on the legal pad he'd seen her use many, many times as she made notes of what he wanted her to do for the day. The pen was just a plain old ballpoint, nothing special, but still he could feel her.

This woman was . . . filling him. There was no other way to describe the wonderful, warm feeling that swelled in his chest.

He studied the pen, and then put it in his pocket as if it was some intimate treasure that only belonged to her.

His thoughts were interrupted by a squeaking, frantic scratching of nails on glass.

He turned to see Dippy. The hellhound clawed again at the glass door that led to Tristan's office, the action frenzied, feverish.

Tristan walked to the door, not moved by the mutt's panicked behavior.

He pushed open the door, and Dippy barely waited until he was inside with the door closed to blurt, "Finola has gone out with the mail room staff."

This was why Tristan was here? Because Finola had gone out with some of the mail room workers?

"Dippy," he said, stepping past the crazy beast, "I think you are spending way too much time worrying about your self-absorbed owner."

Dippy trotted after him. "She isn't my owner. Satan is my owner."

Tristan shot him an irritated look. "Fine. But in this scenario, she is your owner, and frankly, I think you are just getting far too worked up about what she's doing. So she's gone out with these people. So she thinks she's going to get close to them, figure out what their greatest desires are, and then attempt to get them to sell their souls. That's what we all do. And if she succeeds, who cares? She's just done our work for us. Your real owner isn't easily duped, you know that. We'll just take credit for it, and Satan will be happy to have more damned souls. Why are you making this more than it needs be? Frankly, this is a good thing."

"You don't get it," Dippy insisted, so intense in his concern that he was practically under Tristan's feet. "She was happy to go out with them."

Tristan stepped into his office, holding the door for the dog to go inside ahead of him.

"So she's pleased with herself because she thinks she's got some plan to get Satan to notice her again. Like I said, we will take credit for her work."

Or rather I will, Tristan amended to himself. Dippy was

never going to be his equal in this venture. But there just didn't seem to be a way to get rid of the awful animal completely. Otherwise, Tristan would happily do it.

"Tristan, she wasn't happy about that. She was genuinely happy to be with them. She's . . . changed."

Tristan stopped at his desk, glancing at the white, fluffy yapper. "Well, all the better. Maybe finally she's realized she isn't in control here, and she is content with her new position just gathering souls."

"Tristan, you know that is not Finola's nature. She seems to actually like these humans. Especially one called Eugene."

Tristan didn't believe that. But he didn't bother to state his opinion. Clearly Dippy wasn't listening. And clearly he was also blowing everything out of proportion.

"I'm telling you, something is happening to her," Dippy said, his tone a low growl.

Tristan didn't respond. God, there was nothing worse than a drama queen on four legs. Tristan strolled around his desk to sit. While he was here he might as well work a little. On the magazine. Because even with a drama queen hellhound and an apparently happy demon diva to contend with, he still had to run the magazine to keep up this façade.

He pressed the on button of the computer to check his e-mails. He still had to be sure the fashion spread for the July issue was ready to go. And that the articles on fad diets and the most popular colors for fall were done. If he got this stuff done now, he could spend more time tomorrow just enjoying Georgia.

Maybe he could even take the afternoon off and they could go somewhere nice. A picnic in Central Park perhaps. He wondered what the weather was supposed to be like tomorrow.

"Just like something is happening to you," Dippy said.

Or maybe Peaches wasn't a picnic kind of woma—

Tristan finally registered Dippy's roughly muttered words. "What do you think is happening to me?"

Dippy stopped his puppy pacing and looked directly at Tristan.

"You are obsessed with that mortal woman. And don't bother to pretend you don't know who I'm talking about or to deny it. I can see your obsession. Truthfully, I can smell it."

Tristan didn't doubt the mutt could smell his attraction to Georgia. After all, Tristan could smell arousal. So what was to say a hellhound couldn't smell his attraction, too?

But he wasn't obsessed.

"What does it smell like?" Tristan asked, curious and also trying to prove a point. He *wasn't* obsessed.

"It smells like trouble," the hound stated dryly.

See, the silly, worrywart canine didn't know what he was talking about. Smelling his obsession—just ridiculous.

"You must get control of your worries, Dippy," Tristan said. Then he added, "That's why I haven't yet approached Lucifer about you being my official co-leader. How can I take the chance of giving you so much power when you are forever flying off the handle about everything?"

Maybe the mutt's obnoxious fretting had a silver lining. That argument certainly sounded believable to him. He was sure it would to the silly mutt, too.

But instead, Dippy sat down and peered at Tristan with those beady, soulless black eyes.

"You are going to have to get a handle on yourself and on Finola, or I will go to our master myself. Whether that leads to my co-leadership or not. He needs to know something is amiss here."

Tristan narrowed an irritated stare back at the white fluff ball. "I don't like threats, Dippy."

"And I don't like seeing all our hard work jeopardized because the demon in charge is too damned horny to see what's going on in front of him," Dippy said calmly, clearly not intimidated by Tristan's low, angry tone.

"I'm not horny," Tristan said, which was a lie, of course. "Or obsessed," he said.

Dippy didn't stop watching him, nor did he respond.

Tristan gritted his teeth and returned his attention to his e-mails.

He wasn't obsessed.

Tristan reached into his pocket and curled his fingers around the pen there, holding the ridged plastic tightly.

Chapter Twenty-six

Gabriel watched as Finola White entered Eugene's office, sashaying into the plywood cubicle with a flirty smile on her lips. She'd been carrying a cup of coffee and a bag of donuts, clearly meant for the unassuming head of the DIA.

Gabriel knew he shouldn't do it, but he found himself leaving his desk to get closer to the small door, to hear what was going on inside. These two had been flirting for over a week.

Gabriel looked around him, wondering why other members of the DIA hadn't noticed, or if they had, why they weren't concerned. But the "mail room" seemed to be carrying on as always. Everyone was working on his own specific task for the DIA, and oblivious to the fact their leader was being seduced by a demon, right in their midst.

"Finola, what is this?" Gabriel heard Eugene say, drawing his attention back to his eavesdropping.

Finola laughed, a twittering, yet seductive sound. "I just wanted to thank you for last night. I had no idea how much fun you and my co-workers could be."

Gabriel frowned, looking around the busy mail room. Did other DIA staff know about this meeting? And which co-workers had joined them?

"It was a good time, wasn't it?"

Gabriel could hear the smile in Eugene's voice.

"Like I said, more fun than I could have ever realized."

"I'm glad," Eugene said, his usually deadpan voice full of sincerity. "I'm glad you feel a part of us."

A part of us. How could a demon, a very powerful, evil demon, ever be a part of them?

Unless it was the other way around. Was Eugene becoming a part of the demon world? Had Finola lured him over to her side? It was an outrageous thought, but Gabriel knew demons had ways of swaying humans to the dark side. Possession worked in different ways. Sometimes possession was as simple as an individual allowing evil into his life, seeing it as an acceptable part of existence. Eugene certainly didn't seem concerned with Finola's presence, or about the demon rebellion at all.

In fact, for the last week, Eugene had seemed more interested in associating with Finola than worrying about the demons' potential world domination. Was that because Finola was already possessing him, controlling his thoughts?

Gabriel's chest tightened at the idea. That would explain all of Eugene's inactivity over the past week. Really, when he thought about it, Gabriel had never seen his boss show the proper concern he thought this whole rebellion warranted. But Gabriel stood by the man, backing his decisions because he believed that if Eugene occupied this place of power, he must be very good at his job.

But now Gabriel had his doubts, serious doubts. He'd never actually laid eyes on the demons Eugene had purportedly reformed. He didn't even know how Eugene had supposedly accomplished this miraculous task. Nor had he seen Eugene slow down the rebellion. All the power players were still power players: McIntyre, White, and several other formidable underlings. And he'd certainly never seen Eugene save a damned soul.

Gabriel tried to pull in a calming breath. Maybe Eugene

wasn't really working for the DIA, but against it. He hated to doubt his higher-ups; it went against his slayer training, but things weren't making sense.

Finola giggled again at something Eugene said, the low, quiet giggle of a shared, private joke.

No, this was not making sense at all.

He listened as the couple flirted a little longer. Then he shrank back against the side of the cubicle so that Finola wouldn't notice him as she left Eugene's office to go back to her workstation.

Gabriel debated a moment, and then decided he had to talk to Eugene himself. He didn't feel that he could outright confront his superior, but maybe it was time to see what the head of the DIA planned to do. After all, he had every right to talk to Eugene about Georgia Sullivan again. It didn't appear that the woman was going to help them. In fact, she seemed to be under the demon's spell, too. He knew she was spending a lot of free time with McIntyre, and her attraction was almost palpable whenever Gabriel saw her. So it was perfectly within Gabriel's rights to press Eugene for a new plan.

Gabriel rapped a little too forcefully on the doorframe of Eugene's door.

"Come in."

Gabriel entered to find Eugene working at his computer, as usual. But the little smile on the man's lips was not usual. Actually, Gabriel had to amend, it wasn't usual until just recently.

"Gabriel, what a surprise to see you."

Gabriel frowned, not understanding that reaction, but feeling the comment was intended to imply something he didn't follow.

"What can I do for you?"

Gabriel wanted to say, "Stop flirting with the demons

and send them back to Hell. Or let me kill them." That's what he would have done as a demon slayer in the old days.

But instead he watched his tone, keeping it calm and respectful, and asked, "What are we going to do about the plan to utilize Georgia Sullivan? She's had a week to come to us, and I don't see any signs of her cooperating."

Eugene gave him an almost blank stare. His oddly blue eyes were devoid of any emotion or question.

"There isn't any need to do anything with her at the moment," Eugene said. "In fact, things are going very well with her."

Gabriel's awareness rose, prickling down his spine. If Eugene was truly possessed, wouldn't he be pleased Ms. Sullivan was, too?

After all, how could he say things were going well? Nothing, absolutely nothing had happened with Georgia Sullivan, aside from her being obviously smitten with the demon leader. She certainly wasn't helping them find out any of Tristan McIntyre's plans.

"I guess I'm confused," Gabriel said, struggling to keep his voice calm. "I don't see how you can say things are going well on that front. As far as I can see, nothing at all is happening."

Eugene didn't speak for a moment, studying him.

"Well, some things in life you just have to trust. Faith, I believe it's called."

Gabriel's barely squelched frustration rose, making it hard to remain still. Something was not right about this man, and Gabriel wasn't sure whom he should talk to about Eugene's behavior and ineffectuality.

"I'm sorry, Gabriel, but I actually have a lot to get done today," Eugene said, gesturing to his computer. "I hate to cut our meeting short, but I am very busy. And I need to stay focused to be an effective leader."

Gabriel stared at him, stunned at his choice of words, which so closely matched his own mental wording. Ineffectual. Effective. Eugene was eerie.

But Gabriel nodded. He couldn't talk to Eugene anyway. But he would figure out who he could talk to about the DIA leader's weird behavior and lack of action.

As Gabriel turned to the door, Eugene spoke again, "Faith can be hard for all of us. Even me at times."

Gabriel met the man's eerie blue gaze, and nodded again. Oh, he had no faith in Eugene. None at all.

Georgia was just getting settled at her desk when the intercom on her phone buzzed. She set her purse down beside her desk, smiling. How did he do that? Tristan had an uncanny ability to know when she was arriving. She picked up the receiver, knowing full well who was on the other end.

"Hello?"

"Good morning, Peaches," Tristan drawled from the other end, his rich voice seeming to reach through the phone wires to stroke her ear and cheek. "Did you sleep well without me?"

"Well, I was rather tired," she said, not actually answering the question. And telling the truth, for the last week, Tristan had spent most nights at her apartment. And he was insatiable, which made her toes curl in her platform shoes. Last night she had needed the rest. And Tristan actually had had work he needed to get done. Since they'd gotten involved, Tristan hadn't paid nearly as much attention to work as usual. Not that she was complaining; she loved his undivided attention, but *HOT!* didn't run itself.

He chuckled, and again, she felt the smooth, deep sound throughout her body.

"I missed you," he said, and Georgia could have sworn real desperation replaced his naughty, flirting tone.

"Well, I'm right here in the reception area," she said with a slight laugh, although the idea that this man wanted her so much did make her head spin and her heart thump wildly in her chest.

"Too far away. I think I need you to come back and take a memo."

"Oh, not that old cliché."

He chuckled. "Come back here and get naked?"

"Very unprofessional," she said, clucking her tongue.

"Very," he agreed. "But come back here anyway."

Georgia started to say she'd be right there, when a shadow fell across her desk. She glanced up to see Finola White standing there, and Georgia instantly wondered, none too happily, what the awful woman had overheard. It would not be good for either her or Tristan if Finola heard too much and figured out who was on the other end of the line.

"Ms. White," she said for Tristan's benefit. "How can I help you?"

"Oh, no, the evil witch," he said, taking her cue. "I don't suppose you can get rid of her? I'll do something extra naughty, if you do."

Georgia wanted to laugh, but instead she managed to keep a straight face.

"Absolutely, ma'am," Georgia said in an overly polite voice, not revealing to Finola who she was actually talking to, but also letting Tristan know she wasn't taking the bullet for him. "I will let Mr. McIntyre know you are very much looking forward to your meeting."

"Nice. Nothing naughty for you," he said with a sigh. "Although, I will admit that even with you throwing me under the bus here, I'm still definitely looking forward to our next meeting. Send the witch back."

He hung up the phone, but she didn't hang up her receiver right away. She knew that Tristan had never cared for Finola, but it was evident now that he truly disliked her.

She gathered her thoughts, preparing herself for Finola's usual venom.

"Good morning, Ms. White. How may I help you?"

Finola smiled, but it wasn't her usual judging smirk. She actually looked almost friendly. That made Georgia all the more nervous. What was she up to?

"Hello, Georgia. How are you this morning?"

Okay, something was definitely up. This was the first time Finola White had ever asked her how she was. And she'd never addressed her by name. In fact, Georgia would have bet money that the woman didn't even know her name.

"I—I'm doing well. Thank you. Did you want to see Mr. McIntyre?"

"I do, thank you." Finola smiled wider; her pale expression looked . . . sweet. Almost angelic.

Again, Georgia found Finola's kind smile more disturbing than her disdain. At least she knew and expected that; this behavior seemed like some kind of sneak attack.

"You can head right back," Georgia said, just wanting the woman away from her.

"Thank you." Finola smiled sweetly again, but she didn't continue on; instead, she said, "By the way, I love the newest hair color. Your style is so different and funky. I just love it."

Georgia gaped at her. Loved her style? Finola had repeatedly alluded to how awful she found Georgia's fashion sense from the first day she'd started at *HOT!* What was this sudden change?

It couldn't be sincere. But Georgia managed to nod and mumble, "Thank you."

"Absolutely."

Finola gave her another eerily nice smile and disappeared into the back. Georgia watched her go, wondering what the heck she had in store for Tristan.

Chapter Twenty-seven

Tristan dreaded the door opening. His plans of being with Georgia were sadly on hold. That was bad enough without their being interrupted by Finola. *Anyone but Finola.*

"Good morning, Tristan," Finola said as she breezed through the door. Today she wore a white gauzy dress and her pale hair was in a style he'd never seen before. It looked almost demure, in twisted braids across the top of her head.

"What's up with the new do?" he asked, making a confused face. "Are you trying to rock Amish chic?"

Rather than the scathing look Tristan expected, his comment was met by a light laugh.

"Tristan, you are so droll."

Droll? Was that what she was calling it now?

"Finola, can we just cut to the chase? What do you want?"

"That's the problem with you, Tristan. You never just let us enjoy a pleasant chat. You need to relax."

"You'd love that, I'm sure."

She gave him a sympathetic smile. "I *would* love that. Things have been far too tense between us."

"And it's no mystery why," Tristan commented, wishing she'd hurry this up. His cock was bored with the conversation and ready to spend some much more enjoyable time with—and in— Peaches.

"I will admit that I was very bitter about you taking my position as the leader of this rebellion, but I've come to terms with it. In fact, I'm quite content with how things are."

"I'm sure you are," Tristan said wryly.

Finola sighed, not an irritated or frustrated sound, but almost sad. "Okay, I can see you aren't in the mood to discuss our past issues, so I'll get to the point of why I'm here."

"Excellent."

"I thought you should come down to the mail room and see these employees for yourself. Especially Eugene."

Her suggestion caught his interest, and he stared at her. "Why is that?"

"I just think they are the perfect people to help us."

"Mail room employees? Don't you consider them beneath us? Not worthy of being possessed or controlled. Simply just more souls to collect?"

Finola nodded, her expression serene, oddly serene. "I did think that, but now I see how much potential power they have."

Tristan narrowed his gaze. She was up to something—trying to lure him into some sort of trap.

"What kind of power?"

She smiled, her expression sweet and almost . . . gentle looking, her angular features appearing softened somehow.

"They are just a lot more . . . remarkable than I originally thought. They have a certain—I don't know how else to say it—power, I guess, that is amazing."

Her tone sounded oddly dreamy and filled with awe.

Tristan narrowed his gaze more, regarding her closely. This was very clearly some new trick. He'd never heard of one demon being able to possess a whole workroom of humans, but he wouldn't put it past her. Especially as scorned as she was.

Whatever she was up to, she clearly wanted him to go down to that mail room, and he didn't think it was for altruistic reasons.

"I will consider it, Finola," he said, pretending to be distracted by something on his computer screen. "But right now, I'm just too busy."

"I understand," she said easily, and when he looked back at her, she was still sporting that oddly kind smile. She didn't even look like herself and that made him very nervous.

She was definitely up to something. And since this was Finola White, it was definitely something not good.

"I hope you have a good day, Tristan." Her smile widened, but he couldn't detect the usual undertone of maliciousness that usually accompanied the expression. "Good-bye."

She drifted out of the room, and Tristan was even happier than usual to see her go. But he didn't bask in his relief for long, already thinking about another relief that would be far more satisfying.

He reached for his phone. Georgia picked up on the first buzz.

"She's headed back your way," he said, tone sly and conspiratorial. "We both need a little fun after dealing with her."

"Absolutely," Georgia agreed, understanding his meaning and more than willing to oblige. Her eagerness was just one of the many things he loved about his Peaches.

He smiled and hung up the phone, thoughts of Finola already gone

"Seriously? Are you not even concerned with Finola's behavior?" Dippy said, appearing out from under Tristan's desk. "Can't you see something is not right with her?"

Tristan sighed. "It's just another of her silly and desperate strategies to gain control back."

Dippy came close, sitting directly beside Tristan's office chair. "You mean to tell me you don't see something different about her?"

Damn it, that dog was always around. Always.

Tristan wanted to growl, much like Dippy often did. Did he have to have another pointless, irritating conversation with a recalcitrant underling?

"I see a desperate demon trying yet another strategy to get what she wants," he said instead.

"Then you are a fool."

Georgia glanced away from her computer as Finola exited the back office. Usually, her interactions with Tristan seemed to make Finola even more irritable and vindictive, but this time she looked calm and almost happy.

"Have a wonderful day, Georgia," she said on her way past.

"You, too," was all Georgia managed to reply, totally bemused by this sudden shift in her old boss.

She watched the tall, pale blonde head back through the maze of *HOT!* offices and cubicles. Then deciding even the most unpleasant of people was bound to have a good day, Georgia rose, her thoughts going to Tristan.

She headed through the glass double doors to his office. She knew she should feel guilty and concerned about going back to fool around with her boss. But over the past week, they had grown so close, she didn't feel like he was her boss. He was her lover and her friend and a person she felt totally comfortable with against all odds of position and wealth and beauty.

And she was insanely attracted to him. That at least did made sense.

She smiled to herself, realizing she hadn't been this happy

for ages. Tristan made her feel important, made her feel she had an ally, which she hadn't felt in years. She'd had to be the one in control, taking care of everything since her grandmother had gotten sick.

She reached Tristan's door, seeing that he was talking to someone. He was clearly alone, so he must be using the speakerphone. She considered going back to her desk and waiting until he was done, but then changed her mind. He wouldn't care if she was there while he talked. They had even done some very naughty things while he was taking business calls. Definitely unprofessional, but oh-so-much fun.

She carefully pushed open the door and stepped inside the room.

"I don't know what the hell you are worked up about now," Tristan said sharply, and Georgia realized this wasn't a usual business call.

"I'm worked up about the fact that you aren't seeing what is so obviously right in front of you."

Georgia frowned. The voice responding to Tristan was odd sounding, rough and raspy, but it didn't seem to be coming from a phone line. It sounded as if it was coming from right in the room with them.

Which she didn't think could be possible. After all, until Finola had arrived, he'd been cajoling Georgia to come back and play. Even Tristan, who was wildly adventurous with the places they had sex and role-playing and toys—all of which Georgia loved—wouldn't fool around with a client or employee in the office with them.

"And what's right in front of me now, Dippy?" Tristan asked, his voice dripping with condescension.

Dippy? That was the name of Finola's dog. Georgia frowned, also realizing that Tristan's attention was focused toward the ground. As if he was talking to . . . to a small dog on the floor.

"Finola has changed," the raspy, throaty voice said.

"She's changed because she's desperate," Tristan stated.

"No, she is actually changed. Just like you are changed."

Tristan snorted. "I'm not changed."

"You are," the rough voice said. "You aren't even thinking about this takeover."

The takeover again. What did that mean?

But more important, who was Tristan talking to? Very carefully, so as to not draw attention to herself, she sidled into the room. Her heart stopped in her chest.

Finola's little white dog sat perched on the floor in front of Tristan, his head raised, his gaze looking directly at Tristan's dismayed face.

"I am," Tristan said to the animal. "You just don't like how I'm handling it."

"Damned right," the guttural voice said.

Georgia squinted, trying to comprehend what she was looking at. Was Tristan doing some sort of ventriloquism? Was he using the dog as some sort of alter ego? She hadn't noticed anything odd about him, anything that would suggest delusions. But then again, Ted Bundy had a girlfriend who never saw his dark side. Not that she thought Tristan was a serial killer or anything.

"You're not paying any attention to this rebellion," the rough voice said, sounding even more eerie to Georgia as she realized how odd this situation was. "You are too busy being utterly obsessed with your personal assistant."

Georgia's heart stopped again. Was this some bizarre way of breaking up with her or something? Letting her overhear a strange conversation with a dog? If so, this would have to go down as the worst breakup ever.

"I'm not obsessed. And you need to leave Georgia out of this."

"You're right," the raspy voice said. "You aren't just obsessed. You're changing, too. This relationship with her is changing you."

Georgia frowned. Wait, was Tristan actually using this strange dialogue to admit his feelings for her? Was she supposed to be overhearing this? She had to admit it was as odd a declaration of potential love as it was an odd way to break up. But she still liked the declaration of love theory better.

But quickly her opinion was changed again.

The rough voice continued. "Can't you feel the change in your demonic nature? I can."

Demonic nature? What?

"My demonic nature is not in question," Tristan assured him as matter-of-factly as if the . . . dog had questioned his work ethic. "You are just getting agitated because I'm not making you my co-leader as quickly as you would like."

Tristan planned to make a fuzzy white dog the co-leader of his potentially demonic takeover. This was utterly insane.

"I'm definitely not pleased about that," the rough voice stated. "But frankly, I think you aren't capable of running this rebellion, with or without my help. And I think it's time to go directly to Satan and tell him."

Tristan rose at that threat.

Satan was clearly the one they both answered to. Georgia remembered other mentions of Satan in the conversations she'd overheard.

Tristan really believed he worked for Satan. She shifted back toward the door, and then froze as the dog dashed away from Tristan, clearly feeling threatened. Thankfully, neither of them had noticed her. Apparently, shock had turned her virtually to a statue.

"You know I'm Satan's favorite, and he will listen. And believe you me, there will also be very dire repercussions if something happens to me."

Georgia didn't even hear Tristan's reaction to the dog's

threat, because she was too horrified by what she'd just seen. The dog was talking. She'd seen its mouth move, phrasing the words, its face making expressions that were entirely too human.

For the first time, she made a noise. A shocked gasp.

Then she realized both the dog and Tristan were staring at her.

She turned and ran, hearing Tristan's desperate cry behind her.

Chapter Twenty-eight

Georgia ran straight through the *HOT!* offices to the front reception area, not daring to stop. She didn't understand what she'd just seen, but she knew she *had* seen it. There was no denying that.

She wanted to believe her eyes had played tricks on her. Her ears, too, but she just couldn't. That dog had talked. The dog she'd cooed to and cuddled.

And if that was the truth, that Dippy was a talking dog, then it only stood to reason, Tristan was also exactly what the dog had said: a demon.

She frantically pounded the elevator down button again, willing it to hurry up. Then she cast a frightened glance over her shoulder. The blond receptionist at the front desk regarded her with wary curiosity, and Georgia wondered if she knew she was working for the boss from Hell. Potentially for real.

Then more fear tightened her chest. What if the receptionist was a demon, too?

She glanced behind her again to be sure Tristan hadn't followed. Then she gave up on the elevator and headed to the stairwell.

Her heels clomped and echoed through the empty stairwell and she hurried down the steps as quickly as her overly high footwear would allow.

The sound reminded her of a horror movie, that hollow echo as the heroine tried to make her awkward escape, the noise blocking out the killer's more stealthy approach. She paused and pulled the shoes off, snatching them up, and felt relieved as she silently padded down the stairs and couldn't hear any other footsteps.

Maybe you imagined the dog's voice and the movement of his mouth and features, she told herself as she kept up her rapid pace down the stairs.

Maybe she'd imagined the whole thing. But even as she tried to rationalize it, she couldn't. She had seen and heard it all.

Her breath was coming in short, harsh pants as she turned the corner at floor 7. She was over halfway down to the main entrance.

It was not as if Tristan couldn't find her. He knew where she lived. Plus, if he was a demon, he probably could find her anywhere. Not that she really knew what a demon had in the way of tracking abilities, or other powers for that matter.

Dear God, was she really believing Tristan was a demon? This was insane. So insane.

Then her thoughts returned to the things she'd overheard at the gala and when he'd been on the phone. He'd mentioned Satan—or rather the Devil and the Prince of Darkness in those conversations. She'd thought those were figurative terms. Not literal names of Satan himself.

This made her original thought that Tristan might be involved with the mob look pretty damned tame.

The mob. Her thoughts turned to the mail room guy, Gabriel. He'd told her that Tristan was very dangerous and involved with the underworld. Hence, her deduction he'd been referring to mob connections.

But Gabriel might have meant *the* Underworld. Literally.

She glanced at the door she was passing. Floor number 4. She could stop at the main level and flee the building, or she could go down one more floor to the mail room to find Gabriel.

Of course, he was very likely as much of a nut job as Tristan was apparently turning out to be.

Or Gabriel could be her only hope for help. After all, how was she going to protect herself from Tristan? He could just come to her apartment. Maybe Gabriel knew how to make sure Tristan didn't hurt her or her grandmother.

Making her decision, she bypassed the main level and headed to the lower level and the mail room.

Georgia's first instinct was to burst into the mail room. But she contained her fear and agitation, carefully pushing open one of the swinging double doors at the end of the hallway.

Several mail room employees noticed her quiet entrance, but they didn't stop their work. Somehow that made her feel better. If this was a den of demons, wouldn't they all descend on her?

Like she knew. Until fifteen minutes ago, she hadn't even believed demons were real.

She cast a gaze around the room, trying to locate the tall, handsome blond. She spotted Gabriel on the other side of the room. Of course. She was already a wreck without getting herself farther away from the exit. What if this was a trap, too? What if Gabriel worked for Tristan?

She took a calming breath, telling herself she had very few choices here. And right now, as unlikely as it might seem, Gabriel was her best bet.

She strode toward him, trying not to seem overly panicked. Given that every movement around her, the sorting machines, employees pushing mail carts, even people just walking by, caused her to start, she suspected she wasn't pulling off casual in any way, shape, or form.

But after what felt like traversing a harrowing ravine, she made it to the giant blond.

"Gabriel," she whispered, her voice escaping as little more than a croak.

But he heard her, looking up in concern. Concern for her? Or for Tristan?

"Ms. Sullivan," he said, and she almost found his formality amusing under the circumstances. Or she would have found it amusing if she wasn't so scared.

"Are you okay?" he asked, positioning himself to shield her from the room.

Oddly, she didn't find the action intimidating, but rather comforting.

"What is Tristan?" She didn't see any point in beating around the bush. If Gabriel knew the truth, he would tell her.

"He's a demon," he said without hesitation.

A wave of nausea washed over her, stealing her color and her strength. She sagged against his worktable.

He placed a hand under her elbow to steady her, and she didn't pull away, feeling the need for human contact. If this man really was human.

She studied his face, trying to tell. How would she know a demon if she hadn't even realized the man she'd been having sex with was one? Clearly, demons didn't look like they did in movies.

"How?" she finally said, having no idea what else to ask. How had this happened? How did demons exist? How?

"Come with me," he said, looking around. Maybe he was afraid Tristan would appear, too. Or maybe he knew others in the mail room were demons as well. Whatever the reason, she found herself following him.

He led her toward a rather rustic-looking cubicle made of plywood in the middle of the room. Then he seemed to change his mind and led her in the other direction. The sudden change made her a little nervous, but she still followed, again feeling she had no other choice.

He led her to what was clearly the employee break room; one wall was lined with small rectangular lockers and the main floor littered with round tables and uncomfortable metal folding chairs. A water cooler gurgled in the far corner.

He closed the door behind them, and then gestured for her to sit. She did, although just on the edge of the cold metal, feeling she'd never relax again.

He sat, not looking any more relaxed than she was.

"I know what I'm going to tell you is going to sound totally crazy," he said.

"I just saw a talking dog," she told him. "Nothing is going to seem crazy after that."

"A talking dog?" He gaped at her.

"Great, my crazy is already outdoing your crazy."

He frowned, clearly still considering what she'd just said. Then he refocused on his explanation.

"You are safe down here," he told her. "I work for an organization called the DIA, the Demon Intelligence Agency."

She blinked. She had to be dreaming. Things were just getting weirder and weirder.

"The Demon Intelligence Agency?"

He nodded. "It's a government agency that was established decades ago to locate and counteract demonic activity."

She shook her head slightly. The government knew demons existed?

"I know it's hard to process," he said, his voice low and sympathetic.

"Next you will be telling me there's really government alien cover-ups?"

He made a pained face. "One paranormal creature at a time."

She groaned. Aliens, too? Dear God.

"We have been working down here to watch the employees of *HOT!* We discovered about two years ago that Satan planned a demonic revolution by infiltrating the fashion industry."

Georgia glanced at her dolly platform heels, which now rested on the table in front of her. "Fashion can be pretty hellish."

Gabriel nodded, although she got the feeling he didn't really understand her comment. Then again, what did men know about high heels, Spanx, and all the other implements of torture women were expected to use and wear in the name of beauty?

"It was easy to get people to sell their souls for beauty and success and wealth in this industry. The demons played right into humans' desire for all of these things."

Georgia could see that.

"Finola was the first leader of the rebellion, but she made some mistakes and Satan then placed Tristan in her place."

Georgia couldn't believe this. She'd been working for demons. And she never had any idea. Hell, she'd been sleeping with a demon.

Talk about being unaware.

"Eugene, who is the head of the DIA, asked me to talk to you about spying on Tristan to find out who he was meeting with and what contracts he was making. Because that is how they are spreading their poison. Making deals with designers, other fashion editors, even department stores and boutiques. They are spreading their power throughout the industry."

Georgia thought about all the huge fashion industry people Tristan met and worked with. Were they all involved?

"Well, I can't help now. Tristan knows I know what he is. Or at least he must be pretty certain. I didn't exactly make a casual exit after seeing the talking dog."

Gabriel shook his head, clearly amazed. "I had no idea we also had a hellhound in our midst."

"A hellhound? That white, fluffy ball of fur?"

"Hellhounds can disguise themselves," Gabriel explained. "Just like demons."

So Tristan was in disguise. Well, he'd picked a good one.

"So what do I do now?" she asked, not able to think about how duped she'd been by Tristan, on every level.

God, she felt like a fool. She had actually thought she was falling in love with the man. Or rather, the demon.

Gabriel didn't answer right away, and again she sensed reluctance in him that she didn't understand.

"I guess I have to talk to Eugene. I'll get him. You just wait here."

She nodded, still feeling she had no other choice.

Gabriel was actually surprised how well Georgia was taking all of this. He suspected it was mostly shock that had her acting so calm, and the truth would sink in eventually.

Hell, he'd never even seen a hellhound in all his years of slaying. Seeing a talking dog had to be pretty damned weird. Even if the hound was disguised as a bichon frisé.

He slowed his pace as he approached Eugene's office, still not sure what to do. He didn't trust Eugene. His behavior had just been so weird with Finola.

But honestly, he didn't see any other alternative. Georgia needed protection. And Gabriel could only provide so much.

He reached Eugene's office, gathering his thoughts and

what he'd say. He wanted to be sure Eugene finally understood how dangerous the situation was getting, especially to Georgia Sullivan.

He knocked.

"Come in."

Gabriel entered, resolved to see something done. Something real.

"Sir, Georgia Sullivan is down here. She knows Tristan McIntyre is a demon. And apparently Finola's little white lapdog is actually a hellhound."

Eugene looked at him, raising an eyebrow as if only mildly interested. "A hellhound. We missed that, didn't we?"

Gabriel wanted to point out that Eugene seemed to miss a lot, but knew sniping would serve no purpose. Right now, he had to focus on seeing that Georgia remained safe.

"Well, has Georgia agreed to work with us now?"

Gabriel knew he should keep the shock out of his expression, but was Eugene kidding? How could Georgia work for them?

"Sir, you must be joking," Gabriel said, realizing his voice didn't sound calm in the least. "Sending her anywhere near Tristan now would be insane. Beyond insane, outright deadly."

Eugene smiled then. "And we just talked about having faith. I don't need her to do much. Just to get Tristan down here. And the hellhound, too."

That sounded like a whole lot to Gabriel. And why did Eugene need Tristan down here? Gabriel hated to admit it, but his first thought was that Eugene, if he was working with Finola, just wanted all the most powerful demons congregated in one place. That would make it easy for the demons to attack the DIA, right on their own turf.

"Gabriel, you have always been one of my best men. Loyal to me and the agency. Why the hesitation now?"

Gabriel stared into Eugene's eerily blue eyes. "I just don't think sending a defenseless female mortal out to bring us a very strong demon, basically Satan's right-hand man, is a wise choice."

"But she's the only one who has the power to do so," Eugene said. "Faith."

Chapter Twenty-nine

"You want me to what?" Georgia gaped at Gabriel. "Eugene said you need to get Tristan to come down here. And the hellhound, too."

"He's a demon," Georgia said, not believing her ears. Hadn't he told her once that Tristan was dangerous?

"I know." Gabriel sighed as if he didn't think this was the best plan. "Listen, let me get Eugene. Maybe he can explain his reasoning."

Georgia watched as Gabriel left her again in the sterile, unwelcoming break room. She looked around, her mind abuzz as it had been ever since witnessing Tristan's conversation with Dippy.

Tristan. A demon. She couldn't really believe it. She kept feeling that there had to be another explanation. Surely the man who'd cooked dinner with her, watched *Murder, She Wrote* with her grammy, made love to her as if she were the most precious thing he'd ever touched could not be a minion of Satan.

She didn't understand. She didn't understand why he'd go to the effort of treating her so well. Clearly, Finola had had no such compulsion. Until today.

Which seemed weird, too. What was going on with her? She'd been down here in the mail room. Maybe this Eugene had done something to her.

She just didn't know. It was all too much. What she did know though, was that she felt a heaviness in her chest. Now that the shock had diminished to incredulity, she realized she felt betrayed. She'd been falling in love with Tristan.

And maybe that was why he'd been so sweet to her, so adoring. Maybe making women fall in love with him was his evil power.

But why?

She was afraid of him, but she wanted answers. And she wanted to be sure that ultimately she and her grandmother would be safe.

After a few moments, the break room door opened again, and this time Gabriel walked in with another man. He was average height, with mousy brown hair in a rather bad-looking haircut. He wasn't unattractive, but not particularly handsome either.

But when she met his gaze, she was surprised by the vividness of his blue eyes. They reminded Georgia a bit of the bright brilliance of Tristan's. Of course, all of Tristan was stunningly beautiful.

Still those blue eyes made her a little wary.

"Hello, Ms. Sullivan, I'm sorry we are meeting for the first time like this. I'm sure you must be very confused and scared."

"Yeah," she agreed, seeing no reason to pretend otherwise. "I'm pretty freaked out."

"Understandably." The man's voice didn't actually reveal that he understood. It sounded completely unemotional, which didn't do much to reassure her about him as the head of this DIA, or about his plan.

"I'm sorry you aren't confident that we are truly here to help you. I cannot blame you for that doubt either. But as I told Gabriel, you are the only one with the power to bring Tristan McIntyre to us."

"Why me?" she asked, wishing someone else could deal with this, because she was scared to see him, and not just because he was a demon.

"Because you are the only one he will listen to."

She doubted that.

"We won't send you alone. Gabriel here will follow and watch from a distance. If anything appears to go wrong, he knows how to handle it."

Well, if the tall blond knew how to handle it, why not just send him?

But she didn't ask that. She didn't say anything for a moment. Then she nodded. How weird to discover there were real demons in the world, and within just minutes of finding this out, be told you had to help bring them down.

"Okay," she finally said, feeling a bit like one of those reluctant heroines in movies who felt no choice but to do what was asked of her, or all humanity would cease to exist.

It was hard to believe that if she didn't get Tristan to these people—the DIA—then he would bring about the fall of society.

But apparently that was the case. A stunningly handsome metrosexual man and a fluffy white dog could be the end of them all.

"I'll do it."

"Thank you," Eugene said.

She glanced at Gabriel. He just looked worried. Not exactly the huge sendoff she thought she deserved before going off to fight a demon. Or to lure a demon to a mail room.

Yeah, this plan made no sense.

Tristan glared at Dippy. He'd tried to follow Georgia. To explain. Explain what exactly, he wasn't sure. But the damned hellhound had twined around his feet like a cat, slowing him down, until she'd disappeared through bustle of the *HOT!* offices.

"Don't give me that look," Dippy said with the complete lack of remorse of a cat, too.

"I needed to talk to her," Tristan stated.

"And that is exactly what I've been trying to show you. You aren't thinking you need to find her to stop her from telling the truth about us. Or to get her soul, then cast her into Hell. Or even that you have to kill her, which is probably the safest plan at this point."

Tristan shot him a look. The hellhound had been lecturing him endlessly ever since Georgia had disappeared.

Dippy shot a look back. "No, you are more concerned with finding her to . . . what? Explain? Smooth things over? Convince her that while you are a demon, you're not one of *those* demons?"

Tristan didn't respond, because that was exactly what he'd planned to do. And he still would, if he could find her. He'd go to her place. She had to go back there sooner or later. She must be worried about her grammy and what a demon and a talking hellhound could potentially do to the old lady.

Of course, the idea of harming Grace made him feel ill.

He paused. When had he started worrying about the welfare of old women? When had he started trying to persuade his personal assistant that he wasn't one of the bad guys? Sure, Georgia was more than an assistant now. She was his lover—his only lover.

That in itself was strange, but he didn't care to think about it right now either. He told himself his interest in Georgia wasn't a big deal. "I'm going to find her." Tristan sidestepped the animal.

"I'm going with you," the hellhound stated, and Tristan didn't bother to argue with him. He didn't care if the annoying mutt went with him or not. Tristan's mind was on one thing and one thing only. Making sure that Georgia understood he would never harm her, and that somehow he took away that terrified alarm in her beautiful dark eyes.

How are you going to do that? he asked himself as he strode through the *HOT!* hallway toward the main reception elevators. And how are you going to make her understand without jeopardizing the work you've done here?

Dippy had already threatened to go to Satan, and Tristan had no doubt the four-legged snitch would. But even with that inevitability, Tristan didn't care. He cared only about finding Georgia. Somehow. And making things right with her. Getting back the look that had always been in her eyes when she'd gazed so longingly at him before today.

He reached the elevators, receiving lots of curious stares from employees as he punched the down button.

"Are you looking for your assistant?"

Tristan turned to see who'd spoken to him. The gorgeous blond receptionist stood from behind her desk. At one time, Tristan's libido would have surged to life at the very sight of her. But this time, when he looked at her, his only interest was in what she knew.

"Yes. Have you seen her?"

"She went down the stairwell about twenty minutes ago. Maybe half an hour."

He nodded his thanks, not taking even the time to speak. He bolted to the stairs, with Dippy right behind him.

When he stepped through the heavy door, he paused just inside the stairwell, trying to detect any sign of Georgia.

Dippy had already started down the stairs, but stopped when he saw Tristan wasn't following.

"She went this way," Dippy told him, gesturing with a jerk of his furry head. "I can still smell her."

Tristan couldn't smell her. Her arousal he always scented, but not her fear. He couldn't. Or wouldn't. But he nodded and hurried after the dog.

They spiraled downward, Tristan feeling certain she must have gone to the main entrance level. Once she made her escape out to the busy streets of Manhattan, Dippy would lose track of her.

The idea depressed Tristan, causing a heavy weight on his chest.

You can go to her apartment, he told himself, except he wanted to see her now. To fix this now.

He followed the dog, not realizing right away that the hellish canine hadn't stopped at the first floor.

"Where are you going?" he asked when he finally noticed that they'd passed the main level.

Dippy looked over his shoulder, exasperation clear in his beady dark eyes.

"She continued down here."

Tristan hesitated a moment longer, then decided he had to trust the mutt. Why would Dippy bother to lie about this? The hellhound wanted to find her for a different reason, Tristan knew, but right now all that mattered was finding her. He could deal with the mutt after he'd seen and talked to Georgia.

He continued down, right behind the beast.

The heavy metal door opened to a sterile, gray hallway that led to the mail room.

"Are you sure—" Tristan didn't even get to finish his thought before one of the swinging double doors at the end of the hallway was pushed open and, to his shock, Georgia stepped through. Tristan noticed that a tall, muscular blond was behind her, but he remained in the mail room, and the door swung closed to block him from view.

Tristan didn't think about the man or who he might be. All his thoughts, his attention, were on Georgia.

She froze when she saw him, only to glance nervously over her shoulder at the now shut door behind her. Then she looked back at him, her dark eyes enormous behind her glasses. Today her glasses frames were red to match her red baby doll dress. He loved how she coordinated her eyewear to her clothes.

"Georgia," he said, his voice sounding hoarse. Hoarse with emotion. He didn't love the fear in her eyes. God, he'd never hurt her.

"Tristan," she said, her voice shaky. She was terrified. Could he blame her?

He took a step toward her, and then stopped. He didn't want her to run again.

"I know you don't understand what you saw," he said, not even sure what he planned to say. He just needed to talk. He needed to keep her there. "I know this all seems incredibly bizarre."

"That's putting it mildly," she said, her wide-eyed stare shifting to the dog standing by Tristan's feet. Tristan glanced at him, too, fighting the urge to kick the little animal. He didn't want Dippy here. The damned beast wasn't a part of this.

But there was no getting rid of him, not right this minute. Tristan did step away from the hellhound as if that would somehow show Georgia that he wanted nothing to do with this creature.

Her eyes returned to Tristan, wary.

Tristan stopped, wishing he could just pull her into his arms.

"Georgia, you need to know that I would never, never hurt you."

Georgia stared at him, her face ravaged by warring emotions. Tristan could see she was scared and uncertain, but he also could see she wanted to understand. That she still had feelings for him. That realization buoyed up his own overwhelmed feelings.

"Tristan," she said, her voice still quavering, "what . . . what are you?"

He hesitated, for the first time in his whole existence ashamed of what he was. But she deserved the truth.

"I'm a demon."

She released a shaky breath, the sound something between a cry and a disbelieving laugh.

"But I would never hurt you," he repeated.

Behind him, a sigh sounded from Dippy. "This is all very touching, but you need to fix your mistake, Tristan."

Tristan didn't look at the mutt, although he wanted to shout at the hound to just shut up.

Again, Georgia's attention was on the animal. Her pink cheeks had gone a disturbing white.

Damn it, Dippy needed to go.

"Georgia, please listen," Tristan said, his voice sounding desperate to his own ears. But he didn't care. This woman had become his world. He couldn't lose her.

"I'm sorry I didn't tell you any of this up front, but I didn't realize how much I would come to care for you."

Behind him, Dippy made another noise.

"Can demons care?" Georgia asked, her own tone desperate and heartbroken.

Damn, he felt like shit. He'd never wanted her to find out about him like this. In reality, he'd never wanted her to find out at all. He knew the truth would kill all feelings she had for him.

"I do care about you. More than anyone I've ever met."

She stared at him, and he could see she wanted to believe him. That encouraged him to continue.

"I am a demon, but I don't want—"

Tristan had been about to admit that he didn't want to be a demon. He stopped in shock. He'd always been a demon; he'd always liked being a demon—until this moment.

"I don't want you to be scared of me," Tristan said instead. "I want you to trust me like you did before."

For some reason, those words seemed to affect her in a

way his others hadn't. She stared at him for a moment longer, and then straightened.

"I will trust you," she said. "But only if you trust me."

He studied her for a moment, and then nodded. He did trust her.

"Okay," he agreed.

Georgia didn't speak for a moment again. "I need you to come with me."

A flare of warning flickered inside Tristan, but he was determined to do whatever Georgia needed him to do to make her realize she could honestly trust him.

"Okay." He stepped toward her.

"Are you fucking crazy?" Dippy growled behind him. He darted between Tristan and Georgia, facing Tristan. "You're going with her? Don't you see this has to be some sort of trap?"

Tristan looked from Dippy to Georgia. Her eyes were still wide and her skin snowy pale.

"Why do you want me to go with you?" Tristan asked, a moment of doubt making him uncertain.

"Because—because I want to talk to you. Away from that." She bobbed her head toward Dippy.

Tristan couldn't blame her for that. Dippy unnerved *him*; he could only imagine how the talking hellhound must affect her.

He moved forward again.

"This is a trap," Dippy repeated, more insistently, but Tristan kept his gaze on Georgia. He trusted her.

Tristan stepped around the dog, just wanting to be near Georgia.

As he got closer, he saw more uncertainty in her deep brown eyes. But he continued toward her.

Once close enough to touch her, he controlled himself. He knew moving too fast would probably just scare her off.

But he wanted to feel her heat and her smooth skin. To pull her soft body against his.

"Where do you want to go?" he asked instead.

She swallowed and he could see she was very nervous.

"You honestly do not need to fear me. You'll never need to fear me."

Her eyes met his, and he saw confusion and pain there.

"Where do you want to go?" he asked again.

She glanced over her shoulder. "In here."

Her voice shook and he knew it was going to take a lot to convince her she was all he cared about. But he'd do it. Nothing else mattered.

Then he touched her, gently caressing her cheek. She didn't pull away like he thought she would. She just stared at him with those beautiful wide eyes.

"Let's go," he said, gesturing to the double doors behind her.

She didn't move.

Then she said almost brokenly, "Why are you so willing to go with me?"

He didn't hesitate. "Because I love you."

He'd never said those words in his whole existence, and now that he had, he felt somehow different. Warmth filled him, a feeling he'd never experienced. Warmth and contentment.

"Because I love you," he repeated. Then he took her hand and pushed open the mail room door.

Georgia wanted to stop him. He'd said he loved her, and despite what she knew about him, that he was a demon from Hell, probably a master of deception, she'd believed his words.

She'd seen something in his vivid green eyes that had been so real, so honest, she couldn't help but believe him.

And now she was leading him into his adversary's lair.

For the first time, she wondered what the DIA intended to do to him. Would they kill him?

She couldn't let that happen. Demon or not, she had seen goodness in Tristan and she believed it was real. She *knew* it was real.

"Let's just leave here," she said, but it was too late. He'd walked through the door.

He smiled, not his usual naughty grin, but a beautiful, sincere smile that stole her breath.

"I don't want to leave. Let's just talk this out now."

She followed, and because she was lost in that sweet smile, she didn't see all the mail room staff—or rather DIA staff—standing in a group, waiting for him. Not until they were in the room, and the door closed behind them.

Only when Tristan saw her alarmed expression did he turn to see what she was gaping at.

His gaze moved over the crowd, clearly trying to understand the scene.

Gabriel moved closer to them, his stance protective, but Georgia knew she didn't need protection. Not from Tristan.

Tristan's roaming gaze finally landed on Georgia, a confused frown creasing his brow.

"What's going on?" he asked, and Georgia was devastated by the look of betrayal on his face. She'd led him here, and she didn't even know what was going on, or what was going to happen to him.

She moved closer to his side, feeling the need to protect him, in the way Gabriel had clearly felt the need to protect her.

"Hello, Tristan."

To Georgia's shock, Finola White stepped out of the crowd. Her white blond hair and pale skin seemed to glow in the fluorescent lighting.

"Finola?" Tristan sounded as confused as Georgia. Why was Finola here? Was this some sort of elaborate trick set up by the female demon to get her position back as leader of the rebellion? Had Georgia been duped? Had she just delivered Tristan on a platter?

"I knew you'd end up here eventually," Finola said, although her voice wasn't laced with satisfaction or malicious glee.

"What's going on?" Tristan asked. He sounded as strong as he always did, unshaken, but Georgia knew he was nervous.

"We are just gathering to welcome you," Finola said, and Georgia grew even more confused. She glanced at Gabriel and he appeared just as bewildered. That could not be a good sign.

Then another figure approached, coming from near Eugene's makeshift office. But this man wasn't Eugene. He was tall and elegant. His hair wasn't mousy brown or his voice average. This man was stunningly attractive, almost surreally beautiful. His blond hair glistened in the artificial light. And his skin seemed to glow golden.

Georgia peered at him. Who was he? And what did he intend to do with Tristan?

"I'm not here to hurt anyone," he said, his voice smooth and almost musical, answering Georgia's unasked question. "I'm here to save you."

Georgia stared at the man, meeting his eyes: vivid blue eyes. This being was Eugene. She knew it. Just as she knew he wasn't simply a man. He was something otherworldly.

Again she glanced at Gabriel, who gaped in shock at the transformed Eugene.

"He can save us," Finola said, her comment directed to Tristan. "He can make us whole in a way we've never been."

Tristan looked from Finola to Eugene.

"What are you?" Tristan asked the golden man, just as Georgia had asked him in the hallway.

Eugene smiled, a beautiful, serene smile. "I'm an angel."

Just as Georgia had known Tristan was not lying about being a demon, she knew Eugene told the truth.

"He's changed me," Finola said, her tone filled with such joy. "Tristan, I feel a peace and happiness I've never known. A contentment we could never achieve as demons. No matter how much we satisfied our vices."

Tristan again looked from Finola to Eugene.

"I already feel that contentment," Tristan said, and then reached for Georgia's hand. She grasped it back.

Eugene nodded. "I know. I didn't need to save you. Your soul mate did that. She gave you a soul."

Tristan's eyes met Georgia's, and Georgia's heart swelled. Eugene had said she was the one with the power. She'd been the one to save Tristan. Tristan gazed at her, his green eyes bright with love and a warmth Georgia hadn't seen before this moment, a happiness that had always been just out of his reach.

"But I do have something to ask," Eugene said to Tristan. "I do need you to help us stop this demon takeover."

Tristan looked away from Georgia to Eugene. He didn't hesitate.

"Whatever you need is yours."

Georgia's heart swelled with pride and happiness. Tristan was no longer a demon. She didn't know how she knew that fact, but she did. He had a soul.

His gaze returned to Georgia, his eyes so full of love.

"As long as I have my soul mate, I have everything I need."

She rose up on her toes to kiss him.

"You have your soul mate," she murmured against his lips. "And I have mine."

Epilogue

"How is Grammy?"

Georgia sat on the overstuffed sofa close to Tristan. He pulled her half onto his lap, so she was draped over him, looking up at his gorgeous face.

"She's doing well. Thrilled that I'm getting married."

Tristan kissed her. "I'm pretty damned thrilled, too."

She smiled. "You're not damned anything these days."

"No, I'm not." He smiled, that contentment she'd first seen in the mail room still clear on his face. "And I never realized how tortured I was until I found you."

She smiled and kissed him.

"A demon of lust," she said, still amazed she'd been involved with a demon.

"Well, that is definitely something that hasn't changed within me. I still lust after my Peaches. But now, only for my Peaches."

And she only lusted for him.

He kissed her slowly, thoroughly. Then he lifted his head and added, "Let me amend that. I only lust for and love my Peaches."

His naughty grin appeared, and she returned it, glad that not all of his wicked side was gone.

"An angel on my arm and a demon in my bed."

Tristan laughed, the sound still supernaturally rich and delicious. "Definitely."

And he proceeded to show her how very devilish he could be.

Gabriel entered Eugene's office. His boss had returned to his average, unassuming self, and he was busy packing up his computer.

"We've gotten almost everything in boxes," he said to Eugene, his tone filled with a new respect.

"Excellent," Eugene said, his tone even as usual.

The DIA was moving to a new location. *HOT!* magazine no longer needed their services, but other places did. Unfortunately, the fight of good against evil never really ended, but at least this rebellion had been thwarted.

"Sir, I owe you an apology," Gabriel said. He regretted ever doubting their leader.

Eugene looked up from his work. "There is no need."

Gabriel nodded, wanting to say more, but not sure what that would be. But he did feel good about the DIA again, and his place in the organization.

"Tell me though," Eugene said when Gabriel would have left the room, "how do you think our newest recruit will work out?"

Gabriel knew Eugene referred to Finola White, who was now working with the DIA as an operative.

Gabriel met Eugene's vivid blue eyes, the only hint of the angel under the average Joe façade.

"I have every faith she will work out just fine."

Eugene actually chuckled. "Very good. Very good. Well, let's finish packing up. We have more work to do."

Gabriel nodded and left the office to get back to work.

★ ★ ★

"You know, the DIA is a real pain in my ass," Satan grumbled, shifting to line up his shot. He tapped the golf ball, and it rolled into the can across the room.

Dippy didn't answer, just sitting obediently beside his master's desk.

"They have reformed some of my very best demons. It's getting highly frustrating." Satan dropped another ball on the brimstone floor. He tapped it as he had the first one, and Dippy fought the urge to chase the little white ball across the floor.

He suspected this was Satan's way of punishing him for not coming to him sooner with his concerns. Lucifer knew he had a weakness for chasing balls.

"Ah, well," Satan said prosaically, "I guess we just re-group and start again. After all, the Devil's work is never done."

Dippy nodded, his gaze on the ball in Satan's hand. He licked his chops.

Satan started to drop the ball, and then paused. "So where do we attack next?"

Now this Dippy had considered already, and he didn't hesitate to give his master his answer.

"Well, the dog show circuit might be a good place."

Satan stared at him, and then laughed, the sound boom-ing through the cavelike office.

"Dog shows. I love it. Make it happen."

Dippy nodded. Finally, he would be the leader of a de-mon rebellion. Who said you couldn't teach an old dog new tricks?

If you enjoy fun contemporary romance with a paranormal twist, you won't want to miss DELICIOUS, featuring novellas by Lori Foster, Lucy Monroe, and Sarah Title. Read on for a taste of Sarah's "Full Moon Pie"!

"Is she out there yet?"

Dan Fields dropped the blinds to the office window at the sound of his assistant's voice. Mrs. Harris came up behind him, filling his nostrils with the sweet powdery smell of her . . . well, he wasn't sure where the sweet powdery smell came from. But it was a smell he always associated with sweet gray-haired ladies of a certain age, which Mrs. Harris certainly was.

Maybe not so sweet.

Especially now, as she pinched the blinds open and gave a knowing "ah."

Yes, of course she was out there. A few days a month, every month, she was out there from late morning until well after most of the businesses downtown had closed. And she always had a steady stream of customers for the entire day. A few days a month, and then she disappeared.

And every day, he looked for her.

Mona and her stupid pink truck.

Apple of My Pie.

Who would have thought that a small town in Ohio would embrace something as trendy as a food truck? But the people of Delicious had always been pretty open-minded, especially when it came to food, and especially when that food highlighted the Golden Delicious apples that made the town famous. Well, famous in Ohio.

Everybody said Mona was a genius with her baking; she managed to create treats that combined cutting-edge flavors with the comfort that only homemade baked goods could provide. She always managed to get the apples to taste just right, even this early in the season.

Not that Dan would know.

"I'm going to go down and see what she has this morning. You sure you don't want anything?"

He knew Mrs. Harris was a professional, distinguished, accomplished woman, so there was no possible way that she had just winked at him. He just grunted at her and returned to his desk.

No, he didn't want anything from Mona Miller. He had spent the past few years very specifically not buying anything from Mona. Not that he wasn't tempted. The first time she came to a meeting of the Delicious Small Business Association, her idea for a mobile bakery was just that, an idea. Dan loved it, at first. He thought it was creative and had great growth potential. And judging by the way his colleagues fell on the samples she brought in, she would be successful. He had watched as they grabbed every last crumb, leaving nothing for him, but he didn't mind. He was distracted.

He had tried to be professional about it, but there was no denying that Mona looked, well, delicious. She was short but curvy, and she had a mass of crazy brown curls that framed her eyes, eyes that were such a pale green they were almost gold. They were amazing eyes. And that smile. When he offered her suggestions on how to file the right paperwork for her permits, she had smiled at him, and her whole face lit up.

That was them, in a nutshell. She had wild, inventive ideas; he had paperwork. Not that there was a "them." Just a smile that made his heart stop, and a business plan that he could, if he was being generous, call erratic.

Normally he made a point of buying local—after all, his accounting firm would never survive without the support of the Delicious business community. "Accounting firm" might be a slight exaggeration—it was just him and Mrs. Harris. But they did all right. They had regular customers and a solid reputation and he was even thinking of taking on a business school intern when the semester started.

So how could he, as a responsible small business owner, one who paid his taxes and his bills and had a lease on an actual building, support a woman who clearly did not take the rigorous work of owning a small business seriously? One who worked frivolous hours and ignored the tremendous growth potential in this town so she could maintain those frivolous hours?

A food truck! She couldn't get a real bakery? And pink! Ridiculous. Branding was important, he got that, but pink? A pink truck and pink shirts—and apples weren't even pink!

And the name—Apple of My Pie. When he had first heard it, he liked it. It had a whimsical quality that suited what he thought were her start-up plans. Apparently, though, whimsical was a way of life for Mona. Every time he heard that business name now, it made his teeth hurt.

He hated the cutesy name and the cutesy truck and the cutesy little pink tank top she wore as she handed out muffins and tarts and pie and . . . whatever else she sold. So far Mrs. Harris had just brought back turnovers and the occasional pie to take home when her grandchildren were in town. Each one smelled amazing, and if the satisfied sighs Mrs. Harris emitted as she ate every last crumb were any indication, each one tasted amazing, too.

But that was not for Dan. He turned back to his e-mail. He had work to do.

★ ★ ★

Mona grabbed a bite of an apple turnover before turning back to Joe Gunderson. She probably shouldn't help customers with her mouth full, but Joe didn't care. He liked a girl who ate, he told her. And if he wasn't eighty years old and half-blind, she would have been flattered.

Frankly, she was still a little flattered. It was nice to be appreciated.

The turnover was good. The golden delicious apples that made the town of Delicious famous were a little early, but they had baked up amazingly well. She shouldn't be surprised; it was a full moon. She couldn't mess it up if she tried. She thought Joe would probably like them, so she threw one into the white box she was loading up with assorted fruit tarts for him. It would be a nice surprise for him when he got home.

She handed Joe his change and tied his box with red-and-white string. That was probably her favorite part of the bakery. She loved that string. It reminded her of small towns and neighbors who liked each other, and it suited Delicious to a "t." She slapped a pink Apple of My Pie sticker on the box and handed it across the little counter that folded down from the window cut into the side of the truck. As soon as she was sure he had a good grip on it (he promised he would never drop any of the stuff he bought from her—but he was eighty, after all), she stood up to stretch her back.

She loved her little pink truck, but leaning over to help all of these customers was rough work. It was better than when she first started out, when she was selling baked goods out of the trunk of her hatchback. That had been one really good thing to come out of her limited interactions with the Delicious Small Business Association. Its members were all really supportive in helping her get funding to upgrade to her dream vehicle, even if some of them balked when she proved that she was serious about painting it pink. Dan the Accountant, known as Khaki Dan among her girlfriends, had been especially . . . not into it. But she knew he saw a food truck as just a stepping stone to a "real" bakery, as he called it. Mona humored him, even though she also knew a full-time business was impossible for her.

Her truck had shelves and refrigeration and she did her best to make it look homey and welcoming. After a lot of false leads, she'd finally found it cheap on eBay. The guy selling it said it was a retired cupcake truck from Chicago, but it smelled suspiciously like falafel when it was delivered. Fortunately, she had had plenty of time in between baking spurts to fix it up. Joe's nephew, Dylan, owned a kitchen supply store and he'd agreed to work on it in exchange for her catering his daughter's college graduation party (fortunately, the party fell on a full moon), and a selection of goodies for his wife's monthly book group. So Dylan ripped out the old gas grill that didn't work anymore and put in a warming oven, and tuned up all of the refrigerators and the solar generator on top of the truck.

Then Mona gave it a thorough cleaning, scrubbing every surface within an inch of its life, scouring out any unsavory old-food smells. When she could move her arms again, she contemplated the peeling paint job, and her future. This venture had to work, and going halfway was not an option. So, despite Khaki Dan's protests, she painted it pink.

And so Apple of My Pie, Mobile Bakery, was born. She still did most of the baking at home, where she had spent all of the money she inherited from her grandmother on a massive kitchen overhaul. The demand for her food was so great that she still relied on insulated shopping bags for the extra inventory, but business was good. Business was really good. So good that she was finally ready to stop worrying about the fact that this venture would only be part-time, because she could finally afford to live on the money she made with her limited schedule.

She checked her watch. The lunchtime rush was about to begin, so she pulled the German apple cake out of the warming oven, then switched it off. Even with the fans going, Apple of My Pie could turn into, well, an oven, especially as the summer sun beat down in the afternoon. She pulled a pink bandana out of her jeans pocket and wiped her forehead, then tied her hair back with it. She had pulled her hair up into a ponytail that morning, but her curly mop was no match for Ohio summer humidity, and she knew she looked like a frizzy mess.

She started slicing the cake into squares and putting them out on the little paper trays she used for plates, then stacked them under the dome of the old-fashioned cake plate she had super-glued to the counter. Apple cake was a specialty of hers, and a lot of her regulars came by just for a slice of it. She laid out a tray mixed with cookies and berry tarts next to it—her regulars could usually be counted on for an impulse buy.

She wasn't sure exactly why she looked up when she did, but, then, it always took her by surprise. There he was, going into the Mom and Pop diner down the street.

Khaki Dan.

She thought he had been avoiding her ever since Apple of My Pie hit the road. He hadn't accepted the invitation she'd extended to the whole SBA when she had her opening day street party. He never stopped by like the other small business owners did. He never even seemed to look at her food truck.

She thought she had done something to offend him, but whenever she saw him anywhere else—in the park, at the library, at the one bar in town—he was nice enough. He smiled and exchanged small talk and she thought she even saw some interest in those piercing blue eyes of his—interest she was definitely willing to reciprocate. But then she would pull up in Apple of My Pie, and it was like she had put a sack over her head. A sack filled with month-old garbage that said "I Hate Accountants." He didn't just ignore her when she worked; he seemed insulted by her.

Not that he didn't have opportunities to be cordial. Every day, like clockwork, he and his well-fitting khakis went into the diner at noon. Every day, according to Marylou, he ordered a turkey sub with lettuce, tomato, light on the mayo, extra pickle. He drank black coffee, never pop, and always skipped dessert.

Which was probably how he stayed so fit.

Truth be told, that was what Mona had noticed about him first. After all, it's not every day that you see a nicely dressed, not-wearing-a-wedding-ring, good-looking guy in a small town like Delicious. She sort of resented that such a catch could be such a jerk. It seemed like a cruel trick on womankind.

But apparently Mona, or Food-Truck-Mona, was his only pet peeve. Marylou said he was actually a very nice guy and a good tipper, and Mrs. Harris, one of her best customers, worked for him and had nothing but good things to say. But he sure didn't like Mona. And she wanted to find out why.

By the time the lunch rush was over, she had almost forgotten about Khaki Dan, but then she heard the distant tinkling of the bell to the diner, and out he came, briefcase in one hand, to-go coffee in the other. Black coffee. Who could drink coffee without anything in it? This was a man who needed some sweetness in his life.

"Hey!" she called out and waved. He looked up, startled, then looked behind him. "Yes, you!" she shouted, then gestured for him to come over. Even from down the street she could see his eyebrows scrunch up in consternation, but he started toward her anyway, his loafers leading his reluctant legs. And what legs they were. Damn, that man could fill out a pair of khakis.

"Hi, Dan," she said as he approached, and leaned out the window.

"Hi," he said back. She noticed that his gaze flicked down to her tank top, but went straight back to her eyes. She appreciated the effort. And she appreciated the attention from Dan a little differently than she did from Joe. A down-low-in-her-belly appreciation.

"I've seen you just about every day and you never come over to say hi," she said.

"Okay. Uh, hi."

"Been a while." She brushed an errant curl behind her ear. His eyes followed her fingers.

"Been busy. You?"

"So far, so good. Is your office around here?"

He pointed to an office across the street. She knew that, of course. It said FIELDS ACCOUNTING LLC across the door. Mrs. Harris came out of there every morning, and every morning she talked about her boss, Dan, and how he would never take a break for a cookie or a slice of cake but that he was just as nice as could be. Worked too hard, so he sure could use a break. She thought Mrs. Harris was either trying to help Mona make a sale, or marry them off. Probably both.

"Ah, Mrs. Harris's building," she said, letting this charade that they didn't really know each other continue.

"She works with me."

Mona knew that Mrs. Harris was his secretary, and that she preferred to use that old-fashioned job title instead of the more twenty-first century Administrative Assistant. But Mona appreciated that Dan said Mrs. Harris worked "with" him, and not "for" him, even if that was technically true. She took it as a touching show of respect.

"Mrs. Harris is one of my best customers," Mona said, as if Mrs. Harris had not been planting the seed for this conversation for the past several years.

"I know," he sighed.

"You want to try something?" she asked. "On the house." His gaze flicked down her body again, then quickly back up to her eyes. *Ha,* she thought. *Do that again,* her belly said.

"No, thanks, I'm not much of a sweets person," he said as his eyes lingered over the fruit tarts.

She shrugged. "A little sugar could do you some good."

"Why are you only out here once a month?"

It was a question she got a lot from customers, and she was pretty good at deflecting it. But most people just asked out of polite curiosity or because they wanted her to feed their sugar cravings more often. Ever since she'd started Apple of My Pie—even when it was just an idea and a hatchback—Dan had been up her butt about making it more permanent. He just wouldn't let it go, and here he was again. He didn't even know if her goodies were good enough for a full-time business!

It made her hackles rise. It made her defensive.

Because she had a feeling he wouldn't take polite deflection for an answer, that he wouldn't stop until he got the truth.

He couldn't handle the truth.

The truth was, she was cursed.

It had to do with the moon. Every full moon, she baked. No, that was an understatement. Her baking skills erupted into an almost maniacal inspiration around the full moon such that she could not ignore them, compelling her to bake and bake and bake. She couldn't do anything but bake—she couldn't read, she couldn't check her e-mail, she could barely sleep. She definitely couldn't hold down a regular nine-to-five job—not unless she would be allowed to take a few days off a month. To bake. When the moon told her to.

She was grateful, usually. Her curse gave her a talent that enabled her to do something she loved to make an okay living. But in moments of self-pity—usually about halfway between full moons—she began to feel that maybe her full-moon inspired baking bursts were holding her back. She would never be able to open a real shop, or make more than her modest living. She didn't want riches—although she wouldn't turn down some sparkly jewelry—but it would be nice to know that she could pay both her mortgage and the electric on time without scraping under the couch cushions for lost change.

Sometimes, she just wanted to be normal. Khaki normal.

It didn't matter. Her grandmother had the curse, and *her* mother before that, and they passed it on to Mona's father, who, with typical Dad-efficiency, tried freezing his pies and tarts to be able to enjoy them throughout the month. But full moon baked goods don't freeze well. They don't keep at all. She learned that you just have to get them while you can, and enjoy them while you got 'em.

It took her father a long time to accept that, but it was a lesson he made sure Mona learned. And she had. So, yes, there were times when she wanted to be normal. But her curse had forced her to create a life for herself that was unique and satisfying, one that left her exhausted during the full moon, but with plenty of free time to foster friendships, volunteer around the community, and use her non-baking talents to make people happy. It wasn't perfect, but no life was.

And this guy, she thought as she stared down Dan the Accountant, King of the Khakis, this guy comes up here and accuses me of laziness. That's what he was doing. He wasn't the first one. Her curse wasn't commonly known—

outside of her family, only her best friend Trish knew, and she was sworn to secrecy. A lot of people found it strange that her work schedule was so . . . flexible. (When in reality, it was more rigid than they knew—she was at the mercy of the moon, after all.) But something about this guy, with his obsessive routine and his smart-looking briefcase, really pissed her off. Mrs. Harris told her he hadn't ever eaten anything from Apple of My Pie, at least not that she'd seen. So what did he even care!

And the fact that his blue eyes nearly crackled with fire when he confronted her, that pissed her off, too. Those were some really nice eyes. The nerve of those eyes.

"Wouldn't you make more money if you didn't have such a capricious business model?"

Mona stood up straight. She was short enough that she never towered over anyone, but she towered over him now, her inside the food truck, him on the sidewalk down below.

"What's it to you how much money I make?"

He flushed. Good, she thought.

"Maybe I don't need to make money," she said, leaning back down. "Maybe I'm a baking empire heiress, just slumming in Ohio." Uh-oh, she thought. Her imagination tended to go wild when she was mad. And her mouth tended not to be able to stop it. "Maybe my business is backed by a handsome desert sheikh who tasted a slice of my apple pie and decided he had to have me all to himself, but once a month he sets me free into the world as long as I promise to return to him in his desert lair."

His eyebrows went up. "Desert lair?"

"Yeah, a desert lair."

"In Ohio?"

Stupid logic. She wanted to disarm him, badly. "You think I couldn't get a desert sheikh?"

Down his eyes went, again. She wanted to tease him, ask him if he had a muscle spasm or something. But she sort of liked it. Dan the Accountant did not seem like the kind of guy who was out of control very often. The power to unnerve him was sort of intoxicating.

Not that it meant anything. Despite Mrs. Harris's assertions to the contrary, Khaki Dan was an egotistical control-freak. He wasn't even a customer and here he was, trying to tell her how to run her business. And now there was a line forming behind him.

"Listen, do you want something or not?"

This time his eyes didn't wander. They just honed right in on hers, and she felt a jolt. She wasn't sure of what—recognition? Lust, at least. Definitely lust.

Oh, he wanted something.

She would be happy to give it to him.